THE
TREASURED EGG

Kathy ~
How wonderful it
is that we have reconnected
after all these years—& we can
share & appreciate the stories of
our lives). Thank you so much for your
support ~ I hope you enjoy the
book! Love ~ Phyllis

PHYLLIS MAGOLD
Author of "A Beast No More"

outskirts press

To

My mother,

My grandmothers,

My great-grandmothers,

And to all mothers

And to all women.

We carry the treasured egg.

Chapter 1

. . . .

When I was at home, I was in a better place.

(Shakespeare)

ST. JOHN'S HOSPITAL
CLEVELAND, OHIO
JULY 1, 1988

S creams and moans and cussing reverberated through the otherwise silent halls of Saint John's Hospital on Detroit Avenue in Cleveland, Ohio.

"Aaaauuuuuggghhhhh!" Rosie bellowed.

"Try not to push," Babs said.

"Count backwards from ten," Brigid advised.

"Shut the hell up!" Rosie screamed.

"It's not yet time to push," said Dr. Hannah Manfred, in a gentle, confident tone.

"Really?" yelled Rosie. "Really? Tell that to my exploding uterus! And, hey doctor, why don't you shut up too!" Rosie continued her lament. "I know I said I wanted it natural, but screw that! Give me a shot; give me a drug. Give me anything!"

"OK, now you may push, Rosie," said Dr. Hannah, as she gently turned the placenta-soaked head of baby Scarponi. "One more, Rosie; give it all you got."

1

Babs Turyev-Schwartz dabbed a damp washcloth on the forehead of her dear friend, Rosie Vanetti-Scarponi, as Brigid Nagy held Rosie's hand. Thirty-eight years ago, these three women had been born at this same hospital on June 1. They met later as they attended the same high school, and had remained the closest of friends ever since, despite the geographical distances that separated them.

Babs worked at NASA in California; Brigid taught British Literature at Marquette University; and Rosie lived in Kenya, where she and her husband managed an elephant sanctuary. The women had returned to Cleveland to attend their twentieth high school class reunion, and shortly after the event, Rosie started her labor pains.

Rosie was eight months pregnant, and had planned to return to Kenya on July 2, but her baby evidently decided to be born in his mother's hometown of Cleveland. This was Rosie's third child. She now had three sons. Her other two children—Ricardo, twelve years old, and Antonio, four years old—remained in Kenya with their father, Sam.

Babs and Brigid glanced at each other and stifled a smile. They were accustomed to Rosie's direct way of expressing herself. They stood back, trying to ignore the yelps and language emerging from Rosie's mouth as they gazed in awe at the tiny human being emerging from Rosie's body.

But the baby made no sound.

Silence filled the room.

A few eternal seconds later, after suction to the nose and throat was completed, baby boy Scarponi announced his arrival with a hearty bawl, as everyone exhaled in relief.

"Give him to me. Give him to me," Rosie whispered, her voice hoarse from the grunts of labor.

The baby was a month early, and Rosie had been weary from travel. Worries of complications had dominated everyone's thoughts, so the healthy baby in Rosie's arms, and the exhausted but strong smile on Rosie's face, triggered a tearful response from her friends.

Rosie was especially worried because of the guilt she carried in her heart. Raising two children is not easy under any circumstances, but being so far away from family made it even more difficult. She loved Kenya; she loved the people, she loved the animals, and she loved Sam. But, as middle age began to blitz her body, the strain of caring for the children, her husband, and the elephants was wearing her down. When the tests confirmed this pregnancy, she felt suffocated.

Several months ago, when she had called Babs and Brigid to tell them the news of her upcoming third child, she announced: "I killed another frickin rabbit."

As the nurses continued to clean birth debris off of the mother and child, the mothers of the three friends waited nervously in the waiting area. Rosie's mom, Mama Rose Vanetti, sixty-nine years old, had a sharp mind and a body that had begun to show the wear and tear of life's traumas and dramas. Arthritis, high blood pressure, and angina had slowed her down, but the Italian blood heated her soul. She lived in Cleveland, at the family home on W. 61st and Detroit Avenue, a few blocks east of the hospital. She continued to run the neighborhood market, which she and her husband, Massimo,

Rosie's father, opened when he returned from World War II. Massimo had been a City Councilman and an icon in the westside Cleveland neighborhood where he and Mama Rose grew up and started their business. He died of a heart attack a few years ago, and suddenly Mama Rose had lost her childhood sweetheart and lifelong partner. There was a hole in her heart that would never again be filled. But although she and her husband were devoted companions and lovers, Mama Rose never allowed her own identity to be swallowed up. Her love was his, but her mind was her own.

Dar Nagy, Brigid's mother, was sixty-four, with silver hair that cropped a petite frame. Of the three mothers, she was the most physically fit, which she attributed to her Irish genes and resistance to the temptations of cigarettes and alcohol. Her legal name was Brigid, but Miklos, her husband and Brigid's father, gave her the moniker "Dar," when having two Brigids in the house became too confusing. When Miklos was in the army, he had purchased a gold bracelet for her, but he ran out of money for a full engraving, so "To my darling," became "To my Dar." The bracelet, and the name, became a permanent part of her being. Dar had chosen to forgo any professional career and devoted her life to her husband and family. Six daughters gave her little time to explore any other options, and she was quite content.

Barbara Turyev, Babs's mother, at fifty-nine, was the youngest of the three. A brilliant NASA scientist, Barbara researched and contributed to the moon landing and Mars explorations. She was privy to the most secret and challenging endeavors of scientific studies — a confidant and adviser to astronauts and the builders of rockets.

It was her husband, however, who gained the fame and recognition. Richard Turyev was a world-famous astrophysicist whose name became synonymous with space exploration. He was seventy-five when he passed away, leaving behind a legacy of celestial and earthly achievements, not the least of which were his daughter, Babs; his son, David; and wife, Barbara. Mother and daughter remained close. Although they communicated through letters and occasional phone calls with David, he had chosen an artist's life of isolation in the East Village of Manhattan.

Barbara had not fared well since her husband's death, and her brilliant mind was slowly withering to a worrisome loss of cognizance, often resulting in irrelevant or inappropriate comments. (During this visit to Cleveland, Babs had taken Barbara to be evaluated by a renowned psychologist, Lisa Steinway, at the Cleveland Clinic. Dr Steinway confirmed that Barbara was in the early stages of Alzheimer's Disease. She recommended a diet change to help with brain health, and provided the name of a nutritionist, Megan Zamusta, who specialized in that area.)

When Brigid and Babs entered the waiting area, Mama Rose leaped from her chair as quickly as her body would allow, and moved close to them. The nerves she was hiding spewed into a babble of questions.

"That girl was never on time for anything in her life, and now she delivers her baby a month early! How is she? How is the baby? Did the doctor do everything right, or do I have to hunt her down and show her what happens to someone who messes with my daughter?"

Babs respectfully interrupted the barrage and gently put

her hand on Mama Rose's shoulder, silently relishing Rosie's decision not to have Mama in the delivery room.

Babs reported, "You have another perfectly handsome grandson, Mrs. Vanetti, and Rosie is doing just fine."

Mama Rose softened with relief. "I was so worried. Away from her husband. Only in the eighth month. Thank God."

Brigid had walked over to her mom and Barbara, and warmly hugged them. They chatted amiably while they waited to see Rosie and the baby.

Dar began the conversation. "Hard to believe thirty-eight years ago, we were in this same hospital, giving birth to our oldest girls. Who would have guessed we'd all be back sharing the joy of Rose's grandson?"

Mama Rose responded, "It is a marvel how quickly lives have changed. We've seen the good and bad together, haven't we, ladies? These daughters of ours have been our greatest joys, and our biggest pains in the butt. So glad you two are still with me, 'cuz I'm sure there's a lot more pains in the butts to come."

Barbara, who sat quietly detached from the conversations, interjected by saying, "Babs looked like Don Rickles when she was born."

Mama Rose was the first to enter Rosie's room. She held Rosie's hand and began to cry. It wasn't a sob; it wasn't a weep; it was a gentle flow of a worried, relieved, loving mother's tears.

"Oh, Rosie," Mama sighed. "I was so worried when you started labor early. But I'm so happy to be able to be here with you. It's been so painful to be so far away from you when you had your other kids. And when you didn't make enough effort to be at your father's funeral, it just made me realize how distant we've become. I'm gonna hold this baby every minute you are here."

Rosie thought, *Zapping me with loving guilt — my mother's specialty.* She observed the genuine care and bonding between grandma and grandchild as Mama Rose cuddled the baby in her arms. She reflected on the pain and joy that Mama had lived through because of, and with, her family. When Rosie's father died, Rosie did, in fact, try desperately to come to Cleveland for the funeral, but she was pregnant, and the doctor advised her that the trip would be dangerous for both her and the baby. She remained in Kenya, knowing that her absence added to Mama Rose's grief.

Before leaving Kenya for this reunion, she and Sam had begun to discuss that it was time for their children to experience, firsthand, this familial bonding of love and joy … and sometimes, pain. There were job opportunities for them in Cleveland, as well as deep roots of family, past and present. Rosie wanted these roots firmly planted in her children's future. Sam's parents were a quick plane ride away in Washington DC, and they, too, were anxious to see their son and grandsons more often.

Rosie, still exhausted from the delivery, spoke quietly.

"Mama, please put the baby down. There is something I would like to tell you."

"Sweet Mother of God," Mama said. "I have heard that comment before from you, and it hasn't always ended well."

Again, guilt, thought Rosie.

Mama wrapped the baby tightly in the blanket, and gently

put him on his side in the crib. (She had read that these days, experts advised that laying the baby on his side helped prevent Sudden Infant Death Syndrome and choking from vomiting.)

As the baby slept peacefully, Rosie took her mother's hand, and began to speak, as lovingly as she has ever spoken.

"Mama, we are naming the baby Massimo, after Dad."

Rosie's mother sat in silence for a few seconds. She took Rosie's other hand, and said, "Never underestimate a mother's prayers. Through everything, God has answered mine." Mama Rose's tears were now a full-throated sob.

"Well, here's another one of your prayers answered. Mama," said Rosie. "I want my children to know you, to know their family, to know their Cleveland roots. I'm coming home."

The three friends and their mothers ogled over baby Massimo, and soon it was time to leave and let mother and baby rest. Mama Rose drove back to her home just a few blocks away, and Dar drove Barbara back to the Nagy's home in Parma. Barbara had moved to California a few years ago to live with Babs, so she and Babs were staying with the Nagys for this visit.

Brigid and Babs were saying their goodbyes to Rosie, who was flushed with exhaustion and emotion. Before they left, Rosie told Brigid that she hoped Brigid would meet someone to settle down with.

"Nothing beats having a loving husband," said Rosie.

The girls chuckled at the irony of Rosie telling Brigid to settle down. Rosie was the wild one of the three. In her teens and early twenties, she sexed, drugged, and rocked and rolled in a lifestyle that almost killed her. She never returned to those habits, and Kenya fed that wild spirit with constructive energy. Rosie adored her husband. She felt a special bond with Babs because they both seemingly had found men who loved them, and who nourished their bodies and souls.

"Wouldn't it be great if Brigid found a guy like ours?" Rosie asked.

Brigid, annoyed, but maintaining courtesy, only because she had just witnessed Rosie's body explode with stress and fatigue, said, "I have always liked Adam. He just seems so right for you, Babs. Smart, and caring.

Rosie added, "Yeah, not many could match up with your intelligence and dedication. You're the perfect couple."

Babs responded. "I'm getting a divorce."

Silence.

"Forget him, you were always too good for him," said Brigid.

"Damn rat bastard Steelers' fan," said Rosie.

Rosie dozed off quickly, and Brigid and Babs decided to drive down Detroit Avenue to their favorite greasy spoon, formerly called The Egg Palace, now called The Big Egg. In high school, and after late nights during college breaks in downtown, the girls would come here and enjoy the grit and grub of vintage Cleveland. It was their place to share hopes and dreams, and heartaches. Tonight, they had much to discuss.

"Good Lord, Babs, what happened?" Brigid asked as the waiter brought the egg-shaped menus to the table.

Babs replied in a straightforward manner, to the point, and unemotional. She was the stoic of the three friends. "After Annie was born, Adam began to change. He criticized my appearance, constantly demanding attention. He, I think, was actually jealous of the baby. His whole demeanor changed."

Brigid,who could cry at a dead ant, became teary-eyed, and asked, "How did you handle it?"

"Well, believe it or not, I tried to appease him. I began to wear make-up, even after an exhausting day. I always made sure the house was clean, and dinner was on the table when he came home. I tried to keep Annie quiet, so he wouldn't be disturbed. I did my work late at night after he fell asleep. I became a damn Donna Reed. When all that didn't work, I asked my mom to come and help, so Adam and I could have more time together. That turned into a disaster, because her mental state was slowly deteriorating. So, I was basically taking care of Adam, Annie, and Mom. It became too much. One night, I took a long walk in a rare, Southern California, heavy rainstorm. The rain refreshed me and cleared my head. I thought it all out and decided to tell Adam that I needed him to be a partner and helper. It was time for him to be the one to step up; I was out of ideas. I needed my soulmate back — as well as my soul."

Dinner of buttered, dripping eggs, toast, and grease-laden bacon arrived, briefly interrupting the conversation. The women, out of habit, said a silent sign of the cross and the grace before meals, as they had done since they learned to speak. Revelers from the Flats, a favorite Cleveland party destination on the Cuyahoga River, started coming in. Brigid and Babs could not help smiling as they silently recalled their own reveling from a couple of decades ago.

"Ah, it was all so easy when we were their age, wasn't it?" sighed Brigid.

"Well, if you discount riots, assassinations, nervous break-downs, and drug overdoses, yeah, I guess it was easy." Babs laughed, and Brigid laughed with her.

The girls enjoyed the food, and each other, and when the coffee came, Babs finished her story.

"So, when I confronted him, Adam confessed he had been having an affair with his Teacher's Assistant. I have to tell you, despite all the warning signs, I was shocked. God, such a common, predictable, male weakness. I thought he was stron-ger than that, or at least had a deeper sense of morality. He actually broke down and apologized, and said he was willing to try again. But my heart was now stone cold. This wasn't the Adam I married, and I had no faith that he would ever be that man again. I had decided early on that I would have a 'no cheat or beat rule.' If he ever cheated, or hit me, I was out of the marriage."

Brigid reached for Babs's hand. They had been friends too long for her not to see the soft, warm pain under the stone-cold heart.

The girls always ended their conversations with a toast. Tonight, they lifted and clanked their coffee cups, as Babs said, "I'm coming home."

When Babs and Brigid arrived back at Brigid's house, in Parma, the mothers were enjoying a late-night Burger King Whopper and french fries. It was grossly unhealthy comfort food. Noticing Brigid's grimace, Dar said, "Cholesterol has been bombarding our arteries for six decades. We have done our best, and now when we have a taste for a burger and fries, gosh darn it, we're going to scarf it up. Right, Barbara?"

Barbara's reality had returned to normal; fog had lifted from her eyes, and temporarily from her brain. She defended her choice of food by reminding the women, "If the astronauts on the Space Shuttle can have beefsteak and sugar-filled pudding, we can certainly enjoy this with no guilt."

Babs was relieved to see her mother enjoying herself. Although the dementia crept in intermittently, she knew that it would not improve, and someday, decisions would have to be made. For now, she simply enjoyed the scene.

Brigid and Babs grabbed a can of pop from the refrigerator and joined their mothers at the table. Miklos, Brigid's father, was working all night at the fire station, so the women could talk as loudly and as freely as they chose. Brigid's youngest sister, Cindy, still lived at home, but was out for the evening. This little bungalow that Miklos and Dar had built in 1950 had weathered storms, both physical and emotional, but the conversations around this table always brought the rainbows.

The chat turned to Barbara and Dar discussing Rosie's and Babs's return to Cleveland. As Brigid listened, she could feel her mother's longing gaze and read the unsaid thoughts of her desire to have Brigid back in town. Brigid had left when she was eighteen, first to college, then to the Peace Corps in India, then back to Marquette University in Milwaukee, where she enjoyed an academic life of lecture and scholarly pursuit.

During this last visit home, she happened to see an old friend, Paul Kantzios, in Parmatown, the city's shopping mall. Paul was a widower who had been married to Brigid's childhood friend, Patti DeSantis. Brigid met him when she was tutoring on summer break between her junior and senior year at Marquette. Today, they decided to have lunch at Teddy's, a mall favorite with good food and an atmosphere that lent itself to good conversation. During their chat, her friend bemoaned the lack of good educators to teach in Cleveland's inner-city schools. He was a principal at a near west-side inner city Cleveland high school, close to where Brigid had attended Lourdes Academy. He told Brigid that truly dedicated, smart teachers who were willing to tackle inner city problems, were getting hard to find.

The words stirred a whirlpool in Brigid's psyche. Her life was idyllic in Milwaukee. She was content with intellectual stimulation, and a plethora of romance and available men. It had everything she wanted.

Except … whenever she came home to Cleveland and Parma, she felt this was where she truly belonged. Nothing in Milwaukee touched her as much as the emotions evoked by Saint Patrick's Church on Bridge Avenue in Cleveland, or State Road Park in Parma, or Shaker Lakes in Shaker Heights, or Edgewater Park on the shores of Lake Erie. Driving down Pearl Road, even the pot holes filled her with nostalgia.

She would always fight these emotions, and rationalize that Milwaukee offered her solid satisfaction. But talking to Paul convinced her of something she had already known. Satisfaction does not equal fulfillment. At thirty-eight years old, she had already achieved many of her life's goals, but mid-life awakened different needs.

By the end of the lunch, Brigid had accepted the job of English teacher and Department Chairperson at the high school. The contract had been finalized the day before Rosie gave birth. She was waiting for the right time to make the announcement. This was it.

So, when her mom was looking longingly, Brigid told her.

"Mom, I was hoping Dad would be here to share this moment, but I have something to tell you."

Barbara, Babs, and Dar stopped chewing and put their food and drinks down on the kitchen table. When Brigid told them the news, all the emotions of the day hit their hearts with a resounding thunder of hope and expectation.

They raised their glasses in the familiar gesture of a toast, as Brigid finished the evening by saying, "I'm coming home."

Chapter 2

. . . .

"There is no greater agony than bearing
an untold story inside you."

Maya Angelou

BRIGID

1974-1988

B rigid Delia Nagy was born on June 1, 1950, in St. John's Hospital in Cleveland, Ohio. She bore the first and middle name of her mother, and her mother's mother, and her mother's mother's mother.

Parma, Ohio, a suburban haven southwest of Cleveland, provided a secure and healthy landscape for her childhood and adolescent years. The quiet, tree-lined streets echoed with neighborly greetings during the day, and the glow of street lights and pollution-free skies during the evening.

Her parents were high school sweethearts, flirting and sweetening their love in the halls of West Technical High School on Cleveland's west side in the 1940s. After Miklos, her father, served his time in the Philippines in World War II, he and Dar married. Then, in 1950, they planted their love in their Parma bungalow, where they still lived. Grandparents, aunts, uncles, and cousins lived nearby and nourished Brigid with ethnic doses of Hungarian and Irish culture.

As Parma grew, so did Brigid. Saint Charles, the elementary school that Brigid attended, became the largest Catholic grade school in the country, burgeoning to an enrollment of over 2500 students by the time Brigid reached eighth grade. The Ursuline nuns taught a rigid Catholicism, which both frightened and strengthened Brigid. She had grown to reject most of the frightening part, but still held onto the strong faith that there was something and someone better and bigger than humanity.

The absence of people of color in Parma did not strike her as odd until many years later.

Most of all, Saint Charles contributed to her love of music. The musical inclinations were also sustained in her home, where her mother was an accomplished pianist. Brigid, her parents, and her five sisters would often sing and dance and jam in their tiny living room — which never really seemed too crowded.

It was at Lourdes Academy High School where Brigid began to comprehend the world and her place in it. The Humility of Mary nuns, and the environment that encouraged young women to soar without sexist restraints, cultivated her love of literature and her curiosity of spirituality.

Lourdes Academy was located in the near west side inner city of Cleveland. Brigid's roots were planted in that neighborhood, and as she was growing up, she frequently visited her father's childhood home on Carroll Avenue, near the West Side Market, across from Saint Ignatius High School. She still harbored resentment toward the Cleveland Diocese that allowed Saint Ignatius to flourish as a leader in all male education, while Lourdes, a beacon of female triumph, had been forced to close its doors many years ago. That was one of many occurrences that spurred her psyche to feminist action.

She would always be grateful for the greatest gift that Lourdes Academy bestowed upon her: the lifelong friendships that began freshman year in 1964 and continued to sustain her through the decades. The most significant of those friendships was Babs and Rosie.

During the four years she spent at Marquette University, she and her friends exchanged monthly letters, and it was this support from Babs and Rosie that succored her through the upheavals of protests, changing theologies, and changing moralities of the late 1960s. The deepest upheaval was the death of one of her dearest friends, Martin Gorman. Martin was killed in Vietnam, and his death left a permanent pang in Brigid's heartbeat.

Her days at Marquette were peaceful compared to the instability on the campuses of Berkeley and Ohio State where Babs and Rosie attended. Brigid participated in some of the protests against the war but became discouraged when the anti-war and racial voices drowned out the feminist voices.

She spent most of her time at college in a normal cycle of studying, dating, drinking, and smoking an occasional hit of marijuana. Her orderly lifestyle earned her the nickname "Saint Brigid" from Rosie, whose lifestyle at the time was anything but saintly.

After graduating Summa Cum Laude from Marquette in 1972, Brigid spent two years in the Peace Corps in Bombay, India, where any perceptions of Western reality withered in the faces of limbless beggars on the streets, molesting men on the train rides, and relentless, ever-present poverty. The political unrest there posed an increasing danger to Americans, and Brigid's group was the last to be assigned to this location. Although she finally settled in to appreciate the beauty and love in the human soul that is found in all peoples, she returned home confused in the dichotomy between the stench of the poor in the cities, and the fresh air in the natural beauty of the Himalayas. Did the same God really create both? As William Blake questioned when writing about the beastly tiger, "Did he who made the Lamb make thee?"

In 1974, the mothers and friends celebrated Brigid's return home with hoopla and hoorays. Babs came in from Indiana, where she was working at the time, and Rosie postponed her assignment to Kenya, so she could share the moment. One of Brigid's deepest regrets was not being present at Babs's wedding and Mr. Turyev's funeral. Seeing her friends, for even this brief amount of time, both refreshed her and depressed her. Brigid needed order and consistency in her life. She had imagined the girls picking up where they left off, but that fantasy was smacked into the real world almost immediately when Rosie and Babs told her they were sorry, but, because of work obligations, they only had one more night to stay. They did manage to spend most of that night at their old favorite restaurant, the Pewter Mug, in downtown Cleveland.

"Even now, it seems strange to order a drink with you girls and not have to dig through my fake IDs," Rosie laughed.

"We lost girlhood a long time ago. We are twenty-four. I'm a scientist; Rosie, you're off to Africa to save a species; and Brigid, you've just returned from a life-changing experience. We're the women of the world, pals. Time to go make the changes we've been talking about for the past ten years."

Babs spoke with the authoritative tone of a young woman whose studies and career continued to break down sexist barriers while pushing mankind closer to the stars.

Brigid sighed. "I'm not sure what changes I'm strong enough to make. Since I've returned, all I want to do is eat and sleep, and try to synthesize the disparities and absurdities I've witnessed over the past year. It pains me that you two will not be here with me."

"Christ," said Rosie. "You're still a damn buzz kill."

"And you're still a foul-mouthed wild woman," Brigid snapped back.

"And I'm still perfect," laughed Babs.

"Mhmmmmm," said Rosie. "I'm curious, Babs. You've been married two years; have you had sex yet?"

In a moment, the years melted away, the laughter erupted, and they were once again teenagers, remembering Babs's vow of chastity and commitment to be a virgin when she married. The memories flooded the conversation, washing away worries and woes, hiding the underlying question: When would they all be together again?

A few months after Brigid returned from India, she received a call from a friend, Donna Mihovk, who worked for the English Department at Marquette University. Donna began the conversation, breathless with excitement.

"Brigid! Hi, it's Donna Mihovk. It's been a couple years since we last talked, do you remember me?"

Brigid, rather startled, slowly recollected. Sounding much more confident than she actually was, she responded. "Of course I do, Donna." *I do remember that you set my hair on fire one time while we rode on a bus home from a beer fest,* Brigid thought. "How are you?"

"Well," Donna said. "The English Department has an opening for a fast-tracked Master's/Doctoral candidate that includes classwork, research, and teaching opportunities. Dr. Berkshire had heard that you recently returned from the Peace Corps and mused that you might be a perfect applicant. I jumped on it and am calling to see if you would be interested."

"My God, yes!" said Brigid, not hesitating for a second, feeling alive for the first time since she returned home.

Brigid applied. Marquette hired her. For the next fourteen years, Brigid called Milwaukee home. She lived in an old, refurbished boarding house, on the second floor, with a bay window that overlooked Wisconsin Avenue near campus. The dark mahogany woodwork, and the thick, leaded window panes created an ambience that embraced her every time she walked through the door. Sitting on the pillowed window seat of the bay window, watching snow fall during the winter months, provided her with solace and spiritual contemplation.

There were four other tenants: a linguistics professor, who was studious, but very amiable and interesting; an old Jesuit theologian, who spent most of his time writing essays about celibacy and secular ministries; a visiting lector from Ireland, with whom Brigid developed a scholarly friendship; and an FBI field operations agent, with whom Brigid also developed a close friendship, which later developed into a relationship. She always wondered how he fit in with the other tenants, but she was not curious enough to investigate. He had asked her not to question his connection with the University, so she was content to be satisfied with the romance and intellectual stimulation they shared. At one point, she had fallen deeply in love with him.

Brigid earned a Master's degree in British Literature, and a PhD in English, writing her thesis on the *Muted Consciousness of Women in the Linguistic Wordscape of Male Dominance.* She obtained full professorship and became a favorite of both students and faculty for her intelligence and down-to-earth approach to literature. An essay on her thesis topic was shared in several literary publications. Brigid's work marked her as a notable feminist literary critic.

Theme of Female Muted Consciousness in: "The Yellow Wallpaper," by Charlotte Perkins Gilman and "To Room Nineteen" by Doris Lessing

Professor Brigid Nagy
Marquette University

The twentieth century has been an era in which the realms of literature have been penetrated, extended, and interrogated by female authors. Sexist barriers in politics, employment, and the arts are consistently being eliminated, as women have become liberated to express themselves in many arenas, including, and perhaps, especially, in literature. This freedom to write has produced mountainous volumes of poetry, prose, short stories, and novels authored by, and for, women. The prolific outpouring of feminine writing has initiated provocative debates regarding the direction of feminine criticism. Feminist critics are attending to the task of addressing the critical question:"What is the difference between literature written by women and literature written by men?"

Elaine Showalter, feminist author and critic, proposes a definitive response to this question in her essay,"Feminist Criticism in the Wilderness," Showalter reviews the current and previous modes and theories of feminist criticism: physiological, psychoanalytical, linguistical, and cultural. She proposes that the most complete mode of criticism is a "gynocentric, cultural, anthropologistical" system. This system retains everything that is valid from the other theories, and studies them within an anthropological and cultural scope.

One of the most stimulating concepts within this theory is that of the "muted consciousness" of women. This concept is based on a model suggested by Oxford anthropologists Shirley and Edward Ardener. Their model addresses the fact that men have historically dominated both the language and power structures. Thus, it has been the male consciousness that has been communicated, leaving the female consciousness"muted" and "silenced," in an unchartered area of communication.

Showalter believes that within this "muted consciousness" lies the uniqueness in women's writing. Many feminist critics, including Showalter, observe two plots or alternating texts written by females. Underneath the literary, linguistic communicated text, is a "silence," a "wild zone," which emerges, sometimes obviously, sometimes after careful analysis. Two literary works which reflect this concept are"The Yellow Wallpaper" by Charlotte Perkins Gilman and "To Room Nineteen" by Doris Lessing.

In "The Yellow Wallpaper," Gilman creates a chilling scenario in which a woman suffers from what now would be diagnosed as postpartum depression. This woman is driven to madness, because her physician husband does not believe there is anything "really wrong" with her. In a "careful and loving manner," he confines her to one room, removing all independent movement or socialization.

The woman is stripped of all creative and self-communicative outlets. Her consciousness is muted to the extent that only madness brings her a release. Specifically significant to female literary study is the woman's thwarted attempt to write. She says, "If only they would allow me to write a little, it would relieve this press of ideas and rest me." For centuries, women were unable to "relieve the press of ideas."

Relief in "The Yellow Wallpaper" is achieved through insanity. A woman, confined to a room where her only "company" is a hideous yellow wallpaper, begins to peel off and sometimes devour the wallpaper. As she does this, she "sees" another woman creeping behind the wallpaper, clawing for freedom. As the lady behind the wallpaper begins to creep, the woman also begins to creep. Soon the story is filled with women "creeping aimlessly"—in the garden—in the streets—in the room with the yellow wallpaper—inside the yellow wallpaper.

When viewed within the concept of Showalter's premise, the main character is an example of a muted consciousness, so thoroughly suppressed by her husband's dominance and society's dictations, that her only mode of expression is madness. Looking deeper into the story, we see an even more frightening example. The women who have supposedly gained "freedom," and are able to "escape" from behind the wallpaper are still "creeping aimlessly." This indicates that even when attempts are made for female expression, women's consciousness can, and are, still be crushed or hushed.

Doris Lessing, in her short story "To Room Nineteen," also portrays a silenced woman, but in a much more subtle manner. It is this subtlety which disguises the ironic situation of the heroine; she seems to have everything, but she is miserable. The following passage is indicative of this subtle, matter-of-fact tone, through which Lessing tells her story.

"They lived in their charming flat for two years, giving parties and going to them, being a popular young couple, then Susan gave up her job, and they bought a house in Richmond. It was typical of this couple that they had a son first, then a daughter, then twins, a son and a daughter. Everything was right, appropriate, and what everyone would wish for."

It is this *"matter-of-fact," "this is how it should be"* tone which permeates the story and follows Susan through her mandatory obligations of being a perfect wife and a perfect mother. These obligations eventually lead her to become selfless, depressed, and suicidal. Lessing successfully engages the reader in a serious struggle of discovering exactly why Susan is so miserable. Susan addresses the struggle:

"All is quite natural. First, I spent twelve years of my adult life working, living my own life. Then I married and from the moment I became pregnant for the first time, I signed myself over, so to speak, to other people. To the children. Not for one moment in twelve years have I been alone, had time to myself. Now I have to learn to be myself again."

Susan's *"finding herself"* is the core of this story. We witness Susan's self-exploration through the lens of Showalter's contention that there is an expressed consciousness and an unexpressed consciousness.

At first, Susan does all that is expected from a *"perfect wife."* This ranges from meekly accepting her husband's infidelities (*'It was banal when one night Matthew came home late and confessed he had taken a girl home and slept with her,'*) to sacrificing her career (*"because children needed a mother around up to a certain age. That, they both agreed on."*) These were the parts of her consciousness that she expressed.

In reality, the true feelings of her self remained silenced. When her husband was unfaithful, her thoughts were filled with "bitterness" and "absurdity." But she suppressed these thoughts and offered the obligatory "forgiveness" and "understanding." When her depression led to "bad temper and resentment" toward her children, she was not able to express it... "Why is it I can't tell anyone; why, why not?"

Lessing brilliantly leads us to examine the unexpressed, unconsciousness of a woman who has it all ... except herself. Susan finds temporary relief in a rented hotel room where she can be completely alone and anonymous. But when her husband learns of her retreat, she can no longer be at peace. Her consciousness can only escape the frustration of silence by ending it. She commits suicide.

As women penetrate deeper into the realms of literature and personal freedom, the female "muted consciousness" will eventually be expressed and articulated. Until then, Showalter proposes that women must question the insanity in "The Yellow Wallpaper," and avoid being tricked by what is considered normal in "To Room Nineteen," always considering that, "women have a duality, as members of the general culture and partakers of the women's culture."

Brigid quickly learned that being published, while gaining academic recognition, did not automatically get approval from friends and family.

After the article was published, she received a curt note from Rosie, which said: "Not all marriages are a trap, you know. Some of us are very fulfilled in the role."

Her mother took the time to call her to say, "Brigid, what have your father and I ever done to make you think that being married was so horrible?"

She tried to make them understand that the stories were other women's perceptions, not her own. But to no avail. *God help me*, she thought, *if I ever write a novel.*

The fact was, that Brigid had the highest regard for marriage. Men danced in and out of her life, but while some received her love, none had earned her trust. She had always enjoyed the romance of dating. However, when she returned from India, she noticed some interesting changes in the custom. In the 1960s, when she first tasted being a female in the dating game, the men paid for everything. Men held doors for women, walked on the sidewalk nearest to the street, and in general, tapped into a modern code of chivalry. Her mother had once told her that the behavior stemmed from ancient customs where the women were revered because they contained the "treasured egg," the power of fertility and reproduction. In fact, her mother once admonished her for delaying marriage and pregnancy because the "treasured egg" does not last forever — a comment that produced drink-spitting, nose-choking laughter from Babs and Rosie. Her mother, in delicate terms, advised her that the custom of modern-day chivalry was a beckoning prelude to sex.

Now, in the late 1970s and early 1980s, apparently women did not need much coaxing to give up their treasured egg, so the wooing and chivalry were not as needed. Brigid was conflicted, because she did like the courtship rituals, but embraced the freedom that came with not being bound by social expectations of female behavior.

Her relationship with the FBI tenant in her building, Jay Vargo, brought her close to marriage, but their time together ended abruptly when he made a choice she could not accept.

She often thought of the conversation that destroyed her trust ...

"Brigid," Jay said. "I forgot to mention that I will be out of town next weekend."

"Business?" she asked.

He laughed. "No, I am going to Las Vegas. You know my best friend is getting married in a couple weeks, and his bachelor party is in Vegas."

Brigid did not hide her disappointment. "You are traveling across country to a city where strip clubs abound, prostitution is rampant, and stag parties are notorious for sexual exploits? Do you expect me to be OK with that?

"Well, I'm certainly not going to be with a prostitute, Brigid. Christ, have some trust," Jay snapped.

Brigid did not let up. "But the strip clubs, stag parties, and topless shows are on the agenda?"

Jay was visibly annoyed. "Yes, that's what we do. It means absolutely nothing. It's a bunch of guys having fun and letting loose. I love you, for God's sake. I never dreamed you would take issue with this."

"OK," she murmured.

When he called her from Vegas that weekend, in slurred, uneven diction, he said how much he missed her. She could hear sexy strip music and tittering girls very close by, accompanied by Jay's friends shouting crass remarks and lewd invitations. *No*, she thought. *I do not want a man who thinks this is OK.*

In a rare burst of vulgarity, she responded, "I do not give two squirts of piss if you miss me. Enjoy your good ol' boy fun. We are through."

Now into her thirties, Brigid realized that her standards might be too high — in men, in student performance, in music, in everything. As she reflected on her life, she felt an overwhelming sense of how much has been afforded to her. Her father, though flawed, loved her mother and his family unconditionally. He was genuinely proud of his wife's achievements and never felt diminished if she outshone him in any environment. He did not mind when men occasionally flirted with her, because he knew her, and he trusted her not to return the affectations. His masculinity did not rely on endeavors with the "guys," or prideful struts of male prowess. What made him a good man was his integrity and commitment to his wife, his family, his job, his community, and most of all his God. Physically, he was strong, well built, attractive, and the proverbial handyman who could fix anything. But his true strength emerged from his spirit. Would she ever meet a man who met those standards? And could she ever accept less?

Brigid's educational opportunities were a blessing and a curse. Academically, the Jesuits at Marquette, the Humility of Mary nuns at Lourdes Academy, and the Ursuline nuns at St. Charles provided her with outstanding teaching, strict discipline, and enlightened encouragement, which resulted in a superb education in liberal arts, as well as a humanistic call to service.

Finally, the music. From her early education in the band and orchestra at St.Charles, where nothing short of superior achievement was expected, to her witnessing Judy Garland in concert, to her playing in a jazz band with highly skilled musicians, Brigid always had a taste of the best. She now felt a growing disdain for the popularity of the heavy metal sound and the highly suggestive lyrics of rock and roll. She recalled Babs's father's constant warning of the battle between the beast and the spirit that rests in the souls of all people. She questioned which of these the current bands appealed to — although she knew she would always love rock and roll, beast or not.

Those were the blessings.

The curse was that the blessings made it difficult to accept anything less than those standards from her students, her peers, her friends, or her men.

During her time there, Marquette afforded Brigid opportunities to explore various academic interests, including, and especially, the role of women in literature, particularly Irish literature. In 1981, she spent the summer studying at Trinity College in Dublin.

Her mother had never taken much interest in her scholarly endeavors, but a trip to Ireland put her into a state of delirium. "You must go to County Mayo to walk the roads of our families who stayed behind. Maybe you could visit the gravesites of the O'Malleys, many who didn't make the move to America. And oh, you must look up some of my distant cousins who are still there! Oh, me mudder will be dancing in her grave."

Brigid's "mudder" rarely broke into the Irish brogue, but when she did, no matter what the circumstance, it made Brigid smile. That bond to her matriarchal roots was cemented early on when her grandmother (also named Brigid), took her to the Cleveland downtown parades on Saint Patrick's Day, and sang Irish songs, loud and clear, on the bus rides, not caring what the "heathens" were thinking. Brigid also had a vague memory of chasing her great-grandmother (also named Brigid), down W. 25th in Cleveland after she "escaped" from a home for women suffering from dementia. These memories served to deepen her love for Irish women.

When she looked out the window of her plane to see the sunlit, lush greens of the Irish countryside, she stifled the gulp of tears that was moving from her heart to her eyes. She could not help herself. She was no longer the college professor; she was the great-great-great … infinite greats granddaughter of the proud Brigids of Ireland. She felt each of their joys and sorrows float up from the mists of the dazzling blue waters and the green hues of the land, with a metaphysical, kindred embrace.

Brigid quickly settled into the beautiful campus of Trinity, and frequently lost herself in the historic splendor of its long hall in the library where ancient manuscripts and millions of books and literature found a majestic dwelling place. Viewing the medieval beauty of the Book of Kells and the Book of Durrow interconnected both the physical and spiritual essence of her senses and mindfulness. The transcendence of the experience was clearly stated in the institution's motto: *Perpetuis futuris temporibus duraturam*: ("It will last into endless future times.") She would later refer to time at Trinity as "an infinite gift."

Her classes, too, were intellectually stimulating, an incomparable academic oasis of thought and literary insight. But the true education and learning was nurtured outside the classroom, in the nooks and crannies of the Irish landscape, and cooks and brandies of the Irish people.

In addition to the classroom lectures, Trinity had arranged tours for students to explore literary locations. Sligo, the scene that captured the soul of her favorite poet, William Butler Yeats, was the first, and one of the most rewarding, of the planned excursions.

Brigid's first sight of the Lake Isle of Innisfree, the inspiration for Yeats's poem of the same name, was a disappointment. The landscape was not vibrant, and although she observed numerous species of birds and fauna, she saw nothing remarkable. It reminded her of her first trip to the western United States, where she wrote to friends, "The mountains are rocky and the desert is sandy." *What a fool I was*, she thought.

As in much of Ireland, the beauty often rests not only in the visual wonders, but in the spirit. The group was permitted to walk around independently, and in a small, quiet restaurant on the coast, she could indeed hear the "lake water lapping," as she imagined Yeats escaping from the "pavement grey," to find the peace in his "deep heart's core." It awakened both the scholar and the nature lover in her. She soaked in the history of the isle and her ancestral roots that lived in the mystical fog with tales of sprites and fairies. The area had not yet succumbed to the distractions of heavy tourism, so the lake, and thoughts of Yeats, and connections to her mother, and grandmother, and great-grandmother, warmed her, while she walked in the chilly mist.

The trip to Glencar Lough, a few miles north of Sligo, presented a deeper verdant vista which swept her up in the whispers of Yeats's poem *The Stolen Child* ... "where the wandering water gushes from the hills above Glencar."

As with any exploration and study, there are serendipitous discoveries that can alter a person's worldview and foster a profound appreciation of the connection among cultures.

It was the Irish pubs where she experienced a more intense understanding of the links between peoples. Liquor, lingos, and lyres combined to feed her soul in a manner no curriculum could ever achieve. Such was the case when Brigid visited Thomas Connolly's pub in Sligo, one of the oldest pubs in Ireland.

Brigid entered the pub alone — the Trinity group had decided to stay in their hotel bar for the evening. She was comfortable being alone; she actually preferred it. There was a table in the back where one man was sitting, also alone, and she asked if she could share the space with him. The man was subdued, but friendly, and in an accent that was definitely not Irish, he said, "Ukeh, certainly."

Curious, but not wanting to be intrusive, Brigid did not initiate a conversation. Instead, she relaxed and reveled in what was resonating from the stage, particularly enjoying the sounds of the fiddle, and the beat of the bodhran, both of which reminded her of the music in the jazz bars of New Orleans. Her first love was the written word, but the universal truth that emerged from music, forced its soulful power, connecting the body and the spirit. Traditional Irish music and American jazz, to Brigid, captured what she called, "the swing of the universe," a connection between the sounds of heavenly spheres and the sounds of earthly souls. There was angst yet hope; sensual pleasure yet mystical satisfaction; and sometimes, an inescapable humor that either gently or viciously laughed at the human condition.

She noticed that the man seated at her table began to slowly rock back and forth and tap his feet. He smiled at her, and she used this communication as an opening for a chat.

"This is so enjoyable, isn't it?" she said, while thinking, *Perhaps that is the lamest conversation starter ever.*

"It is very nice," he answered politely.

"Are you visiting, or do you live here?" she asked, undaunted by his seeming reluctance to engage.

He sighed, realizing there was no escape from the parley.

"I live in the United States. I am from the Choctaw Tribe in Oklahoma. My name is Nashoba. There is a group of people here who, like the American Indian, have been treated poorly, and I am here to meet with them to discuss common problems. My people are in the process of constructing a Constitution. We have a long history with the Irish. I have become friends with the Irish; we share many tales of sadness and hardship. Now, I have been sent here to explore ideas regarding the treatment of indigenous peoples, in particular, the travellers."

Brigid was dumbstruck. She did not know anything about a history between the American Indian and the Irish. And who were these Irish travellers, indigenous people with whom he wanted to meet? She had read about them, but never pursued their story.

Before she could start asking questions, the band had taken a break, and the fiddler came to the table.

"It's amazing how you Yanks always manage to find

each other," he said as he embraced Nashoba, and winked at Brigid.

Brigid always found the authentic Irish brogue charming, and she relished the fiddler's attention. "How did you know I was an American?" she asked.

"Well, I wish I could say I have the second sight, but the truth is, I heard you talking with the other Yanks outside the hotel a while ago when I walked by. And from the stand, I saw you gravitate to the Chief over here. By the way, he doesn't like to be called a Yank or a Chief, but he is my buanchara, and we joke and kid each other, knowing we are forever friends. By the way, my name is Logan."

Nashoba smiled, and, shedding the shield of caution he had previously exhibited in his interaction with Brigid, he began to explain.

"Logan is brother to my soul. We met several years ago during my first trip to Ireland. I had learned that our tribe, after our darkest moment following the Trail of Tears, sent money to the starving people of Ireland during their time of famine. I desired to learn more about these people, who like my tribe, have suffered at the hands of imperial domination."

"This bloke is not a fan of cultural domination for sure," chimed in Logan, "but he respects his native land in the States and seeks peace with everyone."

Nashoba continued. "Your former president, Richard Nixon, helped the American Indian gain some independence with the support of the The Indian Self-Determination and Education Assistance Act of 1975. We have been trying to heal and govern our tribes with this freedom. A freedom that we do not consider a gift, but rather a fractured duty."

Brigid cringed at the thought of giving credit to Richard Nixon for anything. Thoughts of Rosie waving anti-Nixon signs on the Ohio State campus flashed through her mind. Nevertheless, the conversation intrigued her.

"My first visit to this isle was in 1976, and I immediately walked in harmony to the tune of my Irish brethren, and their love for the land. I recalled the words of Frederick Douglass, on his stay in Ireland, when he said, 'I have spent some of the happiest moments of my life since landing in this country. I seem to have undergone a transformation. I live a new life.'"

Brigid, somewhat embarrassed, sighed, "I never even studied Mr. Douglass' visit to Ireland. And I certainly did not know of your people's generous gift to the Irish people."

Logan looked intently at Brigid. "Your books and your institutions only tell one perspective of history, lassie. Seek out the truth in the words of common peoples, not the words of oligarchs."

The remainder of the evening passed by with the fiddler and his bandmates playing the tumultuous and tender tunes of the Irish hearts, while Brigid listened both to the music and the voice of the American Indian, who could now not be silenced, knowing that Brigid was hungry for the manna that his story was serving. Before the night ended, the fiddler, the Indian, and the professor had made plans to drive the highways and byways of the Irish countryside to meet the travellers.

Brigid returned from Ireland with a fresh perspective on the acquisition of knowledge and a deeper connection to national and global humanity. One of the trendy practices in 1980s education was to substitute personal reflections and journals for scholarly essays. She did not like the practice because she thought it severely diminished critical thinking and academic excellence. She read students' "feelings" about how they "felt so sorry for Grendel's mother" in *Beowulf* that they could "barely read the gory details of her death," or how Chaucer was "so mean he should be banished from the literary canon."

Use of the first person was ubiquitous, and toxic to an English professor. "I think." "I feel." "I want." "I need." The absurdity of dwindling down the cosmic significance of literature to the dribbling ruminations of libido-driven eighteen-year-olds drove her to the brink of drink.

However, *One can always use the system for one's own benefit,* she thought. So when the department chair asked her to write an academic article about her class at Trinity College, she requested permission to write a personal reflection instead. They heartily approved.

⌒

Traveling with the Travellers in Ireland
A Personal Journal presented by Brigid Nagy PhD

The dictionary describes a traveler as one who goes on a journey, one who seeks, a wanderer, an adventurer, one who travels, a member of a community having an itinerant way of life. In Ireland, I met all of these types of travelers, and I am the richer for it.

Trinity College in Dublin was my home base, a splendid and beautiful place filled with history, and a feeling of esoteric knowledge hidden in millions of books.

The women attending the lectures were part of one of the first groups of females who were permitted to have residence on campus. Yes, previously women were allowed to attend classes, but were required to leave after five o'clock p.m. How refreshing that I was permitted to sleep at the same institution that was now offering lectures on Women in Literature.

I was afforded the distinct pleasure of meeting Professor Annette Jocelyn Otway-Ruthven, who is a pioneer of integrating women into the academic community of Trinity. She is retiring this year, and made it a point to speak with and nurture female students of all ages on campus before she left. She gave us a fascinating view of the battles women faced in academia over the past century, but also gave hope from the current triumphs, and to those that are yet to come. Hers was a journey through the maze of intellectual misogyny and sexism — a journey that will be continued by other travelers whose goal is to shift paradigms.

The lectures exhibited paradigm shifts as well. When one earns a doctoral degree, one tends to get uppity, thinking that perhaps, he or she resides in a realm of supreme knowledge and expertise. I confess, I fell prey to that pride. And yet, here I was, discovering a previous coterie of women writers I had never come across in my studies: The Irish Women Writers' Club. This was a group of women from the 1930s who for twenty-five years celebrated and promoted Irish women authors. They were activists who met regularly to support women writers who most likely would have been, and, in fact, were, being ignored in the literary circles. They met monthly, developing a formidable force of intellect and know-how, readily competing and succeeding on the men's turf, while creating their own fertile blooms on female soil. Elizabeth Bowen, Kate O'Brien, and Teresa Deevy were three of the authors whose works we studied. Elizabeth

Bowen's short story, "The Demon Lover," had always been a favorite of mine, but the works of Kate O'Brien and Teresa Deevy
were new to me, and through their words and works I gained new
insight into Catholicism and the power of women in a masculine-
dominated sphere of authority. Deevy, who was deaf, was a brilliant
dramatist, dismissed by the critics, and disregarded by the public.
O'Brien's "Land of Spices," is one of the most fascinating novels I
have read exposing the innermost thoughts of women. Both Bowen
and O'Brien spent much of their lives away from Ireland, so, unlike
men, such as expatriate James Joyce, who were welcomed home after
living in various countries, these women were often judged as being
not Irish enough to be considered true homeland authors. Being an
expatriate and a world traveler was acceptable for men, but not for
women.

Other participants in the class, all women, also relished and welcomed these fresh, yet old, literary faces who expressed the female
consciousness, into the canon of literature. I was surprised and de-
lighted to observe the cosmopolitan flair of both my colleagues and
the city of Dublin itself. Dublin was rich with Italian and Polish
restaurants, and a hidden gem serving Nigerian cuisine not far from
the College. All were integrated into the Irish urban culture, which
I found to be welcoming and distinctly multicultural. Two colleagues, Jing Li from China, and Karina from Latvia, accompanied
me many afternoons and evenings through the shops and eateries of
the Dublin streets. One afternoon in July, we happened to be dining
at a restaurant several blocks from Merrion Street, where the British
Embassy was located. These are the happenstances when one learns
more about a people than is found in hallowed libraries and colleges.

In an instant, our casual luncheon was interrupted by the
sounds of shouting, chanting, objects breaking, and what was

obvious mayhem. Having lived through the turbulent protests of the Vietnam War, and the civil rights upheavals in Cleveland, I recognized the foreboding cacophony of a riot in the making.

Jing Li and Karina turned pale with fear, for they, too, knew the sounds of rebellion: a pro-democracy movement seething through the streets of Beijing, and the cries for independence smoldering in the underpinnings of Vilnius. We all agreed we wanted no part of what was going on in Dublin, so we walked swiftly, as far as we could from the ruckus, finally hailing a cab that took us back to Trinity. Later that evening, as I conversed while walking through the old and enchanted grounds of Trinity with students and colleagues, I learned that thousands had convened near the British Embassy to protest the deaths of several hunger strikers imprisoned in the Maze Prison in Northern Ireland. Several hundred in the group confronted the police, and a riot did indeed break out, with hundreds injured, including women and children. According to the British Broadcasting Company, most of those who required treatment in hospitals were police.

The event led to an eye-opening discussion of suppression across Asia and Europe with Jing Li and Karina, providing intense insight into life under the rule of a communist society. I briefly lost touch with the Irish culture that surrounded me, as I became more in touch with a global culture.

A few visits to some pubs soon swallowed me back into the flavor of the Irish experience. It was in a pub where I met an American Indian, Nashoba, of the Choctaw tribe, who revealed to me an ignored history of America, as well as an historical and present demographic in Ireland. Some drinks of whiskey, and a conversation with Nashoba and the fiddler, Logan, from the band, and I was intoxicated with Irish life and liquor. Nashoba was in Ireland to talk with an Irish population called the "travellers," people who roamed the highways and byways and cities, begging, doing odd jobs, and living in wagons or wherever they found shelter. I struck up a friendship with my two new acquaintances and made plans to travel a bit together. We ventured through a day trip, driving past the thatched cottages and vast green pastures of Ireland, mainly stopping to converse with the travellers we met along the way.

Each of us had different motives for wanting to meet with these people. My Choctaw friend gained much information regarding the seeds of organization that were forming to help with education and health for the travellers. The Choctaw and the travellers were similar in that they were being oppressed by peoples on their land to which they had ancient ties, while their language and culture were being systematically destroyed. A "Commission on Itinerants" in 1963 was forcing more of the travellers into assimilation.

Unlike the Choctaw, however, the travellers wanted recognition from the government, whereas the Choctaw wanted autonomy; they wanted, demanded, their own government. In this respect, Nashoba identified more deeply with the Irish people in general, who had been oppressed by a foreign government, Britain, for many years. The biggest difference between the travellers and the Choctaw was, as Nashoba observed, "We revere the land on which we live; they do not. They roam."

The nomadic lifestyle was one reason travellers were alienated from the Irish main population. Ties to the land ran deep in the Irish soul, as well as in the soul of the American Indian.

Although they were wanderers, the travellers enriched many aspects of Irish life. Logan stepped in tune with the fiddlers in the camp, as he admired the whistles, banjos, and fiddles, created from tin. Many of their household items and crafts were made of tin, *which led many to refer to these people as "tinkers." Spoons and accordions added rhythm and harmony, as the travellers entertained us with old Irish ballads, reshaped into the group's culture. Logan joined in the music at several camps, and his skill was appreciated by even the most skeptical eyes and ears.*

And skeptical they were, these Irish gypsies. My reason for joining Logan and Nashoba, besides thoroughly enjoying their company, was to soak up the customs and traditions of a people whose culture I had not known. The study of language is an intriguing endeavor, and it was fascinating to observe a culture that did not have any written record. Their history is revealed fragmentally through oral tradition, and they are not eager to share their stories with "buffers" (non travellers). In fact, they have developed a secret language that only a traveller can understand. (Later, I learned from Jing Li that Chinese women also had a secret language, known as Nushu.)

The main language of the travellers has many different names, but Cant seemed to be the one most referred to. It has its own lexicon and syntax, and unless it is studied or used frequently, Cant is incomprehensible to a buffer. We were not looked at like the Irish population buffers, and as a result we received better hospitality. At one camp, the woman invited me into the wagon, which was adorned with religious statues and various pictures and figurines of the Blessed Virgin Mary. It was obvious that they were Catholics. I managed to understand her say that her husband built the wagon with his own hands and had kept the family safe through many a storm. At another camp, the group lived in tents, with less ornamental trinkets, and less sanitary habits. It became obvious that although the various groups shared common traditions, like any society, one group is not representative of all groups.

The travellers extended hospitality to us, I believe for one reason:

we were foreigners who most likely had money. One common circumstance at each camp occurred when we were leaving. I asked to take a picture, and on each occasion, the woman or sometimes a child, would say to the father, "Make them give you a bob or two."

Entrepreneurship at its finest.

On our return drive to Dublin, through the narrow roadways of the Irish countryside, I sat in silence, contemplating the wonder of the human spirit, the universality of music, the human instinct of survival, and the importance of familial roots.

The final lecture at Trinity provided a peek into ancient Celtic culture, focusing on the role of women. From the reign of Macha Mong to the rules of marriage under Celtic law, a vibrant, yet contradictory history of women emerges from the stories and legends of the past. Like my time with the travellers, the lectures at Trinity enriched me, and made me yearn for more.

My grant provided an extra week of stay and discovery after the final lecture at Trinity, so during my last few days in the Emerald Isle, I became a tourist. Nashuba, Jing Li, and Karina returned to their homelands, leaving me alone with an Irish guide, as I visited the wondrous scenes of Glencar Lough, Sligo, The Rock of Cashel, numerous castles, and the Moher Cliffs, among other sites. Although I did not have the opportunity to visit the towns of my ancestral Brigids, I did manage to pray at St. Brigid's Well, and their spirits surrounded me.

My journey enlightened me intellectually, academically, and spiritually, with a connection to humanity that will change me forever. There is one dominant commitment that sears my soul: I shall travel to Ireland again.

∽

Administration enjoyed the reflection but required Brigid to write a more scholarly and researched article suitable for academic publication. She wholeheartedly agreed and added that perhaps the University should require similar standards for the students.

Marquette awarded Brigid with tenure, and within the next few years she published numerous articles and gained national recognition for her curriculum design for Women Writers of Great Britain and Ireland, and her aid in developing curriculum for Black Studies. However, the voices of women and black activists were becoming an enigma to her. In the early days of her civil rights activism, the goals had been integration and inclusion. Now there was an emerging factor of separation. Instead of changing the curriculum to include all peoples in the study of American culture, the dominant voices were demanding to detach from the main curriculum of American history and add courses that focused exclusively on African-American history and Women's Studies.

In addition to studying American history, there was now a month dedicated to Black History. Brigid discussed the matter with her black colleagues and students, who replied intelligently and emotionally.

"We have been degraded or ignored for three centuries. African American History is different from European American History. Until we catch up on informing people of the richness that African culture offered America, and the suppression that has silenced us, and still silences us, we will be just a footnote in texts still submerged in the white perspective. Our voices have been silenced, often violently, and now, we must shout."

Brigid understood and agreed. However, she remained concerned about the inclination to divide rather than unite. In a similar way, the women's movement was undergoing the same leanings. While doors of opportunity were opening, they were still being opened by men. Throughout the past several years, she had served on literary, academic, and political committees that were dedicated to acknowledging the contributions of women. All of the committees were governed by men, and although strides were being made, it was still quite clear who had the power. The feminist voices dominating the conversation in academia were demanding separate courses – not integration into the main courses.

A nagging harbinger lingered in Brigid's fears. Lessening of standards, unqualified applicants gaining employment and scholarships, women and black men being given consideration over more qualified white men — these practices were not what she and her activists were seeking. Equal opportunity, not unfair opportunity, was what she had hoped for. Although she understood that these policies were designed to right the wrongs of the horrendous treatment of the minority populations, she argued that two wrongs do not make a right. "There are a plethora of qualified female and minority applicants; we do not need, nor should we encourage, tokens."

Brigid and Rosie would occasionally correspond regarding the current events. Rosie's response was always intellectually stimulating. She closed her last letter saying, "Screw the man, Brigid. It's time to let them eat the rotten fruit they planted, and let them see first hand what happens when a dream is deferred.(I'm sure you like that Langston Hughes reference, being the egghead you still are.)"

When Brigid replied, telling Rosie that beautiful language is more empowering than vulgarity, Rosie began to close her letters saying, "Screweth the man."

The 1980s seemed to bring a sense of optimism to the United States. The economy was booming for many (not all), and for the first time that Brigid could remember, American flags were ubiquitous. The wounds of the Vietnam War were slowly healing (although Brigid was forever pained by the loss of Martin), brave American hostages were welcomed home from Iran, and freedoms were becoming more evident in music, fashion, and language. It appeared that the movements of the 1960s had helped America become freer and more productive.

And yet ... The "freedom" in music, fashion, and language began to manifest itself in vulgarity. *Feminism,* thought Brigid, *while moving us forward toward equality, seems to have moved us backward to an even more disturbing level of being sex objects.*

She also sensed a growing tide of upheaval. During the 1970s and 1980s, terrorism was spreading throughout the globe, most notably with the Olympic Munich massacre and later the assassination of Lord Mountbatten in England. Lebanon, Greece, and Rome fell victim to random attacks. There were tinderboxes everywhere, and this threat of violence increased Brigid's longing to be close to her family. Babs and Brigid communicated frequently and saw each other during a few Christmases at the annual family get-togethers at Mama Rose's house in Cleveland. Sometimes Brigid would travel to the West Coast and make time to share some coffee, or a glass of wine, or a bottle of wine, or two bottles of wine, or three bottles of wine, with Babs. World problems were seldom a topic. Babs's focus was on her scientific world, and Brigid sat in awe while Babs detailed her work on redesigning the optics for the Hubble telescope and other astronomical endeavors. She also loved watching Babs's face light up when she spoke of her daughter, Barbara Ann Schwartz, whom she called Annie. Babs seldom mentioned Adam.

Communication with Rosie was less frequent — phone access was sporadic in Kenya, and the nine-hour time difference made it more difficult. Brigid and Rosie corresponded through letters, with few in-person meetings during the past ten years. Brigid missed her friends more than anything else in her life.

Her discontent with academia, coupled with the hole in her soul that she could not yet name, filled her with a desire for change. Added to the funk, were disturbing signs of early menopause. By 1988, when she went home for her twenty-year class reunion, Brigid knew that it was time to move back, so she could move forward.

Chapter 3

. . . .

Until one has loved an animal, a part of
one's soul remains unawakened.

Anatole France

ROSIE

1974-1988

R ose Margaret Vanetti Scarponi was born on June 1,1950, in St. John's Hospital in Cleveland, Ohio. She bore the first and middle name of her mother, and her mother's mother, and her mother's mother's mother. She was called Rosie.

Rosie's parents, Mama Rose, and Massimo, like Brigid's parents, were childhood sweethearts and like Brigid's parents, they deepened their love while attending West Technical High School (a few years before Dar and Miklos). Together, they raised a family and owned a neighborhood grocery store on W. 65th. The neighbors elected Massimo their city councilman, a position he held until his death in 1981.

The neighborhood nourished Rosie with Italian *amore e passione*, and cultivated a wild streak that shunned intellectual pursuits, while fostering a primal connection with nature and all living things. While other children were rushing to school, she was examining caterpillars and squirrels that came across her path. Her love of animals would finally lead her to her life's accomplishments, but the road to those accomplishments was filled with wrong turns.

On a carefree afternoon in 1954, while playing with her younger brother, Ricardo, Rosie helped him climb the ladder of the sliding board in their backyard. The watchful eye of her grandmother, and the careful steadying of Rosie's hand could not prevent tragedy. Ricardo slipped through her fingers, and he somersaulted to his death. That was the infliction of a wound that would take a lifetime to heal.

At Lourdes Academy, the healing was aided through her friendships with Brigid and Babs. The three, though vastly different in their approaches to life and lifestyles, appreciated each other's uniqueness. Brigid would share literary insights and rail against unfair treatment of women; Babs would discuss rockets and interplanetary space travel; Rosie would discuss the dogs on the Russian spacecrafts. They were seekers of knowledge in different realms, which Lourdes allowed them to explore freely. Rosie, however, explored other avenues of knowledge more thoroughly than her two friends. At fifteen, she became pregnant, and soon after, miscarried. Her friends and family helped her through it, but it was another layer of guilt that she would carry for a long time.

Her summer jobs at the Cleveland Zoo allowed her to escape into the world she loved the best — the world of animals, especially elephants. She had helped with a baby Asian elephant named Aspara and watched in awe at the maternal care and affection that the female elephants unselfishly offered. Rosie's experience and discussion with other zoo workers awakened her to the horror of trophy hunting, whaling, poaching, and other atrocities that were endangering and possibly annihilating animal species. She knew early on that her calling would be to help preserve and aid the wondrous beings in the animal kingdom. But first, she would take a path that would lead her into her own personal jungle of sexual and drug-infested exploits.

After participating in radical and violent anti-war protests during her enrollment at Ohio State University, and spiraling into a world of narcotics, Rosie left home to travel the West Coast, moving from commune to commune, and engaging in the basest of behaviors. She ultimately landed in California, near death from hepatitis and venereal diseases that systematically zapped her health and immune system, as well as her self-esteem. Massimo and Mama Rose, devastated and shocked, took Rosie home, and nourished her with love and forgiveness. They paid for a psychiatrist to find the root of Rosie's problems. The deaths of Ricardo, Martin, and her unborn baby emerged as the leading causes of her descent. Babs and Brigid visited her as often as possible and provided the care and humor that only friends could offer.

Rosie recovered, stayed drug free, and graduated from Cleveland State University a few years later. She earned a job in Washington DC with the Humane Society where she would investigate horrific abuses of animals. She also worked with the McGovern for President campaign, where she saw first-hand the dirty tricks from the Nixon campaign, whom she called the "Nixon motherfuckers." While she was reveling in the downfall of Richard Nixon, she met a graduate student studying Journalism at Georgetown University, Samuel Scarponi, whom she called Sammy. After one date, the electric dynamics between them suggested that they were a perfect match. Securing a grant to investigate the ivory trade in San Francisco's Chinatown, Sammy and Rosie traveled the West Coast and grew in love for each other, while deepening their commitment to save and conserve the elephant population and habitats. They were married in 1975, and soon after, moved to Africa in 1976, where Sammy would write articles for a conservationist magazine, and Rosie would eventually work in Nairobi National Park, caring for elephants.

When they touched down in Nairobi, Kenya, after a bumpy flight, and an even bumpier landing, Sammy looked at Rosie, and said, "Are you ready for this?"

To which Rosie replied, "I've been ready for this my entire life."

They walked into the airport, greeted by smiling, ebony faces, and were directed to the bus that would take them to Nairobi National Park, where they were to meet Daphne Sheldrick, whose husband had just been appointed director of the park.

Mrs. Sheldrick now lived in Nairobi National Park, having recently been transplanted from her beloved Tsavo. Although she was very kind and overwhelmingly caring to the animals in the park, she carried a hint of melancholy that she told Rosie and Sammy was a result of her recent move. She and her husband, David, had lived in the Tsavo National Park since 1955 and had built, modernized, and transformed Tsavo into a haven for orphaned animals.

She also informed Rosie and Sammy that as a result of this recent relocation, the park was not yet prepared to employ

Rosie. However, she did arrange for them to spend one week at Tsavo, during which time they could decide where to go in Africa until Rosie's employment could be settled.

"Well, this is another fine mess you've gotten us into," Sammy laughed as he and Rosie settled in their tent late that evening, with sounds of roaring lions and a yelping rhinoceros echoing in the not-so-distant surroundings.

"It is what it is," Rosie said with an anxious sigh, feeling extremely defensive. "At least we get to spend time in Tsavo and I can get a taste of what still might happen and you can write and then we can travel through Africa as you write your articles and I can observe and learn and maybe in a while when things get more organized here we can go back to our original plan and come back here and live happily ever after and oh my God, Sammy, I am so sorry. Screw me."

"With pleasure," Sammy said.

They spent their first night in Africa consummating their arrival.

The week that Rosie and Sammy spent in Tsavo confirmed that their decision to work and live in Africa was a choice that fed their souls. While Sammy wrote about the vast, lush landscape of the Kenyan terrain, and the vibrant colors of the sunrise, Rosie deepened her innate ties with the elephants that lived in this sanctuary. The Sheldricks had built a haven for animals and humans, and never before had Rosie felt so close to the spirit that transcends through all creation.

In one of her first letters to Brigid (with a preface that

Brigid put away her red pen — Rosie never did master neither good grammar nor correct word choice) she wrote,

I always thought that we did such a good job at the zoo, helping the animals feel like they were in their natural habitat, but oh my God, to actually see them in the wild and so close, nothing compares. I watch them turn on faucets with their trunks, and lift the tiniest of fragments from the ground. And they actually know the personality of each worker, and though their skins are leathery tough, they are so sensitive to touch that they can feel a person's mood through the person's fingertips. They sway to the beats of the caretakers' hums and drums, and they sense danger and love better than humans. And yet these magnificent creatures are still poached and hunted and their numbers have been reduced and there is fear they may be hunted to oblivion. People like the Sheldricks are sacrificing everything to nourish and care for these elephants who have been orphaned by either human cruelty or drought or abandonment. My heart cries with both joy and sadness.

Screweth the man,
Rosie

The week-long stay at Tsavo seemed brief, but Rosie and Sammy absorbed every minute and observed both the beauty and the dangers of life in the African wild. Rosie was especially fearful of the giant red ant hills that dotted the land, and the snakes that slithered around them. Sammy was very cognizant of the thorny bushes and thick brush that remained untamed around the sanctuary so as to deter the man-eating lions and other animals not always friendly to humans. However, the sight of the workers bringing in wounded elephants and rhinoceroses from the wild, and weaning them back to health, was enough to cement the Scarponis' commitment to remaining in Africa and helping to save these creatures, these ancient, evolutionary wonders of life.

On the night before they were to leave Tsavo, Sammy once again needed assurance from Rosie. "We are about to travel through some dangerous territory. My next assignment is the areas around Lake Victoria — I'm not sure what we will need to do to get there. You didn't sign up for this part of our journey, Rosie; are you totally sure you want to go? Lions are not the only things we may encounter."

"Lions?"

"And tigers."

"And bears."

"Oh my!" They laughed in unison.

They drifted into peaceful slumber in each other's arms, confident that whatever Africa had to offer, they would enjoy or conquer, together.

During the following months of 1976, Africa extended to Rosie and Sammy its tender, boundless beauty, and wild, distinctive dangers. They dodged the dangers of Ebola in Zaire, and the uprisings in Soweto, as well as the fallout from the terrorist raid on Entebbe. Every turn had a danger, but the magnificence of the land and the friendliness of the peoples far outweighed the political and health hazards.

Rosie was grateful for the surprisingly moderate climate

with temperatures not rising higher than eighty-five degrees.

"Didn't you do your research?" Sammy asked. "Summer months are the best times to travel."

"No, I didn't," said Rosie. "That's why I married you; I don't like to read. But I have seen enough picture books to know a lion when I see one, and there is one not too far from the Jeep, and I'm really not too anxious to cuddle with it. I much prefer elephants."

Sammy stopped the Jeep and zoomed his camera to get a clean picture of the lion. His assignments ranged from writing about the wildlife and the peoples, to the various geographical features of the continent. Rosie loved every minute of it, but the lions did raise the hairs on her arms in fright. Despite Rosie's fears, they arrived at their destinations without supplying any lions a feast of human flesh.

One of their first lodgings was The Mountains of the Moon hotel in Fort Portal, Uganda, which awarded the couple with a spectacular and mystical panoramic view of the Rwenzori Mountains. The mountains dazzled with blazing white snow caps on the highest peaks, complemented with exuberant foliage and trees on the slopes. Sammy wrote, "The vast and all-encompassing greenery of the bountiful landscape rivals the verdant glow of Ireland."

Can't wait till Brigid reads that, Rosie thought.

There were several European guests at the hotel, including Irish and English tea plantation owners. The Irishmen scoffed at the comparison to their homeland, but the Englishmen commented that the lush acres of the tea estates created a verdurous image that was second to none.

One of the Brits, as the English were called, struck up a

conversation with Rosie and Sammy. He relished in telling tales of African folklore and the history of Britain's relationship with the African countries. The Ugandans called him Bwana Roger, and Rosie and Sammy enjoyed his stories and his seemingly endless knowledge of the continent. Bwana Roger was also well connected, and by the end of the evening, he had introduced the couple to Bob Astels, a chief administrator within the regime of Idi Amin, the Ugandan leader. Rosie shuddered at the mention of Amin; she had heard the rumors of his atrocities against civilians, and the support he had given to the terrorists who hijacked the Jewish travelers, giving them permission to land at Entebbe. Astels invited them all to dine at the presidential palace in Kampala, and before Rosie could decline, Sammy replied with an adamant, "Sure!"

It was the first major argument of their young marriage, carried on in their room later that night.

"This guy is a madman and a ruthless killer, and an anti-semite, and as racist as Hitler. How could you agree to meet him, never mind eat with him? He has massacred his own people, expelled the Asians from the country, and he's not very fond of white people. God knows what, or whom, he will serve for dinner! Porca puttana!" Rosie resorted to Italian cussing when English just would not do.

Unfazed, Sammy said, "There is Pulitzer material in my article if I get to interview or see first-hand who and what this guy is. Kampala is a few hours away and was our next stop anyhow. We will have a safe journey with Astel, and along the way, see an abundance of animals, including your beloved elephants. Meeting Amin is the chance of a lifetime;

I really didn't think you would object. We usually share the same attitude toward adventure."

"Next time, ask," Rosie shouted, as she threw a blanket and pillow out of their bedroom, onto the cot in the living room where Sammy would be spending the night.

The next day, as they drove the murram roads to Kampala, the villages of Kyegegwa, Kyenjojo, and Mubende provided a spectacular array of zebra, topi, eland, elephant, buffalo, waterbuck, bushbuck, reedbuck, and sitatunga sightings. Rosie kept a list of everything she saw. On the way, they stopped to help in the rescue of a baby elephant who was stuck in the mud. The flailing and wailing of the creature deeply affected Rosie. After the rescue was complete, the team told her that they would be sending the elephant to the Sheldrick place. Apparently, Daphne Sheldrick was working on a special milk formula that was shown to be successful in nourishing the rescued animals. She whispered to Sammy: "This is what I'm here for. I just keep sinking further into the spell of this place. It is all just awesome."

"Does this mean I can sleep in a bed tonight? Sammy purred.

"Yeah," Rosie replied. "You can sleep with Amin."

Upon arriving at the palace, four armed Nubian mercenaries ushered them quickly to a large bathroom-like area where they could wash and change. Rosie had insisted they would not spend the night in the palace. (Many years later they discovered that several locations, including the palace, were the scenes of torture and grisly persecutions ordered by Amin.)

Boneless tilapia covered in white sauce and rice, roast goat, cassava, and millet bread filled the tables of Amin's dinner spread, along with hundreds of oranges. Other dinner guests included Fiat car dealers, upscale diesel repairmen, and a small group of women. These women wore beautiful colored robes, with v-lined openings that reached their navels, and slits up the sides that swayed with every movement, leaving nothing to the imagination as to what lay beneath.

When one of the guests asked why there were so many oranges, Amin grinned with a wicked smile, and answered, "They make my whopper grow big, very big. Makes boinking better."

A nervous laughter filtered through the room. Amin waved an arm, and one of the girls brought in a large, jewel-bedecked box that was filled with sex toys of every imaginable size and shape. Amin described the uses and details of each one. Sammy leaned over to Rosie, and said, "Forget the Pulitzer; we are out of here as soon as dessert is finished."

They spent the night at a nearby lodging. Rosie was the first to climb into bed. When Sammy reappeared from the bathroom, he found Rosie wearing nothing but a devious smile, as she placed an orange on his pillow.

Rosie and Sammy traveled the wonders of several African countries. Sammy was well paid for his articles, which included insightful descriptions and stories of the vast vistas and curious cultures of each. After a year of these adventures, Rosie received word from the Tsavo administration that they now had a position for her, and she could return to Kenya anytime before October to begin her new job. She wrote to Babs:

July, 1977
Babs,

Well, here I am writing from the heart of Africa. I feel freer when I write to you, because with Brigid I always have a vision of her marking up my words with her professorial red pen. Love that girl. Currently, I am in Ankole on a tea estate in Western Uganda, overlooking the greenest landscape you can imagine. Babs, Africa defies description, but I will try. In the past year I have traveled through Uganda, Rwanda, Mozambique, Zimbabwe, and Zaire. Didn't spend too much time in Zaire because the roads were so bad. We learned from our British friend that the Belgians did not take good care of their colonies so Zaire was far behind in modernizing and comforts. But man-made things are not the attraction here. While traveling around the equator it left me breathless to see snow capped mountains and forests within the same blink of an eye.

In Rwanda, everywhere I looked was amazing. It is called the Land of a Thousand Hills. You can guess why. But you have to see it to believe the beauty of the rolling hills and the five volcanoes with their dark, black crust. And the coffee, served by beautiful, ebony women in beautifully colored clothes would make you swoon. I will never have Maxwell House again. Rwanda is also the place where Diane Fosse has her gorilla safety zone. Oh, Babs, the sight of these gorillas touches me so deeply, and the poaching of these, as well as the elephants, sickens me to the core. It is rampant. I wish people could just see and understand these magnificent animals. But animals aren't the only beings that are being destroyed. Sammy did an article on the Twa pygmy population. Farming and the land destruction is beginning to take away much of the forests where they hunted and gathered their food. I was able to talk to them through an interpreter, and I understood that they only took from the land what they needed to survive. The first conservationists. They were as close to ancient humans as I will ever get.

We have also traveled through bamboo forests. It's hard to believe these are grass and not trees. When I see you again, I will be filled with tales and share Sammy's photos. Elephants are the reason I came to Africa, and though I've been swallowed up by all of the other wonders of this place, I am happy to report that I will be finally going to Tsavo in October, and that's where we will be settling down. Although I will miss traveling, I am looking forward to being in one place. Oh, and one thing I keep seeing in elephant herds is something called "all mothering." That's a behavior in which all female adult elephants take care of each other's pups.

So here's why that's important:

Babs, I am pregnant!! I am due in December. It hasn't affected our plans until now. I'm very tired and am getting a big belly. The people at Tsavo said they are excited to have a birth of a person for a change! Hahaha They will all help with the care of the baby. A human all-mothering.

Sammy is still under contract to write about different locations so I definitely will need help. Who knows, seeing how slow mail is, by the time you get this, I may have already had the baby.

Please share the news with Brigid. Lord, I wish you two could be here. We are near a phone now, and I'm about to call my mother.

Love you,
Rosie

Phone service was not widely available in the countries Rosie visited, but Sammy went out of his way to find one, and

Rosie called her mother. The connection was filled with static, but that was no problem for this Italian family who did not know the meaning of speaking softly. They each took turns grabbing the phone.

"Mama! Mama — it's Rosie!"

"Oh my God. Hey everyone, Rosie is calling from that place! Where are you? You are not near Ebola, are you? Or that awful cannibal Idi Amin? Are you safe? Is Sammy treating you well? Are you getting enough pasta?"

"Mama, I am in Uganda, and I don't know how long the connection will be. I have to tell you something important!"

"Rosie, this is Robert. I got a part in the school play. Can you come home to see me? I miss you, but it is great having my own room since you left."

"Hi, it's Rebecca. Cousin Beth got a ticket for driving under the influence. Big family scandal. She said now she's gonna stick to pot."

"Please, get Mama back on the phone."

"OK, it's your mother. Did you have something to tell me? If you're going to tell me how happy you are there, I don't want to hear it. There's a lot going on here; you should be home."

"Mama, please listen for just a moment. I am pregnant."

If ever there was something called a pregnant pause, this was it.

"Oh, my little Rosie. That is wonderful. And I assume you will be coming home to have the baby and be with your family now. I'm emotional right now. How are you feeling? When are you coming home?"

"Mama, I am staying here to have and raise the baby. This is my home now."

"It might be where you live, dear daughter, but it is not your home."

"We are going to get disconnected soon, Mama; I will write more in a letter. It is so nice to hear your voice. I will be back in Kenya soon, starting my new job; it will be easier to write from there. The baby is due in December. I am happy here. But that doesn't mean I don't miss and love you all so much."

"She's hanging up now, everyone," Mama said, with obvious sobs in her throat.

"Good-bye Rosie, we love you!"

"Please," Mama said faintly. "Please keep in touch and be careful."

"I will, Mama. We will talk again soon."

The line went dead, and mother and daughter fell to their chairs as heavy tears fell from their eyes.

Ricardo Samuel Scarponi was born on Thursday, December 15, 1977, weighing in at seven pounds, seven ounces. A torrential rainstorm, and Rosie's swift uterine dilation, prevented the planned trip to the Nairobi hospital, so Ricardo came into the world at the hands of a mkunga, a Kenyan midwife. Rosie's occasional piercing grunts were drowned out by the steady pounding of the rains on the makuti-thatched roof, and the distant, thundering sounds of the Kori bustard bird whose howls accurately predicted the heavy rainstorms. The natural birth was a fitting beginning for Rosie's first son, who would spend his childhood in an environment surrounded by the natural beauty and sounds of the wild.

Sammy stayed in the birthing room, and his macho

manliness melted away as he held his son. The household was exuberant with the news of the new human baby who would share their love and their home.

Rosie was hired not only to assist in the care of the animals, but to establish education programs for the villagers as well as any Western visitors. As a result, she was afforded a staff and private residence. There were two maids and a part-time cook. The animal keepers often came in to ogle over the baby, as they hummed the rhythms of their tribe. Rosie healed quickly, and after two weeks, Sammy was comfortable leaving for his next assignment. They were bidding each other farewell, when one of the staff entered the room and informed them there was a special guest waiting on the veranda.

When they reached the veranda, a slight shockwave shook their bodies. There stood Mama Rose, frozen in fright, as a dik dik licked her heels.

"Get this creature away from me, and let me hold my grandson," she bellowed.

Mama stayed for a week, during which time she handled all late-night feedings, and sang the songs that she had sung to Rosie when she was a baby. The melodies of "You Are My Sunshine" and "Jesus Loves Me" echoed through the house, as Mama gently rocked and cradled Ricardo. Rosie was well rested and smiled at the sight of her mother holding her child.

"My first baby's first baby," Mama would whisper to the dik dik, of whom she grew quite fond.

A deep joy permeated her soul when she learned that Rosie had scheduled a priest from Nairobi to visit Tsavo and baptize Ricardo. In just one week, Mama was able to witness a fulfilled daughter, a magical homestead, and the traditional ceremony of her first grandchild being welcomed into the Catholic faith. Every evening as she watched the pink and orange laced sunset, she would thank God for her many blessings. She jokingly, or perhaps not so jokingly, told Rosie that if the baby hadn't been baptized soon, she would have taken him to one of the water holes and baptized him herself — with the elephants as witnesses. Rosie didn't think that was funny as she watched Mama Rose's unrepentant smile.

When her mother was preparing to leave, Rosie said, "This meant so much to me, Mama. Thank you. Thank you. Thank you. It was wonderful seeing you and all of the notes and cards and news from my family. I love the Cleveland Browns pajamas for Ricardo. And yes, I remember that my brother Ricardo wore similar Browns outfits. I know that nothing about this could have been easy for you. You helped me in more ways that I can say."

"I'm proud of you, Rosie. This place is rugged but beautiful. The animals are amazing, and already I can see the love you have for them and they for you. And Sammy is a mother's answer to prayers. I feel much better now that I see all of this."

"Thank you, Mama."

"But I still want you home."

"Of course."

Rosie delved into motherhood and her work with her characteristic vigor and compassion. Her professional duties alternated between care for the elephants and various orphaned wildlife that entered the sanctuary, as well as providing education to visitors on the importance of preserving the habitat and eliminating the outrageous poaching that was pushing some animals to extinction. Her housemaids taught her how to swathe Ricardo in a cloth that tied around her body to hold him firmly on her back. She was surprised to hear how antagonistic the Kenyan women were regarding prams, or strollers.

"Baby must feel the mother," they would say. "The baby moves with the rhythm of your hips and feels your warmth. Prams are bad. What you call playpens are also bad. Babies need to be free. No cages."

As a result, the elephants came to know Ricardo, and would gently nudge or even coddle him with their trunks when Rosie fed and washed them. When Ricardo learned to crawl, he would play in the veranda surrounded by keepers and mongoose and the croaking of hundreds of tree frogs which filled the air with musical chimes and soothing rhythms, along with other not-so-soothing sounds of monkeys scurrying through the trees. By the time Ricardo was one year old, he could point and identify giraffes, rhinos, elephants, and zebras.

Sammy was traveling the continent but was never gone for more than two weeks, and returned from his trips with stories of both animal and human cultures such as the lion populations in Mozambique and the Tutsi population in Rwanda. While he was home, he doted on Ricardo and Rosie, bringing trinkets and relics from the places he visited, and helping with the animals and chores of the household.

In February of 1979, Rosie received word that Babs and Brigid would be in Cleveland for professional seminars, which by chance were scheduled on the same dates in March. She had also received letters from her brother, Reynaldo, that seemed to express an angst that worried her. Rosie and

Sammy discussed her leaving the baby and her job, and there seemed to be no obstacles that would prevent her from leaving for one week. Four of those days would be travel days, so that left three days for an actual visit. Nevertheless, she felt it was worth it, and it would be wonderful to spend time with her friends and family. Within a week, she was in Cleveland.

Reynaldo met her at Hopkins International Airport. He gave her a hearty hug and she held back tears, observing how much he had changed in such a short amount of time. She felt anxiety in his hug, as she did in his letters. But the airport was always an exciting place for Rosie, and she would wait for a serious conversation with her brother. For now, as she walked through the terminal, she smiled as she felt the familiarity of home. Browns and Indians shirts and paraphernalia filled the shops along with the Cavaliers basketball merchandise. Books about the Cleveland Orchestra and Art Museum were on display in every shop.

She remembered that in high school, on dateless Friday nights, the girls would dress up and walk through the airport, just for something to do. On nights when they had dates, they would be parked outside the airport, "watching the planes" as they steamed up the car windows with adolescent foreplay.

By the time they reached the car, Africa was already fading in the distance in her mind, but she made it a point to send a telegram to the Nairobi station to inform Sammy that she had arrived safely.

As they were driving to her family home at W.61st and Detroit, Reynaldo began to confide.

"Rosie, I am very grateful that you are here. Things have

been difficult for me, and I just have to break loose before I head for New York."

"Moving to New York isn't breaking loose enough?" Rosie laughed, trying to lighten a mood that suddenly grew very dark.

"I'm just going to say it. It's not easy."

"Jesus, Reynaldo, are you sick? Is it Mom? Dad?" Rosie's angst now matched Reynaldo's.

"Rosie, I'm gay."

"Pull over," Rosie said quietly.

A bead of sweat dripped from Reynaldo's brow. Rosie was the one person he thought he could count on for love and support. He turned down Denison Avenue, hindered by orange barrels and fluorescent cones. Finally, he parked on the side of the road, and looked at Rosie with hopeful anticipation and a bit of dread.

Rosie hugged him as warmly as anyone has ever hugged. She looked in his eyes and said, "I wish I could think of a million ways to say what I feel. But all I can think of is to say, I love you. I love you so much, Reynaldo."

"I don't need a million ways," Reynaldo said. "Those words are more than enough."

They remained parked as Reynaldo told her of the teasing and sometimes violent behavior that came his way at Saint Ignatius, the all-male Catholic school on Cleveland's West Side. Saint Ignatius was nationally known on all levels of achievement: academics, athletics, music, and scholastic excellence. Obviously, though, it wasn't perfect.

"I never came out, but I felt the wrath anyhow. The wrath of someone who didn't meet the criteria of a macho Wildcat.

My years at Cleveland State University were a little easier because I found a niche of friends with whom I could share and be myself."

"Have you told Mom or Dad?" Rosie asked.

"Nope, gonna do that when we get home, with you by my side," Reynaldo smiled.

"You must know it's all going to be OK."

"One thing I've learned is that you never know. I have a couple friends who came out to their liberal parents, and now they are pretty much banned from their family gatherings."

"Not gonna happen," Rosie said. But Reynaldo's words echoed in her thoughts: *But you never know.*

When they turned on to 61st Street, a barrage of whooping and hollering met them. Aunts, uncles, cousins, and Rosie's other siblings, Rebecca and Robert, held up multicolored "Welcome Home" signs, adorned with drawings of the flags of the United States, Kenya, and Italy.

"Is this another one of Mama's ploys to make me feel guilty? Rosie asked Reynaldo.

"No, I think it's a genuine 'we are happy to see you' sentiment."

"I think you might want to wait for your coming-out party."

"Good call."

Rosie loved the attention and laughed at the familiar beckonings of "Eat some more pasta, you've gotten so skinny." And the sincere, expected inquiries: "Where the hell is Kenya, anyhow?"

After dinner, everyone gathered around the photos of baby Ricardo Scarponi and the awesome sights of the vistas of

Africa. The day ended with tears and laughter at the statue of Saint Ricardo, imported from Italy, and placed in the garden by Grandma Clemente, Mama Rose's mother, a few months after the death of Rosie's brother, Ricardo.

When everyone went home, Mama and Rosie and Papa Massimo sat at the dining room table where so many meals were shared in joy and sadness. As memories flooded the conversations, Rosie felt a slight pang of regret that her family in Kenya would miss these firsthand connections of familial roots. The hours sped by, and at midnight, Reynaldo appeared with a bottle of wine. He spoke firmly and lovingly, with no apprehension.

"Mama and Papa, I can no longer wait to share something with you. It is life-changing, and I simply must tell you before I go to truly start my new life in New York. It will most likely change how you look at me or even perhaps be a disappointment, but ..."

"Reynaldo, what?" Mama demanded, as Papa sat with obvious concern.

"I am a gay man. I am gay, and all that entails. I am comfortable with it, and I hope you can understand, and I ..."

Mama took his hands, and gently responded, "My sweet boy, did you think I didn't know?"

Reynaldo buried his tears in his mother's palms. When he looked up, he saw his father smiling strangely.

"Papa?"

Papa walked over and put his hands on Reynaldo's shoulders.

"Forgive my smile, which I'm sure looks out of place. But I'm not as astute as your mother. I was afraid you were going to tell us you got a girl pregnant."

Now, half sobbing and half laughing, Rosie and her brother, and her parents, spent the rest of the night reminiscing about Reynaldo's childhood and how he would coax his brothers and sisters and cousins into performing in his theater productions, and how he loved to play house, and how he softly would console others during hard times when the rest of the Italian brood was fraught with loud emotion and hand-wringing.

Reynaldo had never felt so loved.

The next day, Rosie, Babs, and Brigid met for a late dinner at Don's Lighthouse on Lake Avenue in the Edgewater neighborhood that they all loved. Rosie was anxious to get back to Africa, and Babs and Brigid were visibly stressed from their work at their respective conferences downtown. Their anxieties dissolved into the comforting solace of their friendship. Brigid gave updates on her career and romances. When she relayed the story of Jay Vargo and her breakup because he went to a bachelor party in Vegas, Rosie couldn't resist.

"Brigid, seriously, you are going to be an old maid if you don't give the men in your life some slack."

Brigid responded, "You mean you would be OK with Sammy cavorting with whores, and engaging in lewd conduct with topless lap dancers?"

Rosie looked at Babs and shrugged her shoulders. "Where the hell does she come up with this stuff? 'Cavorting with whores, lewd conduct,' good Lord, who talks like that!?"

She turned to Brigid and said, "Well, I wouldn't dump him, I would just rip his balls off. By the way, that's testicles in Brigid-speak. Forgive and forget — and make him pay. That's what good marriages are made of."

Always the pragmatist, Babs offered her take on the subject. "Being married is different than just being in a relationship. The commitment is deeper, and the obligation to work things out is more profound. You are freer to dump a guy, for whatever reason you want, when you're single. Both of your solutions work for me, each within its own particular circumstance."

"God, how the hell did I ever survive with you two eggheads?" Rosie laughed.

"The three women took a sip of their drinks, Rosie with a Merlot, Brigid with a Bacardi and Coke, and Babs with a Margarita. When Babs and Rosie heard the news about Reynaldo, their reaction was a spontaneous outpouring of support and encouragement, as they shared stories about his talents as well as the troubles he must have suffered through. Then Rosie shared the photos of Ricardo and Africa, and the night became saturated with oodles of awws and ahhs. It ended with a toast to their upcoming June birthdays and their final years in their twenties.

When it was time to go back to Africa, dozens of the Vanetti and Clemente clan walked Rosie to the airport gate, each hugging and whispering advice.

From Mama: "Come home."

From Papa: "We are always a plane ride away, if you need something."

From Uncle Sam: "Never forget where you came from."

From Uncle Johnny: "Stay away from cannibals."

And from cousin Beth: "Send me some of that banghi."

Reynaldo was the last one to whisper: "Thank you," as he hesitated to let go of his hug.

⌒

Sammy and Ricardo were waiting for Rosie when she landed at Nairobi airport. No servants or helpers made the trip; Sammy and Rosie wanted alone time as a family. On the bumpy ride back to Tsavo, Rosie shared the news from Cleveland. She had called Sammy's parents, who still lived in Washington DC. They said to tell Sammy how much they missed him, and how they enjoyed the photos of Ricardo that Sammy had sent. She also reported that his father was suffering from gout flare-ups, and that his mother had her cataracts removed. Simple reminders of the mundane family life they left behind, but still missed.

Ricardo snuggled with Rosie on her lap for the full four-hour trip to Tsavo.

"So," Sammy said. "It sounds like you had a wonderful time. Still no regrets about moving so far away?

Rosie reached her free hand to Sammy's. "It was a very special time, and I enjoyed every minute of it. But I will try never to leave you or Ricardo again. I do regret that our children won't know the warmth and insanity of their extended family. But I belong here. My heart ached every night thinking of Ricardo missing me, and you in our empty bed."

Relieved, Sammy laughed, "Well, I kinda liked not having a leg kicking my back all night."

"I will make up for it," Rosie said, as she kicked his calf.

They made it back to the sanctuary with no human or animal obstacles, and life quickly went back to a normal routine of feeding, washing, and communicating with the animals. The keepers and staff started calling Ricardo "Ricky," and that was the name he now answered to. Life at the sanctuary breathed a fresh spirit of the natural marvels of creation into Rosie and Ricky.

When Ricky was three years old, Sammy began to take him on excursions through the many forests and woodlands that were less than a day's drive from the sanctuary. Ricky's favorite place was Lake Nakuru, where millions of pink flamingos would gather to eat the algae from the alkaline waters. The blanket of pink that covered the water was a spectacle that soaked Ricky's consciousness with a love for birds, as well as deepened his connection with the balance of nature. The black rhinos that roamed the area also filled him with awe, and at three years old, he already walked to the rhythms and sang the melodies of the natural world.

These father-son excursions provided Rosie with solitary freedom to nurse her elephants. Each one had a name, and each had its own personality. Sometimes the Tsavo wildlife rangers would find a mother elephant riddled with poison dart wounds and other evidence of poachers slouching through the Park. She would try desperately to care for her pup who clung close by. The elephants were hauled to the sanctuary where Rosie and the keepers would try to mend the wounds and feed the pup. Often, the mothers would not survive the ordeal, and the other female elephants in the sanctuary would rally to care for the little one. There was friendly competition among the baby elephants who vied for Rosie's attention, and more rigorous competition for territory and affection among the older elephants. Rosie used these human characteristics to educate the human mothers of the villages on the need to respect these wondrous beasts who had feelings and needs similar to their own. Feelings of motherhood transcended the animal-human connection. Rosie often wept when a baby elephant she had nurtured had grown and matured, and left the sanctuary to live in the wild. The elephants were succored by the human companionship and returned the affection, but eventually, one day, they would go to the distant waterhole, and never return.

Despite the demands of the sanctuary, Rosie managed to teach Ricky the basic curriculum of preschool and first and second-grade reading and arithmetic. Many British children attended the boarding school in Nairobi, but Rosie and Sammy could not bear the thought of Ricky leaving their care, so they made a commitment to make sure he knew academics, as well as the workings of the natural world that surrounded him. Once a month they traveled the two hours to Lake Nakuru to attend Mass and have Ricky attend catechism classes. In May 1984, Ricky received his First Holy Communion. Mama Rose had sent him a Communion Prayer Book, a rosary, and a scapular. Babs and Brigid chipped in to buy Rosie and Sammy a videocassette recorder and a camera to record the event. From that time on, Ricky's progress and the activity in the sanctuary were recorded and sent on video cassettes to the families and friends back in the States. Once a month, the Vanetti family in Cleveland would gather for "movie night" and sit with glee as they munched on popcorn, watching their Rosie and her family live amongst the wonderland that was Africa.

The Cleveland families also sent cassettes to Rosie. Ricky was enthralled to see his grandparents and the extended family of Italians who were very different from his peaceful friends in the Sanctuary.

Rosie began to observe something more startling, however. Mama Rose and Massimo would send videos when they visited Reynaldo in New York, and both Rosie and Sammy noticed how thin and tired Reynaldo looked. Massimo also did not have his characteristic vigor and lively step. The grayness of his pallor was worrisome.

One night in June, Sammy woke to find Rosie crying, alone in the living room, watching the latest cassette of her mother and father and Reynaldo walking through Central Park. Mama was between the two men, at times appearing to hold them both up by the elbows.

Sammy put his arms around Rosie, and when their eyes met, he said, "You have to go."

"Thank you, Sammy. I dread leaving you and Ricky, but yes, I feel if I wait any longer, it may be too late. But there is something I have to tell you. I'm two months pregnant. I was going to wait one more month to tell you. Since we have had so much trouble getting pregnant again, I wanted to wait to be sure."

"Rosie, Rosie, Rosie! I had just about given up. Please tell me you are as happy as I am."

"Of course I am, numb nuts. I'm beyond happy."

After a moment of silence, as if thinking aloud, Sammy said, "But it does add a bit of worry to your making the trip, doesn't it?"

"Yes. I will have an examination by the doctor in Nairobi, and if all looks good, I will schedule the trip as soon as possible."

Two weeks later, after a bumpy, muddy ride to Nairobi in a torrential rainstorm, Rosie's doctor gave her the OK to travel. The flight to New York was smoother than the ride to the doctor's office. When she walked down the ramp to the gate at LaGuardia Airport, she was jolted into euphoria when she saw Babs and Brigid through the windows, waving frantically, and carrying signs that said, "Welcome Home, Dr. Doolittle!"

The girls hugged and giggled like children, as they explained to Rosie that Mama Rose had told them of Rosie's visit. They were only in New York for the day and had made reservations for lunch. It would have been a special reunion under any circumstances, but it was also in the month of June 1980, and they would once again be together to celebrate their birthdays — this one, the big 3-0.

After the greetings, Rosie said, "Well, it looks like I am again cavorting with whores, and possibly engaging in lewd behavior."

To which Brigid replied, "Hopefully, that will be more enjoyable than cleaning up elephant excrement. Oh, by the way, that would be shit in Rosie-speak."

The laughter and gaiety continued through their lunch in the Windows of the World restaurant, on the 106th floor of the World Trade Center. The food was surprisingly mediocre, but the stunning view of Manhattan, and the ambience of fanciness, provided the atmosphere that the women needed to celebrate their special day. The conversation made a turn, however, when Rosie began to talk about Reynaldo.

"I don't know how much my mother told you, but Reynaldo has what they call AIDS, Acquired Immune Deficiency Syndrome."

"Damn. No, she had not told us," Babs said. "It is rampant

in the California gay community. Horrifying in so many ways."

Brigid added, "I'm so sorry, Rosie. From what I've read, it's a terrible disease that they don't know what to do with."

Rosie continued. "It is ravaging large sections of Africa too. They are saying it may have originated from eating meat from infected monkeys. The virus was transmitted from the blood of the monkeys to the meat. It then spread from the monkey meat to the hunters, to the wives, and to the children. I have heard the keepers at the sanctuary say that the prostitutes, truckers, and soldiers, have infected thousands throughout Africa. Sammy said that he has seen the ghastly effects across all of the western countries of the continent." Rosie's eyes filled with tears as she concluded. "And now. And now, it is destroying my little brother. And my mother and father are there to witness their son's descent into decay. It is devastating... and I live seven thousand miles away."

The women remained silent as each of them absorbed the sadness of the moment, and the torment of their friend.

Finally, Brigid spoke. "You are here now, Rosie. You will offer them a reprieve and an oasis of comfort, knowing that you traveled those thousands of miles to be with them. Your presence will be a much-needed gift. Even more special than as if you would have been here all the while. Because you have not been part of their darkness, you will bring in light."

Again, a hush.

"I miss you," Rosie sighed.

"Ditto," said Babs and Brigid in unison.

"Well, I hope this lightens the conversation," Babs said. "I'm pregnant. Four months."

Squeals emerged from the thirty, going on fifteen, year-olds.

"So happy for you," Brigid shrieked.

"Oh my God, you had sex," Rosie laughed as she patted Babs's stomach.

"Haha, yes a few times," said Babs.

Babs and Rosie exchanged pregnancy anecdotes, but Rosie did not share her present condition. This was Babs's turn.

Soon, time flew, as it always does. Another hug, another goodbye. Babs and Brigid hailed a taxi to LaGuardia, and Rosie decided to wheel her suitcase down the long walk to West Greenwich Village where Reynaldo lived. She trekked along Hudson Street, enjoying her alone time, even though she was surrounded by busy New Yorkers. Normally, she would be tempted to venture off the beaten path to see the sights on the cobbled streets of Washington Mews, but today her thoughts stayed focused on her families — the one she was returning to, and the one she left. Her heart already panged for Sammy and Ricky, as she fantasized about the growing embryo she was carrying in her womb. She imagined the crib that her house helpers would build, and the gentle lessons about fauna and foliage that big brother would share with his baby sibling. She remembered the elephants' bewildered, and then protective reactions to sharing her affections with a tiny human when Ricky was born. These musings carried her halfway to the Village. When she reached the halfway point, her thoughts turned to what awaited her in a tiny apartment on W. 10th. A feeling of dread came upon her as she drew closer. Even the atmosphere began to change, as suits and ties on the men, and dresses and heels on the women, gave way to jeans and headbands, and leather vests and sandals. She reflected upon the notion that if this was a different occasion, she would be soaking up the free-spiritedness and audacious lifestyles that floated across her path as she reached the Village. Today, however, all she envisioned was the deteriorating body of her brother and the weary tenacity of her parents.

The long walk exhausted her, and when she reached Reynaldo's building, she barely summoned up enough energy to walk up the steps to his second-floor apartment. As she approached closer, she could smell the garlic and spices of oregano and basil that seeped through the door. *Mama Rose is here,* she thought, smiling to herself. Rosie knocked, and before she could catch a breath, her father opened the door.

"Rosie!" he shouted, taking her luggage with his right arm and hugging her to his chest with his left. "It is so good to see you!"

Rosie's eyes surveyed the scene, and stopped when she saw the thin, pale body of Reynaldo reclining on the gray, worn couch. She walked over to him, conjuring up the strength not to break down in tears at the sight of the frail ghost that lay before her.

"Hello, sister," Reynaldo whispered.

"My dear, dear brother," Rosie whispered back.

Mama Rose was watching from the kitchen with her tomato-stained apron, hair frizzed from the steam rising from the boiling water into which she would soon pour her homemade pasta. She walked over and embraced both of her children, holding them close to her still-voluminous breasts. Rosie noticed in sadness that her mother's face had lost the pinkish luster that previously exuded vibrancy and vigor. Instead, the olive skin tone of an aging, Italian matriarch, revealed a mother whose life was being sapped by witnessing the slow, fading life of her son.

They, at first, ignored the shadow of death and sorrow that encompassed the room. Rosie shared the photos of Ricky and Sammy and the wonders of Africa. Massimo and Reynaldo examined each photo as if they were holding a treasure of great worth. Although they had seen numerous videos, there was an intrinsically more personal connection when touching and holding an actual piece of Rosie's life. Both her father and her brother were especially moved as they held the photos of Ricky.

"Am I imagining that he looks so much like our little Ricardo who lives with the angels?" Massimo asked.

"No, Papa, I think of that often. Even though baby Ricardo was only two years old when he died, and I was only four, there are times when my Ricky will smile, and I feel that I am looking into the face of my baby brother."

Mama interjected, "God blesses us with reminders and connections to our loved ones who are no longer on this earth."

"Good to know," added Reynaldo. And for some strange and perhaps supernatural reason, that comment spurred them into laughter — laughter shaped with sorrow.

The afternoon passed with conversations that ranged from family gossip to deep eschatological discussions about life and death, and the afterlife. Dinner was served in the tiny kitchen, at a small, round oak table that snugly fit four wobbly chairs. Rosie was surprised and pleased to see that Reynaldo could muster the strength to sit at the table. Mama's rigatoni and famous sauce was nectar to Rosie's taste buds, but she felt saddened as she watched Mama and Massimo feed small portions of wedding soup to Reynaldo, whose hand could not hold the spoon steady.

After the dishes were finished, Massimo and Reynaldo napped, Massimo on a chair close to where Reynaldo slept on the couch.

Rosie began a conversation that she anticipated her mother would not like.

"Mama, I have reserved a room for you at a nearby hotel in Chelsea. Everything will be paid for, including dinners in the hotel restaurant."

Mama Rose opened her mouth to speak, but Rosie continued. "You and Papa look exhausted, and I think it bothers Reynaldo to know that he is wearing you out. I will be here for three more days. I would like time alone with my brother. I carry a hefty guilt for being so far away, and I think it would do everyone good if you and Papa got some good, genuine rest. You can stop by for an hour during the day if you'd like, but the remainder of the day and night will belong to me. Also, I am aware that Reynaldo's partner would like more time here too, and he feels that he is intruding when you are here. So, going away, close by, is just a good thing."

Mama Rose slumped onto the kitchen chair that wobbled under her weight.

"I want to argue. I want to stay by my boy's side every minute of every day. But you are right, Rosie. Papa and I need a break. We need air. We need to be alone. And this has weakened Papa so that he can barely stand. I must tell you though that Reynaldo often needs to be lifted and carried to his bed

80

or the bathroom, and sometimes he doesn't make it, if you know what I mean. You must know what you are in for."

Rosie teared up at the thought of Reynaldo's plight and the sadness they must all feel watching him fade.

"I can handle it, Mama. I've moved elephants and cleaned up after hippos. Now go pack, and when Papa wakes up, I will call a taxi, and you two will get some rest."

During the three days that Rosie spent with Reynaldo, she learned of the contentious attitudes and unkind behavior that he suffered, in addition to his illness. Dann, Reynaldo's partner, visited often, and told Rosie that people in the apartment put up signs in the laundry room saying that he and Reynaldo could not use the machines. Carryout services refused to deliver to the apartment, and when Reynaldo had been well enough to go to work at the television station, he was made to use a separate bathroom. The stigma and lack of information about the disease made everything more intolerable. Even the wrath of Mama Rose on those who insulted her boy had no effect on the atmosphere of hate and confusion that surrounded their lives. Dann also told Rosie what her parents could not, but what she had already guessed; Reynaldo did not have much time left.

Rosie scrubbed the apartment, cooked, and shopped as much as she could. But most of her time was sharing memories and singing Broadway musical songs with Reynaldo. He told Rosie that she was better than the myriad of pills he swallowed daily. He especially, deeply appreciated that she was willing to share childhood memories with Dann, who entrenched himself in the knowledge of Reynaldo's past.

"Mama and Papa try too hard to be optimistic," Reynaldo said. "They talk about the future. They won't admit that I don't really have a future, even though they know. Thank you, Rosie. As always, you keep it real. I truly love you. And, please, I know you won't be able to come back for my funeral. It's OK. I'll be dead and won't notice."

Again, the bittersweet laughter of loving sorrow.

The days disappeared, as time does when it is most needed to be seen. After three days, Mama and Papa returned, looking refreshed and well rested. During their absence they called twice a day, but never visited. Rosie was right; it was good for everyone.

Goodbyes were prolonged and filled with tears, Rosie, fully aware that it would be the last time she hugged her brother. She finally made it to her plane and settled in for the long flight back to Nairobi. She had hidden her pregnancy from the family and friends, knowing that even though they would be happy, it would have just added another worry to their already worried worlds. She had disguised her morning sickness and fatigue as jet lag and motion sickness. The fourteen-hour flight home was a welcome reprieve, as she slept through most of the journey.

When Rosie greeted Sammy and Ricky at the airport, she immediately noticed a slight hint of sadness in both of their faces. Ricky ran to her, putting his arms around her and squeezing her with a warm strength that momentarily pushed her back.

"Mommy, Mommy, Horton is dead," Ricky cried. "They killed him, Mommy. We tried to save him, but we couldn't. The other elephants are sad. Daddy said all things die. We are all sad."

Horton was Ricky's favorite elephant. They named him after Doctor Seuss's famous elephant, a character in *Horton Hears a Who!*, a bedtime story that they read to Ricky every night.

Rosie held tight to Ricky as she glanced over at Sammy, who sadly shrugged his shoulders, and whispered, "Ivory hunters."

The massacre of elephants and other animals continued throughout Africa, and although sanctuaries were beginning to sprout across the land, the illegal ivory trade and vicious slaughters still ravaged the populations, often condoned or ignored by corrupt governments and greedy businessmen. It was a fact of life that was difficult to explain to the innocent, loving minds of young children who coexisted with the awesome creatures.

Children, however, do eventually recover from loss, and soon Ricky resumed tasks with Rosie — feeding, weaning, and caring for the elephants, new and old, who found safety in the sanctuary.

In August, a telegram arrived informing Rosie that Reynaldo had passed away. Although she had been expecting it, the news filled her with sadness. She was just beginning to feel better when, two months later, another telegram arrived, this time with unexpected news, that plummeted her into the abyss of depression. Rosie shook as she read it aloud to Sammy:

DON'T HAVE TIME TO WRITE MUCH STOP
YOUR DAD HAD A MASSIVE HEART ATTACK STOP
DIED INSTANTLY STOP FAMILY IS A MESS STOP
CALL YOUR MOTHER STOP
BETH

Rosie, now six months pregnant, and fighting fatigue and hypertension, knew that she could not make the trip to her father's funeral. She traveled to Nairobi every day for the next two months to phone her mother and speak with her brothers and sisters. The bills climbed to hundreds of dollars, but Sammy never complained. He delayed travel plans so he could remain in the sanctuary to share the responsibilities of caring for Ricky and the animals, until Rosie recovered.

On January 21, 1981, Rosie, Sammy, and Ricky welcomed Antonio Raymond Scarponi to their family. Rosie's depression temporarily melted away as she saw Ricky holding his baby brother, and singing "Jesus Loves You," closely guarded by daddy Sammy, whose pride was evident by the grin that dominated his face.

Sammy's parents arrived on January 25. It was the first time they had met Ricky, and for the week they were there, they alternated between Ricky and Antonio, Grandma and Grandpa taking turns spoiling, cuddling, and playing with the grandchildren whom they missed so deeply.

Ricky relished the attention and the family ties. He introduced them to the mongooses, who played around the premises, and to the two dik diks who settled in the gardens surrounding the area, and who would often walk around the veranda where Ricky played. His excitement reached a peak when Grandpa and Grandma watched how he interacted with the elephants, holding their water buckets and petting their enormous legs. He could report about the boreholes and water holes and wild areas where the elephants would roam and return to the sanctuary. Ricky basked in the comments of "You are so grown-up, Ricky," and, "My goodness, how smart you are," that gushed from his adoring grandparents.

In the evening, Mr. and Mrs. Scarponi shared photos of Sammy when he was a little boy. Both Sammy and Rosie treasured these moments and the familial connections they brought to Ricky.

For the next few years, Rosie and her family lived peacefully but cautiously in the sanctuary. Rosie worried about the political leader, Daniel arap Moi, who was ruthless and intolerant of those who disagreed with his policies. In 1984, rumors of what would later be called the Wagalla massacre spread throughout Kenya. Moi had ordered the torture and killing of thousands of Somalians, and Rosie feared that his brutal tactics might spread to the sanctuary, because there was evidence that Moi profited from the ivory trade.

Nevertheless, her family flourished, and Rosie played a significant role in helping the Foundation in expanding services, lobbying for improved roads and water conservation, and most importantly, adding resources to care for the hundreds of animals that now called the sanctuary home.

Meanwhile, Sammy traveled to almost every country in Africa, often taking Ricky with him, even to distant locations, sometimes being away from Rosie for two months at a time. By the time he was ten years old, Ricky had sailed on the Mediterranean and Red Seas, as well as the Atlantic and Indian Oceans. He saw the peaks of Mt. Kilimanjaro, and the endless sands of the Sahara Desert, always under the tutelage and overprotective paternal eyes of his father and the African guides that led them around the particularly perilous and unhealthy environments that dominated the volatile political and geographical landscapes. His favorite visits were along the Nile River, where his insatiable curiosity about birds was fed with new sightings of spoonbills, sunbirds, egrets, and herons.

When he returned home, he would share bird feathers with Antonio, and the brothers would frolic and wrestle, while Ricky constantly chattered to his mother about his adventures in what he called the most beautiful places in the world, often interjecting words from the Bantu languages that he picked up along the way. He called his brother umfowethu, and he called Rosie umama. Although his travels were extensive, he was home more often than not, and Rosie had hired a British tutor to assure that he stayed on task in his reading, writing, and arithmetic. Despite her worries about the wilds of Africa, she knew that the education he received traveling with his father was far more authentic than the pseudo education of rules and tests — and yet, she did not want him to fall behind in the traditional world of United States schools.

The Scarponi family was firmly settled in their second homeland when in 1987, after eleven years on African soil, Sammy received a classified letter from his publisher, informing him that the magazine had been sold, and they had been forced to terminate his contract. It arrived on the same day that Rosie informed him that she was pregnant with their third child.

A soul-searching discussion reached into the dark African night within the echoes of screeching hyraxes, restless cicadas, and eerie winds that resounded from the rocks and hills. All of creation seemed to reflect the restless communications between Rosie and Sammy as they were compelled to decide their future. The dawn emerged with its soft hues of pink and gold, piercing through the blackness of the night.

Rosie and Sammy, asleep in each other's arms on the swing in the veranda, had made the decision to leave the motherland of civilization and return to the forestland of buckeyes.

Chapter 4

· · · · · · · · · · · · · · · · · · · ·

For my part I know nothing with any certainty,
but the sight of the stars makes me dream.

Vincent Van Gogh

Babs

1974-1988

arbara Ann Turyev Schwartz was born on June 1, 1950, in St. John's Hospital in Cleveland, Ohio. She bore the first and middle name of her mother, and her mother's mother, and her mother's mother's mother. She was called Babs.

Babs grew up in Shaker Heights, an affluent suburb of Cleveland. Shaker was a short rapid transit train ride from downtown Cleveland, providing Babs with the benefits of big-city proximity, as well as suburban peace and idyllic landscapes and lakes. Although the early history of Shaker was marred with racist housing codes, it eventually evolved into a multicultural haven of excellent schools, fine dining, and high society. The world-renowned Cleveland Clinic was close by — a life-saving advantage when Babs was struck with juvenile rheumatoid arthritis. Wracked with pain and immobility, Babs suffered greatly in her early childhood years. When she was a young girl, she had what she has always considered a supernatural healing, in a shrine dedicated to Mary, the mother of Jesus. When her faith waned as she grew older, she always tried to keep that moment close in her memory, holding on to the strong feeling that there was indeed a God, and God was always with her.

Unlike Brigid's and Rosie's parents, Babs's mother and father met when her father, Richard, was a professor at John Carroll University where her mother, Barbara, was a student. Their intellects served as the magnetic attraction that culminated in marriage.

Richard was a German Jew, born in 1900. By 1930, he had established himself as a prominent physicist, and as a result, was privy to the ominous secrets that swirled through the Nazi mindset of anti-semitism and world domination. His parents remained steadfast in their determination to suffer the slings and arrows of the evils that menaced their homeland, believing that the German people would resist and conquer the vile rumblings that threatened their souls. But Richard knew the threat was too pervasive to be conquered. He also knew that if he remained, he would be forced into helping with the development of the rocketry and weapons that would be used to diabolical ends. He journeyed away from his homeland and his parents and entered the United States, where his reputation preceded him. A stellar career ensued, during which time his intelligence placed him on center stage with astronauts, astrophysicists, presidents, and eventually made him a prominent contributor to America's conquest of lunar travel. His success never brought him peace, however. After a long search for records of his parents' fate, he learned that his mother died of starvation at Auschwitz, and his father committed suicide shortly thereafter. Guilt and grief haunted his spirit until the day his spirit left him, in 1973.

Babs gave a brief but poignant eulogy, which explained her father's approach to life — an approach that influenced every decision she ever made:

As I look out over this congregation, I see men who have traveled to the moon — men and women whose work and vision have made it possible for satellites and ships to travel the stars. My father viewed mankind as travelers through both the corporeal world, and the spiritual world. He continually reminded his children from an evolutionary perspective that we began as animals. But we are animals who have the ability to choose. We can either wiggle and wallow with the wild beasts, or we can aspire and ascend with the angels. Whether it be science, or music, or love, we must always, in every situation, choose to be, as Shakespeare once made reference, a "beast no more."

Babs's mother, Barbara, also excelled in physics and science, and she, too, made significant contributions to the technology of space exploration. NASA provided opportunities for her to conduct research and to aggregate data, which she was able to complete at home. Barbara once told Babs, "Your father receives all of the accolades, while I remain in the background. That is fine with me. I am stimulated by my work but fulfilled by marriage and children. I decided early on that my commitment to my family would always come first."

So, Babs grew up nurtured with love, and invigorated with intelligence. That environment continued in the classrooms at Lourdes Academy, with the added bonus of the friendships with Brigid and Rosie. When she attended Berkeley during the late 1960s and early 1970s, the nurturing disappeared, and for a while she lost herself in the radical ideologies that infiltrated and permeated every aspect of that campus. After her soulmate, Martin, was killed in Vietnam, Babs could no longer maintain her stoicism. She eventually collapsed on the shores in the bay at Cape Cod, while vacationing with her family. Her strength slowly returned, again with nurture and knowledge, but, like Brigid and Rosie, the wound of Martin's death would never heal.

Babs graduated from Berkeley in 1972, Summa Cum Laude, with majors in Metallurgy and Mechanical Engineering. Babs had described her degree to Brigid and Rosie as something that would "provide a thought process through which I can learn about radiation's effects on minerals and other elements with a possibility that I may be able to participate in some altruistic efforts for the environment and humanity."

To which Rosie replied, "Yeah, but have you had sex yet?"

Babs did find what she thought was another soulmate in Adam Schwartz, a Nuclear Physics major at Berkeley. They married in 1973, shortly before her father's death. From the beginning, she felt an intellectual connection to him, and while others engaged in physical pleasures under the star-filled skies in the hills of California, Babs and Adam gazed toward the heavens while discussing these balls of gas and the nuclear fusion that keeps them luminous. Adam joked that they were "the only couple who discussed the Hertzsprung-Russell diagram on their first date."

After warning Adam that she was not a typical cooking, cleaning, ironing kind of wife, Babs settled into married life, while enjoying the academic, yet sexist, life of Purdue academia. Adam had not yet complained about eating out or hiring house cleaners.

They both earned Masters and doctoral degrees at Purdue University, where Babs broke down sexist doors of academia (the doors were broken down, but the glass ceiling was closely guarded). They moved to Los Angeles in 1979, both accepting jobs at the Jet Propulsion Lab, which was owned by NASA and managed by nearby Caltech, the California Institute of Technology.

Babs gave birth to their daughter, Barbara Ann, in 1980. She kept the matriarchal tradition of passing down the name of the firstborn daughter, which was now generations old. However, they called her by her middle name, Annie.

NASA afforded Babs a leave of absence, and she spent a year at home with Annie, who even at one year old, already loved looking at the night sky and picture books of the stars and constellations. Babs's brother, David, who was living in the East Village of Manhattan, would send toddlers' astronomy and planets' books every month. David was an artist, and he had personally illustrated several of the books. When he was a child, he would draw pictures of the heavens. Babs's father once said, "My family studies the stars — except for David; he paints them."

When Annie was a one year old, Babs hired a Nanny to care for her when she went back to work at the lab. She fretted leaving Annie. After a year of full-time motherhood, Babs had found a maternal instinct that she sometimes doubted she possessed. But the lure of planetary exploration still filled her with an insatiable curiosity. The success of the biological experiments on Mars, and *Voyager's* upcoming approaches to Saturn and Uranus were adventures in which she wanted to be a part.

Despite these achievements, the Jet Propulsion Lab was losing favor with NASA and was in danger of losing funding. Much of NASA's funding was diverted to the Space Shuttle Program. When Babs returned, the lab was developing other projects, unrelated to planetary exploration.

Eventually, a nationwide protest emerged from the inner circles of Congress and scientists to save the lab's commitment to exploring the solar system, and beyond. Babs entered this fray with enthusiasm and scientific knowledge and contributed significantly to the *Galileo* mission to Jupiter which was the upcoming endeavor.

Although her contributions were significant, the environment of the workforce was not always welcoming to female scientists, nor was it conducive to marital fidelity. When Brigid came to visit later that year in 1981, Babs shared her struggles as they sipped wine on the patio overlooking the Santa Monica Mountains.

Brigid smiled at Babs and said, "I'm so happy for you. You are a wonderful mother, a successful scientist, and are in a good marriage. This place is awesome. You did it, girl!"

Babs responded, gazing at the mountains, not making eye contact. "I'm struggling, Brigid. There's little respect for women in the lab. Brilliant men, still stoop to crude remarks and suggestive comments. Then there's the lack of morality with so many people sleeping with others who are not their spouses. It's becoming more and more difficult to maintain my faith and my dignity."

"How is Adam?"

"I am with him all the time. At work, at home … but we are making it work. I have to say, right now the problem is me. I love him dearly, but the temptations of working in close contact all day with men who are both patronizing and attractive are very confusing. Their compliments on my work are welcomed, but I know there is an underlying sexual motive almost every time they speak to me. I worry about giving them false signals. And I am simultaneously despising them and flirting with them. For the first time in my life, I am confused. I don't like myself right now."

"Babs, you know me. I don't judge people, especially my dearest friends. But I do judge situations, and you need to talk yourself out of this situation. Remember who you are. For heaven's sake, you've been resisting the temptations of the world since you were sixteen! You are the only one among the three of us, Rosie, you, and me, not to succumb to the dung that men throw our way."

"Easier said than done."

"Imagine Annie in her thirties, coming to you with this same scenario. What would you say to her?"

Babs thought for a moment, then smiled. "I would tell her not to allow the world to shape who she is. I would tell her she is not like other people. I would tell her to be strong in her self-worth and that she should not choose to do anything that would diminish that. I would tell her marital vows are sacred and God would grant her grace to resist temptation … thank you, Brigid."

Brigid lifted her glass, and tapped Babs's to hers, and said, "You got this."

Babs laughed, and said, "You know Rosie would scoff at your use of the word dung."

Another tip of the glasses, while Brigid said, "To Rosie."

Babs continued to work and contribute to the momentous space achievements through the 1980s. The Magellan radar mapping mission to Venus, and the missions called "Planetary Observers," helped lay the groundwork for the Mars *Rover* landing. She never gave into the ever-present temptations of infidelity that surrounded her.

The middle of the 1980s saw a groundswell of preferential promotions for women and other minorities, some deserved, some not. Babs was promoted to lead a team working on the curved mirror that focused the starlight of the Hubble telescope. The Hubble Mission excited her more than anything she had worked on before. The telescope had enormous potential to record extremely detailed images of the cosmos, because, unlike ground-based telescopes, it had significantly lower background light. Although she knew she was not the best-qualified person to lead the team, she accepted the position, and took revenge on the men who had treated her poorly — lording her authority over the lords of the lab.

The project also removed her from Adam's work on Mars exploration. They had been working closely and although the endeavor had stimulating intellectual rewards, the constant presence in each other's work environment eventually crept into their home environment. The change in assignment allowed for a mutual sharing of different domains of knowledge and scientific progress. They could appreciate and even take pride in each other's work, rather than feeling competition.

Babs and Adam would often take Annie on jaunts to their former oases in Berkeley. Their reputations allowed them access to the large telescope at the Leuschner Observatory. Now four years old, Annie would impress and charm the faculty and astronomers with her knowledge of orbits and lunar occultations. The impressiveness came as a result of her knowledge; the charm came when, in the same breath, she would refer to stars as "twinkles." Annie loved the night sky, and the family would spend many evenings star gazing, often driving deep into the night to find a dark sky to observe the planets and constellations.

Adam continued to have moods of antagonism toward Babs and their lifestyle. He often made a sharp turn in his attitude. He criticized Babs for not wearing make-up and derided her for not making an effort to look "better" when he came home from work. He made fun of the few remaining pounds that Babs had yet to shed since the birth, and he constantly bemoaned that their child was consuming their lives. Babs was incredulous. One night, when she finished reading Annie a bedtime story, he blurted out, "You know, Howard Stern was right; once a baby enters a marriage, the husband doesn't matter."

Babs, in a rare loss of control, shouted back at him, "So, now you're taking marriage counseling from Howard Stern? Is this how far you have fallen into male insanity?"

The rest of the evening went on in silence, but later, they had a "make-up" bedtime story of their own.

Before Annie enrolled in kindergarten, Babs wanted to expose her to a different environment, where people-watching was more prevalent than sky watching. They had visited grandparents in Cleveland and Indianapolis, but Babs thought a trip to see Uncle David in New York City would be a unique experience, balancing a perspective between the academic life and the artistic life. So, in the Spring of 1985, Annie received her first taste of the worlds of art, avant-garde, alternative lifestyles — and the New York City of 1985.

They flew to Cleveland and then took a train to New York. There was not much time to visit in Cleveland, but Mama Rose, Dar, and Barbara insisted they meet for a quick lunch at Stouffer's on Public Square, near the Terminal Tower where Babs and Annie would board the train to Penn Station. Although the time was brief, the three older women squeezed in more love and attention than Annie had ever seen outside of her own home. Mama Rose made sure to inform her that when Babs was Annie's age, the Terminal Tower was the tallest building in North America. Dar informed her that Babs, Brigid, and Rosie, would walk from the Terminal Tower to the Cleveland Municipal Stadium to watch the Browns and Indians play. Barbara did not say much but hugged Annie every time she looked at her granddaughter. Annie loved hearing the stories, but she was, after all, five years old, and when they were seated on the train, she lay her head on Babs's lap and whispered, "I loved the hugs the best," as she dozed off to sleep.

Annie awoke to a sight that filled her with awe and trepidation. The walk through Penn Station emitted more human energy than she could ever imagine. She walked doe-eyed, clutching Babs's hand, and observing every sight, smell, and sound that permeated through the paths of travelers and workers.

"This is New York," Babs said, as they scurried through the station, keeping up with the rapid pace of the flow of people.

The blast of blaring car horns and traffic that seemed to stand still while simultaneously managing to turn corners causing walkers to run for their lives, caused Babs, a seasoned city girl, to move with caution. They only had a short walk to the New Yorker Hotel where they would be staying for the next four days.

Brigid's sister, Suzy, one of the Nagy twins, was the Concierge. When Babs first saw her standing behind the desk she felt a rush of emotion which filled her with tears. She had not seen Suzy for several years, and the sight of her as a competent, working woman in a famous New York hotel flooded her with memories of watching Suzy grow up in the Nagy house in Parma.

Suzy, who, unlike Babs, never hid her emotions, ran from her station and yelled, "Oh my God! I'm so excited you are here!"

She scooped up Annie and carried her over to her desk, whispering in her ear, "You will love New York, welcome, welcome!"

She looked at the line forming, waiting for help from the Concierge. "I'm sorry," she said to the people waiting, "But this is my sister's best friend and her daughter, and it's the first time I have met little Annie, and I am just so excited." She asked Babs to wait over by the chairs in the lobby; her break started in a few minutes.

When Suzy returned to the lobby, Annie was gazing at the twinkling, huge chandelier that hovered overhead while Babs studied a map of Manhattan.

"So, I don't know what your plans are, but I can set you up with Ellis Island tours, a trip to the top of the Empire State Building, tickets to a Broadway show, there's a revival of the *King and I* that you would love! And ..."

Babs interrupted and laughed, "Suzy, you haven't changed a bit. You are still the bubble of charged energy that never stops moving — or talking! I hate to burst that bubble, but we are here primarily to visit with my brother, David, and except for sleeping or resting, we will be spending most of our time in the East Village with him."

"Ooh, ooh, ooh," Suzy groaned. "That is the dirtiest, most crime-ridden, drug-infested neighborhood in this dirty, crime-ridden, drug-infested city. And the large number of gay men and intravenous drug users make it one of the hardest hit areas for that AIDS disease in this hard- hit town. I understand if you don't want to do touristy things, Babs, but I really wouldn't spend much time there."

Babs sighed and said, "David warned me about all this, but said there are nice, safe things to do there. He has sent photographs of his apartment and the surrounding art galleries. I trust him. The photos he sent look fine. The purpose of the trip is for Annie to get to know her uncle. And before you ask, David is not gay."

"I actually was going to ask. It's just that the AIDS thing is so scary." Suzy said, her embarrassment visible by the pink hue that suffused her cheeks.

The conversation turned with Babs informing Suzy about

Reynaldo, and other goings-on of family and friends. They shared anecdotes and memories, and soon it was time for Suzy to return to her desk, and for Babs and Annie to rest in the beautiful suite Suzy had arranged for them. They were scheduled to meet David for dinner at 6:00 p.m. at The White Horse Tavern in Greenwich Village. David chose that place because of its history and location, and despite being a popular bar in which to imbibe, it had excellent American cuisine, which he thought would be good for Annie.

Annie ran to David's wide-open arms when they met in the lobby. David's hair had grown to his waist since the last time Babs had seen him, but he looked healthy and at peace, and Babs grabbed his arm to hers, and said, "I love you, you darling anachronism."

Suzy had arranged a much-appreciated stroller for Annie, and Babs and David made the decision to walk the one and a half miles to the restaurant down 7th Avenue to Hudson Street. Annie sat silently, startled as they joined the throngs of the rapidly moving pedestrians, eventually growing accustomed to the blaring of horns and occasional profanity coming from the taxi drivers. The men attacking stopped cars to wipe windows, and then demanding payment was a bit alarming, even to Babs.

"I've always loved the pulse of this city, but honestly, David, I find this rhythm a bit frightening," Babs said, noticing David's eyes, cautiously surveying the scene.

David chuckled. "It's certainly not as safe as when you and your revelers were on the prowl. Drugs and prostitution and a deep vibe of decadence has taken control. I mean, New York has always been a tad decadent, but now it's come out of the dark corners and has spread to the bright lights. But, New Yorkers are New Yorkers, and I trust things will improve. When you visit my home tomorrow, you will see some of the worst of it, but always there is hope in the midst of despair, and I want to share with you my art and friends who radiate that hope."

Dinner time was filled with interesting conversation and eclectic people watching. Babs enjoyed the vintage photos of artists and poets that lined the walls, and Annie took her time peeling off the layers of what she called her "giant cheeseburger," and eating them one by one. The ambience was simple and real, a solid sense of history unencumbered by grandiose flaunting of wealth or self-importance.

Annie was exhausted, and the long walk back to the hotel was out of the question. David hailed his sister and niece a cab and headed back toward his home. He would meet them tomorrow at the hotel and then introduce them to his life.

Before settling into sleep, Babs dialed Adam's number; it was only 6:00 p.m. California time. She handed the phone to Annie.

"Hi, Daddy! New York is exciting and fun and Uncle David is wonderful and Suzy is taking good care of us. It's noisy and dirty and really not so pretty but the buildings are ginormous and there are so many lights everywhere. But guess what, Daddy? When it's dark, and you look up at the sky … you cannot see the twinkles! Are you OK without us? I love you."

"Well, I'm very happy you are getting to see different things, Annie. Thank you for calling and letting me know you are OK. I am OK too. Be careful, and I will see you soon. Give the phone back to Mommy, please."

Babs began, "Hello, Adam. It's been a long day and evening, but seeing old family and friends has been very gratifying. New York seems to have grown dirtier and more dangerous since you and I were here a few years ago, but Annie is enjoying it. How are things on the West Coast?"

"Same ol' same ol'," Adam replied. "I mean, you've only been gone for a day, Babs. By the way, I have several meetings scheduled for tomorrow—not sure I will be home to get a phone call. If we don't get a chance to talk before you head back, please leave a message on the answering machine to let me know that your flight is on time, and I will meet you at the airport."

"I miss you too," Babs laughed, sounding much more jovial than she felt. "We will be sure to keep in touch one way or another. And we'll see you in two days. Don't work too hard. Love you."

"Sorry if I sound curt; it's been an excruciating day of budget fights and some unexpected setbacks in research. I do miss you both and will see you soon. Good night, Babs. Hug Annie for me."

"Will do. Good night."

Babs hung up and made a conscious decision to ignore the indifference in Adam's tone. Her attention was focused on Annie and David, and she would not be distracted by Adam's complacent attitude. She took some brandy from the stocked cabinet, added some ice, and sipped on the night cap as she read a copy of Carl Sagan's new novel, *Contact*. The book would not be available to the general public until September, but a few scientists at NASA received advance copies. Babs relished this first taste of Sagan's genius approach to wormholes, extraterrestrials, and space travel. She continued reading until her eyelids lost the battle to stay awake.

Mother and daughter slept soundly despite the cacophony of sounds that crept up from the streets of Manhattan. They awoke at 8:00 a.m. the next day, ate breakfast in bed, and met David at the Concierge's desk where Suzy was introducing him to the staff. Suzy was off work for the next two days, and this was her last chance to see these people with whom she shared so many happy memories.

David lifted Annie into his arms and carried her into the taxi that was being held for them by the New Yorker doorman. As she peered through the window, Annie remained in awe of the skyscrapers and sidewalks covered with people. Babs and David discussed the day's agenda, which included tea at David's place, a tour of art galleries, in one of which David's work was being featured, and a late lunch at B and H Dairy Restaurant where Annie would have fun twirling on the counter stools that had been at the eatery since its opening in 1938.

David lived on the third floor of an old apartment building on E. 8th, between Tompkins Square and the East River. His place was tiny with one bedroom, a small kitchen, and a smaller bathroom. But the cheery art on the walls, and the floral-patterned couch and chairs, gave it a feeling of warmth and friendliness.

"I have to apologize," Babs said. "I honestly was expecting this place to be a bit dismal. You have always been so distant and solitary, I figured your home would express that."

"Apology accepted. It's true I have always enjoyed a solitary life, but I've also always enjoyed beautiful things, both physical and ethereal. The stars you study are beautifully oth-erworldly to me. That's why I paint them and not study them. And, to me, colors are the elixirs of the universe, whether on furniture, or clothing, or the galaxies. Colors are warm. I often think of Father and how his wardrobe was limited to almost all black and white attire. That's how he saw the world — black and white. My greatest memory of him is when I pre-sented him with my painting of the Christmas night sky of his home town. It was the most emotional moment he ever shared with me. It was the only time I felt his warm colors. When he died, Mother gave back that painting to me, and I treasure it."

Babs remembered that gift, and the Christmas that David presented it to her father. It was shortly before her father died, and it was a beautiful moment for the family. Now, here she was, more than a decade later, sipping freshly brewed green tea, and looking once more at that painting. Annie busied her-self coloring in a book that David had created specifically for her. Each page was a drawing from one of the fifty states, de-picting a species of trees native to that particular state. David painted numerous pictures of trees, which he called "the oxy-gen benefactresses of the earth."

The visit to the art galleries was tainted by the ubiquitous presence of drug users and vagrants, but once inside the gal-leries, the mood became serene and interesting. Both galleries contained some of David's work, and Babs was astounded at the prices. The lowest price tag on one of David's paintings was five thousand dollars. The clientele was a mix of bohemi-ans, Park Avenue socialites, New York University students, and neighborhood onlookers.

"One never knows who has money and who doesn't. But I will tell you that the New York University students are not a popular bunch. They have injected an arrogant, privileged attitude into the neighborhood, and the University itself is gobbling up and destroying historical buildings and valuable land locations. We are bad enough with the dens of depravity that are filtering through our streets without the systemic destruction of history being perpetuated by institutions."

Despite the decadence, there was a charm to even the most deteriorated areas of Manhattan's neighborhoods. Babs continued to be impressed by David's approach to life and art, and felt very proud when friends and neighbors would greet him with obvious respect and fondness as they walked the streets. She also appreciated the way he doted on Annie, carrying her for most of the day. After a late lunch, they returned to David's apartment. Annie napped in the bedroom while David and Babs shared tokes from a joint of East Village's finest weed.

The next day, David met Annie and Babs at FAO Schwartz toy store where Annie became giddy with excitement. David told her to pick out anything she wanted and he would have it sent to her, so they wouldn't have to carry it on the plane. While they were searching through the toys, Babs naturally gravitated to the Science section where she was surprised to see three children's books written by David Turyev.

"God, David, I feel I don't know you at all. I get prouder and prouder every moment I'm with you."

"And I am equally proud of you, my NASA-genius sister."

The conversation ended when Annie came squealing down the aisle.

"I just love this Cabbage Patch doll, Justina Nia, and this Rainbow Bright doll. I can't decide."

This also surprised Babs. She had assumed her daughter would also gravitate toward more educational selections. Before she could respond to Annie's dilemma, David said, "Well, you can have both, of course," as he glanced at Babs with a look that said "no arguing."

The rest of the day was filled with a carriage ride through Central Park, a tour of St. Patrick's Cathedral, and an early dinner at Heidelberg Restaurant on Second Ave. Babs wanted Annie to get an authentic taste of the foods of her German ancestors. Annie obliged by eating the child-size portion of Weisswurst and potato salad. She gave the red cabbage to David, who added it to the Sauerbraten meal for two that he shared with Babs.

They taxied back to the New Yorker and said goodbye with long embraces and tearful kisses. David whispered to Babs, "This meant so much to me. And, I do have to say, we must one day address Mom's mental condition, but I'm glad we didn't during this time. That discussion will be for another day."

"Agreed," Babs whispered back, and hugged her baby brother one more time until they would meet again.

When they returned to California, Babs noticed a palpable difference in Adam's behavior. While they were in New York, he had never answered Annie's calls, but he did leave messages at the desk, telling Annie he missed her and was happy she was having a good time. No mention of Babs.

Adam met them at the airport and listened intently to Annie's observations of New York and her uncle David. Later that evening, he told Babs that he did not appreciate her exposing Annie to the grit and danger of New York, and the questionable lifestyle of David.

After a few months of feeling estranged in her marriage, and even with her coworkers, Babs periodically began to write her thoughts in a journal. Expressing her thoughts helped her make sense of her life, and she took solace in this private place.

June 1, 1985

"The soul chooses her own company, then closes the door on everyone else. She's no longer available to most of the world." Emily Dickinson

Today is my 35th birthday, and I feel like I am at a turning point in my life. Although my daughter brings me great joy and love, the love that I have shared with my husband is slipping away. For a time after Annie was born, Adam went through a stage of what I can only call baby jealousy. He did not want the changes that having a child brought. For the first time in our marriage, he was complaining about dinners, and even my appearance. It is true, things have changed. We worked through it, and when Annie got a little older, Adam began to enjoy taking her places, and we became a family. But we were both working on Martian projects, and the proximity at both work and home started to add to more friction. When our career paths diverged, we shared our research and our ongoing contributions — his, focusing on the exploration of Mars, and the technology that would land and analyze the landscape and biological potential of our sister planet. And mine, on the detailed, fascinating intricacy of building a telescope that would open up a window to the distant galaxies and the hidden wonders of the universe. Things got better. Adam and I would lie in bed, satisfied with what we were doing in this world, and what we were doing with each other.

But now, once again, something has changed. I'm not sure what is stirring, but as I write, I only know that I will do everything to save my marriage — but not at the expense of my soul.

January 28, 1986

Today is a day that has broken the hearts of all America, especially those of us who have worked tirelessly and hopefully on advancing our space missions. Today, the world watched in horror as the Space Shuttle, Challenger, burst into flames above the Florida skies. Our lab stood still in time, everyone shocked and speechless, and then came the moans and tears and hand wringing and embraces. When I composed myself, I left the lab to pick up Annie from school. Because the first teacher ever to go into space was on the shuttle, students all over the country were watching, including Annie's kindergarten class. I went into the building; she is in an Evangelical school. The Catholic schools were filled, and I couldn't enroll her there. Adam and I have both strayed from our spiritual journey, and I thought the Christian atmosphere would be nurturing. I was wrong, but Annie will finish out the year. The older students were in the chapel praying for the astronauts and their families, but the younger students were spared the details of the explosion, just being told that there were problems, and their parents would explain it to them. I was the only parent who picked up her child early. Annie was visibly shaken. She kept asking, "What happened, Mommy, what happened?" I thought of Rosie and Brigid, and their strong faith, and wished they were here to help me deal with explaining such a tragedy to my child. I recalled how soothing my faith was for me through the tragic assassinations that occurred during my coming-of-age years. But the reassurances that God is in control have died in the burning embers of a life surrounded by atheists and immorality. I gave Annie a technical explanation that was neither soothing nor helpful, but it was at least honest. It basically gave her the unsettling message of the mantra of our time ... shit happens.

No mother of the year award for me.

June 1, 1987

Another birthday. I took pleasure today in chats with Brigid and Rosie — all of us wondering how we got to be thirty-seven years old, when in many ways we still felt like we are sixteen, swimming in Ridgewood pool in Parma, or in the not-so-clean waters of Edgewater in Cleveland. We made plans to attend our Lourdes Academy twenty-year reunion next summer. I look forward to that.

Much has happened since I last laid down my thoughts in this journal. After the Challenger tragedy, our Hubble project was put on hold until the shuttle program pulls itself back together. The Challenger was a personal sadness for me, grieving the deaths of those seven astronauts. But the effect it has on the project may be catastrophic. Our launch was scheduled for October, and expectations were high. Now, we're not sure. We can't launch without a shuttle. Although we are taking advantage of the delay by fine-tuning much of our hardware and software, it costs an astronomical amount of money to store everything in a sterile environment.

Adam's Martian exploration project is still moving forward, and he is engulfed in his work. It is ironic that he is actually building on the metallurgical and possibility of biological evidence on the Mars surface — the research that my mother and I laid the groundwork for. The expanse between us has widened, but we are getting much better at pretending. We attend parties together, and even attend church as a family with Annie, but as the Righteous Brothers so woefully sang ... we've lost that loving feeling.

Annie is still in the fundamental Christian School. The Catholic school is still filled. So she gets a dose of fundamentalism during the day, and the Catholic Mass and indoctrination on the weekends. The administration at neither school is happy with me; even in this ecumenical age, Protestantism and Catholicism clash. But money talks, and the school doesn't want to lose the tuition, and the church doesn't want to lose our Sunday contribution. So Annie has made her First Communion in a Catholic Church while attending a school where they scoff at Transubstantiation. She is oblivious to the conflict and relished her special day with my mother and Uncle David who came in for the ceremony. Adam's parents are traveling in Europe and couldn't make it. We attend the Holy Name of Mary Church in San Dimas, in the San Gabriel Valley, and even Adam seems to enjoy the Sunday fellowship. Although, in my heart, I know it's a charade.

I've invited my mother to live with us, hoping that perhaps it will give Adam and me more time to rekindle. We shall see.

January 5, 1988

Adam has moved out of the house. One night, I roamed the streets in an oddly refreshing rare Southern California rainstorm. It was a symbolic cleansing of my psyche and soul. Memories surfaced of my early days with Adam, when I warned him that although my love for him was real and deep, marriage did not appeal to me. Cooking, cleaning, ironing, and all of those responsibilities presented no fulfillment for me. I admitted it, I owned it, and I still do. But I was willing to commit my life to him, if he understood those attitudes.

I do, however, always appreciate women who take pleasure, or at least fulfillment in that honored occupation of being a homemaker. Their role is the foundation of our culture. And I believe motherhood is one of the purest forms of feminism. We alone possess what Brigid's mother refers to as "the treasured egg." I embrace the feminine nurturing and love and responsibility of giving birth and raising children that are instilled in our womanly nature. Even women who do not have children possess a genetic sisterhood with all who do. Aunts are mothers in a different, wonderful kind of way.

I can attest that my love for Annie has always been my first priority, even as I engross myself in the study of the effects of hydrogen on metals and hydrogen explosions in nuclear reactors, as we seek to explore the endless universe.

In the past year, Adam has reversed the attitude toward marriage that he had when we wed. He complained about having a housekeeper, saying that it was my responsibility to keep the house "tidy." He resented my mother's presence, which I admit, has been a burden more than a blessing. But she is a good cook, and she and Annie mutually dote on each other. And I feel having three generations of Turyev women is something good.

So, after my walk, I asked Adam to sit and talk about where we were in our marriage, and our love. I felt I tried to make our home a loving place, but his demands on me were starting to nip away at who I was and who I wanted to be. What can we do, I said, to rekindle what we once had.

And then … the confession. He had been having an affair, for more than a year, with a college assistant. Apologies, tears, promises, all flowed after the confession. But I was done. To me, infidelity and/or physical abuse are the two most powerful swords that give wounds with no healing. No doubt my Christian friends would insist on forgiveness and reconciliation. Forgiveness may come in time, but reconciliation? Never.

After the Lourdes Academy reunion, and the birth of Rosie's baby in 1988, Babs wanted to settle down back in the Cleveland area. However, NASA had asked her to remain at the Jet Propulsion Lab while they still worked on the Hubble and other projects. She agreed, mostly because the salary was very high, and she was saving as much as she could so she and Annie would live comfortably when she did make the move back to Ohio. Adam was living a bachelor's life, but was dependable with his custodial visits with Annie, and did not argue with the large monthly sum of child support. He also agreed to legally allow Babs and Annie to move out of state when the time came, sharing only specific holidays and one month of Annie visiting him in California. Babs secretly held on to the belief that Adam would have little to do with Annie after they moved, but she was happy with the legal arrangements.

The move back to Ohio came in May 1990, a month after the successful launch of the Hubble telescope on April 24, 1990, from the space shuttle *Discovery*.

Chapter 5

· ·

A lot of Middle-Aged Women Are Children, Still Trying to Find their Way

Tamsin Greig

T he three friends had decided to celebrate their fortieth birthday in mid-June, by attending an Indians game and grabbing a corned beef sandwich at one of the few remaining Cleveland downtown restaurants. By the norms that society dictates, they had all aged well. Rosie was strong and tanned with a Mediterranean look of slightly frizzy dark hair, coupled with olive-colored eyes and a face whose thick lips and ample nose expressed both fun and beauty. She never quite let go of her African attire, wearing khaki shorts and a multi-colored tunic-like blouse.

Brigid had the look of a single woman with the time to coif and primp with perfectly applied make-up and stylishly long, auburn hair — and enough sleep. Black capris, a Ralph Lauren green silk blouse, and Gucci leather wedge espadrille sandals gave her the look of an obviously confident, successful woman, with manicured fingernails and pedicured toenails.

Babs, who in yesteryear was the fittest of the three, wore the signs of worry with the look of someone who had much more to care about than how she looked. Caring for Annie and her mother, and the stress of her job, gave her little time to focus on appearance. Her blonde hair was short and a tad unkempt. She wore off the rack jeans and a black tee shirt. Nothing indicated that she was in the inner circle of scientists and astronomers who were reshaping the way humanity viewed the universe.

Brigid was teaching English and Language Arts at an alternative school, Ohio City High School in the neighborhood between the West Side Market and St. Patrick's Catholic Church, where Lourdes Academy students formerly attended their school Masses. She lived in a brick double house on Ridge Avenue in Parma, within walking distance to her parents and Saint Charles Church, and not far from Parmatown Mall.

Babs remained in contract with NASA, working from home, and communicating through the new high-tech internet. She bought a home in Shaker Heights with three bedrooms and a so-called mother-in-law suite, where she lived with her mother and Annie. Annie was enrolled in the 5th grade at Saint Dominic's Elementary School, starting in the Fall.

Rosie and Sammy and her boys moved into an old but completely modernized house on Lake Avenue in Lakewood, Ohio, a few miles from the westside neighborhood where she grew up, and where her mother still lived. She worked part-time at the Cleveland Zoo, providing educational programs about elephants and African wildlife. She visited and cared for the animals whenever she could. Ricky and Antonio were enrolled in Lakewood Public Schools and received their Catholic Catechism at Our Lady of Mount Carmel. Rosie still swaddled Massimo on her stomach and took him to work.

Sammy was making a good living as a freelance journalist. They all seemed happily settled. And yet …

"I can't believe we are frickin' forty years old," Rosie exclaimed, as she sipped a beer at Slyman's Restaurant on St. Clair Avenue in downtown Cleveland.

Brigid rolled her eyes and laughed. "We may be forty, but you still hang on to those adolescent linguistic abominations. And you finally look like the hippy you always wanted to be."

Rosie looked at Babs and shrugged her shoulders. "Nothing better than Mother Earth, with a dab of cannabis, to make a girl look good."

Babs joined in. "Being forty doesn't bother me at all, but the change in Cleveland bothers me a great deal. Pewter mug … gone. Silver Grille … gone. Top of the Town … gone. The Theatrical … gone. Swingo's … gone. Higbees … gone. The list of favorite places that are no longer here seems endless."

"Don't forget Lourdes Academy," Brigid added. "But do you know what? We're still here; we're still together; and we're still kicking ass. We've been all over the world, lived through what the world has thrown at us — and those high school bonds and Cleveland fires are still crackling in our souls."

"Truth," said Rosie. And I'm thankful one of those Cleveland fires is gone forever. Ya know, the one on the Cuyahoga River."

"So, let's catch up," Brigid said, diverting the attention from Rosie's bad joke. "Babs, you've been back for over a month, but this is the first time we could all get together for a good conversation. What's going on since you've returned?"

Babs took a deep breath. "Well, my work at NASA has become globally significant and critical to the success of the

Hubble Telescope. You may have read that the images coming back from the scope are much fuzzier than they were supposed to be. Besides being an indescribable disappointment, the flaw has severely diminished the reputation of the project and NASA itself. It turns out there is, what is called, a spherical aberration, as a result of the primary concave mirror being mistakenly ground in error, by a width less than the thinnest of human hairs. The mirror is only gathering about ten percent of the starlight we were counting on. I'm in constant contact, discussing wide field planetary cameras, mirrors, and possible solutions. It's very stressful. My personal life, however, is very stable. Kind of sad that stability is my goal, but for now I'm OK with it. Annie has met new friends and loves our house. I have a caretaker, who is really a Jill of all trades. She helps with Mother and Annie, and does housework. I pay her well, of course, but the peace of mind is worth it. Mother's dementia is still intermittent, sometimes causing confusion, and other times inappropriate and irrelevant comments, but for the most part, she is under control. She even sometimes offers help with some equations I'm working on. So far, I think the move was a good idea. Being away from Adam has removed a heavy funk from my heart, and although Annie sometimes says she misses her daddy, I think she, too, is relieved to be away from that stress. We'll see how things go."

Brigid looked amazed and said, "Every once in a while, I have to be reminded of what a genius you are. How exciting for you to be involved in this greatest achievement to explore the universe since Galileo. And how exciting for us to be here listening to you talk about it."

"Ditto," echoed Rosie. She took another gulp of her beer

and began her update. "My biggest worry about moving back was the effect it would have on my kids. Antonio seems to be doing OK, and Massimo, who we call Max, is clueless because he hasn't known anything else. The one I'm worried about is Ricky. He is going on thirteen, which is a lousy age anyhow, and he has had to deal with pretty devastating changes. He misses the animals a lot and does not appreciate the captivity of the wild ones being in a zoo. I'm proud of his school work, though. He is doing really well in Lakewood, and he is active in some nice volunteer work at Our Lady of Mount Carmel, but there is a sadness in him, so I don't know. Thanks to Sammy, he has become an avid Indians and Browns fan — and all the pain and suffering that comes with that."

Babs asked, "Is he enjoying the extended family?"

"For sure," Rosie said. "But he often mentions the caretakers we left behind. As for me and Sammy, well, we knew that our financial situation was so uncertain in Kenya that we had to move. He loves the writing he is doing, and I am satisfied with what I'm doing with the zoo. It's only been a year since we've been back. I think we'll be fine. I do love being by my brother and sister, and of course, my mom, and cousin Beth. But even though I'm forty and successful, I still feel like I'm being judged by my cousins and aunts and uncles for my past behavior."

Brigid interrupted. "That's their problem."

"Thanks, Brigid. So, anyhow, that's it for me. You know that Beth is the councilwoman now and she keeps trying to drag us into the fray, but there's no way we are going to be a part of that. She's up for reelection next year, and I'll do the canvassing, and sign deliveries and all that campaign stuff, but after that, I'm done. I do love her though, and she's still crazy like a fox."

"Lord, she bailed us out of a lot of troubles."

"Gave me my first cigarette."

"And our first toke."

They lifted their glasses in a toast to Beth, and then Brigid took the floor.

"It is hard to believe we are forty. It seems like just yesterday we were not trusting anyone over thirty. The cramps in my back, and my sore feet, tell me I am aging, but when I sit here, in a bar, with old friends, I still feel the nineteen-year-old rebel in me."

"You were never a rebel," chuckled Rosie. "But go on."

"Well, one time, I did wear a bandana and peace earrings," Brigid laughed, and continued.

"When it comes to being a rebel, I do bow to you, Rosie. But I did my share of civil rights protesting for women and African Americans, and both of those commitments are still with me today. It amazes me that Parma, despite some efforts—well, mandatory efforts—still only has a handful of black people.

"Maybe if the cops didn't stop every car that has a black person in it, they would feel more welcome," snarled Rosie.

Brigid sighed and continued. "I love teaching in the high school in the old west side neighborhood that we all know and love so well. High school teaching is where I belong. There's such a great mix of students from various ethnic backgrounds and academic levels. Paul, our principal, is the best type of administrator. He puts students first but allows the teachers freedom in their classrooms to meet the students' needs as they see fit. The paperwork is ridiculous, but he knows it is part of the job, and commiserates with us, as he makes sure we get it done."

"Sounds like you have a mid-life crush," Babs said.

"Are you boinking him?" asked Rosie.

"Rosie, where on earth did you pick up that term?"

"I picked it up from Idi Amin. I thought you would prefer it to fu ..."

"Yes, Yes, I do."

After another drink and more laughter, Brigid continued. "I stopped being physically attracted to Paul the moment I found out he was the widower of my old friend. So, anyhow, in addition to the teaching, I do some traveling discussing feminist literary criticism and women writers. I still refuse requests from Harvard, Yale, and Notre Dame, never forgetting those closed doors. If I wasn't good enough for them then, I'm too good for them now."

"That's our girl."

"And, before you ask, Rosie, my love life is just dandy. My youthful enjoyment of dating is still with me, and I have enough men in my life to go out for dinners, and movies, and plays, and academic lectures. And, yes, I do occasionally have a tryst."

Rosie turned to Babs, "Wow, did Saint Brigid just admit to an occasional boink?"

Babs laughed into her drink, "Yes, she certainly did."

The women finished their drinks and dinners, then hailed a cab to the old Cleveland Municipal Stadium, where they sat behind a pole and watched the Indians beat the Milwaukee Brewers, agreeing that Sandy Alomar Junior was their new favorite Tribe man. Although, they did lament that they were now older than all of the players.

The next few months were hectic for the individual worlds of the women and the greater worlds of the entire universe. Babs was in daily consultation with the Jet Propulsion Lab, advising and discussing the tweaking of the Wide Field Planetary Camera 2, which eventually became the savior of Hubble's magnificent photography. She also participated in the conversations about the Corrective Optics Space Telescope Axial Replacement, or COSTAR, which would later become the solution to the complex error of the aberration. Babs was grateful for Annie's strength and ability to adapt to her new surroundings. Her mother's mind was still slipping, sometimes into oblivion, but her periods of lucidity remained dominant. Babs's communication with Rosie and Brigid was minimal, but they held true to a promise of a monthly luncheon where they shared their traditional laughter and love. Her communication with Adam was almost nil, and never pleasant. He feigned interest in Annie, and for now that was all Annie needed.

Rosie, too, was busy. Being a wife, a mother, and an employee, consumed her, and she felt pleasantly fulfilled. They had an outrageously extravagant second birthday party for Max in July, as Ricky and Antonio saw, for the first time, how Italians do celebrations. Her love and advocacy for her elephants never dimmed, and she became highly sought after for advice and fundraising. The aches and pains of middle age manifested themselves in heel spurs, slipped discs, and arthritic joints, for all of which her mother had homemade remedies … none of which ever worked. She looked forward to the monthly luncheons where the friends would laugh at how the conversations had slowly evolved from youthful fantasies to menopausal fatigue. Sammy, too, was content. He had imagined his career would remain focussed on his African adventures. Instead, his contracts became more frequently centered on local color, such as Cleveland's gems: the Cleveland Museum of Art, the Cleveland Orchestra, the Cleveland Playhouse, and the lore and lands of the islands on Lake Erie. These assignments brought with them free access to many events, which he shared with the family. The Scarponi children were seeing the best Cleveland had to offer — a blessing, since in the early 1990s, the best Cleveland had to offer was becoming scarce.

Life in Parma had not yet suffered the demise of favorite haunts that Cleveland was experiencing. Brigid still enjoyed walking to the Parma Theater and grocery shopping at Tal's delicatessen, as well as walking through Parmatown to shop or take in a movie. The Parma Cafe on Ridge Road was still the favorite watering hole for the Nagy clan and Parma people of all ages, where they would gather after weddings and funerals, or to watch the Browns, Indians, or Cavaliers. At forty, Brigid still pumped down the Bacardi and Coke with the best of the clientele. Pipers Three was her favorite suburban place to go when she wanted to hear live music and have a good dinner.

Her close friends and cultural experiences were, however, still in the heart of Cleveland. Peabody's Down Under in the Flats was her "go-to place" to soak up whatever music they were playing. Occasionally, she was even invited on stage to play her saxophone. The venue was filled with famous jazz and rock musicians — including Dizzy Gillespie, who had a celebration of his seventieth birthday there. It was a place of music and poetry — a place that embraced what Brigid continued to call "the swing of the universe."

Ohio City High School also had a swinging rhythm of its own. This inner-city high school allowed her to use the integrated curriculum she had developed for Jazz, English, Art, and Social Studies. Its proximity to downtown made field trips to music and art venues easy journeys. During the past two summers, she also traveled the United States on the lecture circuit, never missing an opportunity to hit the bars and clubs from Los Angeles to Massachusetts. Her Irish-Hungarian genes blessed her with a thirst for life, laughter, literature, and liquor.

During their October lunch get-together at Heck's Restaurant, on Bridge Avenue, Rosie shared that she and Sammy were taking the boys to visit Sammy's parents in Washington DC.

"We decided it was time for Ricky and Antonio to soak up some American History. They know more about Kenya than they do the United States. I thought it also might be fun for them to see where Sammy and I used to work, and where we met."

Babs added, "And where you first boinked?"

Brigid looked at Babs and laughed, "Et tu Brute?"

"No, we'll definitely leave that part out. It will be a historical trip," Rosie replied with a smile, thinking of fond memories.

An unusual lull came over the conversation. Brigid broke the silence.

"Why don't we all make a weekend trip to DC? We have procrastinated long enough about visiting the Vietnam Memorial. It's time we pay our respects to Martin and the rest of those who sacrificed everything for that damn war."

"I've always dreaded seeing his name carved into that black granite. So cold, so dark, so sad ... but I'm in. I'll go," Babs said as she fought back tears.

Even though the country moved on since the '60s and '70s, the wounds of the Vietnam era remained unhealed. The Vietnam Veterans now marched in parades and received some notice and acclaim that was denied them after the war ended. But the pain lingered just below the surface, sometimes manifesting itself in unspoken memories or lingering illnesses both mental and physical. The death of Martin Gorman was the burden that each of these women let fester in their hearts. He was Brigid's dearest friend since kindergarten, Rosie's confidant in high school, and Babs's first and only true love. They held onto the anger, the pain, the sorrow — somehow believing that these things kept Martin alive.

The conversation turned to war with reminiscing about the World War II stories that their fathers told them: Mr. Nagy in the Pacific, Mr. Vanetti in North Africa, and Mr. Turyev's parents in Auschwitz.

Rosie sighed. "And now we're getting ready to have more guys killed, and this time, women too. Bush is gathering the troupes around Kuwait and Iraq."

"Hussein has to be stopped, Rosie. Kuwait has been one of greatest strategic allies in the Middle East. We can't just turn our backs on them. This isn't like Vietnam; it's not a civil war."

Babs concluded the conversation. "True, but war is war, and war is hell no matter what the reason."

They lifted their glasses and toasted, "To the end of war."

Babs decided to take Annie on the trip to DC. David was back in Shaker for the weekend and would take care of Barbara. The Scarponis babysat for Rosie's boys and Annie, while Babs, Brigid, and Rosie visited the Memorial. The visit released emotions that had been buried deep in the women's souls. As they approached the Wall, they simultaneously slowed their pace to a standstill. The quiet enormity of the ebony structure and the steady stream of reverent, hushed visitors overwhelmed them with a somber feeling of awe. They walked slowly, in silence, starting with the first etched name in 1959, gazing with glazed eyes at the seemingly endless names of the rest of the fallen. When they made it to1968, Brigid knelt and cried at the name of John Viktoryn, a friend who attended Cathedral Latin High School, and again at the name of Raymond Garcia from Parma. She thought, *Boys who died on the battlefield while I was having fun in my carefree, high school days. Handsome young men who gave their lives serving their country, never knowing the sweet fruits that life could bring them.*

When they reached 1969, they froze at the sight of the name they came to honor: Martin Gorman. Brigid immediately knelt; Rosie put her hand on Brigid's shoulder; Babs placed both hands on the wall to hold her up, resisting the force of her body's inclination to crumble to the ground. They stayed frozen in those poses for several minutes. Brigid, praying a prayer of thanksgiving to the spirits of these men whom she felt hovering over her. Rosie, silently cursing the war and the politicians who made it happen. Babs, numb with grief, reliving every moment she had shared with Martin.

Brigid finally stood up, put her arms around her friends, and said, "It's time to go."

"I don't want to leave," whispered Babs, as she reluctantly removed her hands from the structure.The women walked, in silence, as they passed the rest of the names, and the Three Soldiers statue. They never spoke of the visit to the Wall again, each relishing memories and each grieving loss in her own quiet space.

Brigid flew back to Cleveland that evening, saying that she had lesson plans to write, and also to make plans for spending Thanksgiving on the East Coast with some friends from the Peace Corps. Babs and Rosie did some sight-seeing with their children. Ricky and Annie began to develop a strong bond, as Annie looked up to him as both a protector and a friend. Babs later told Rosie that Annie had a crush on Ricky.

"An innocent ten-year-old crush, too sweet for words," Babs said.

"Wow, what if …?

"Rosie, let's keep it at a ten-year-old crush. I think it was the trip to the National Bird House that started it all. Ricky knows so much about birds, and Annie was dumbfounded by it all."

"Yeah, that's actually the most excited he's been since moving from Africa. He loves birds and misses the colorful, weird flyers he would see when he traveled with Sammy."

"This city is so filled with treasures; we will have to bring the kids back someday."

"Definitely. We should make Brigid organize a field trip with her students. Although, she would probably want to spend the day in the Library of Congress, looking at books and documents."

In Parma, at that very moment, Brigid was, in fact, looking at books. Medical books. The results of her annual mammogram indicated that she might have breast cancer.

Waiting for test results is perhaps the most torturous stage of a disease. Not knowing. Imagining. Dreading. Hoping. Praying.

Brigid entered the room at the Cleveland Clinic where women were waiting to speak to the doctor after their biopsies. The fact that she was detained was not a good sign. When she was called in, the doctor and a nurse met her at the door. The doctor put his hand on her shoulder and walked her to a seat by his desk. The nurse sat on a chair close to her.

The doctor addressed Brigid in a confident, soft tone. "As you know, Brigid, the reason your doctor recommended a biopsy was because there was a thickening in your breast that he wanted more details on. The biopsy results show that the thickening itself does not reveal any cancer."

Before Brigid could finish her sigh of relief, the doctor continued.

"However…"

Brigid stiffened again.

"You have a condition called Lobular Carcinoma In Situ. It is abnormal cells in the milk glands of the breast. There …"

Brigid interrupted again, not knowing whether to cry in relief or fear. "So is it cancer or not?"

"This condition has only been mildly observed for a few decades and is considered relatively new. There is currently much debate as to whether it is cancer, or an indicator of increased risk of cancer, or definite precursor to cancer."

The nurse gently put her palm over Brigid's quivering hands.

"We consider it stage zero cancer, which means it has not yet spread at all. And, very likely, the cells can be removed with no further present danger. Your doctor contends, and I must say that I share his opinion, that more treatment is necessary to better assure that the condition does not eventually develop into a more invasive type of breast cancer. He has scheduled an appointment with an oncologist who will discuss the options you have. At this point, I am just the messenger. When the results of the biopsies indicate a problem, we share that information immediately so the patient does not have to wonder and worry what may await her. Here is a written copy of everything we just discussed. This condition is completely treatable, Brigid. I cannot offer you any more information than I have already given. Good luck. I have every confidence that you will be fine."

Driving home, Brigid could not quiet her mind. *So grateful it's only stage zero. But I may still have to get preventative chemo or some sort of drug. How will the side effects be? Am I to worry about cancer now for the rest of my life? I should make lesson plans just in case I have to miss school. Oh God, I never miss school. Should I tell my mother? Yes, I will have to, she always knows. Not going to tell Rosie or Babs, they both have so much on their plates. It's just that this is so unexpected. I eat healthy, don't smoke, and drink occasionally. Well, I drink a lot when I drink, but I don't drink often. This isn't really a big deal. It really isn't. But isn't it? The doctor was confident, but obviously concerned enough to treat me like a cancer patient. This isn't like me. I need to control myself. I will. Now I'm just nervous and surprised. Stage zero. For heaven's sake, I can deal.*

Brigid spent the early evening reading in the few medical books and encyclopedias she had in her library in her apartment. There was not much information on Lobular Carcinoma In Situ. She drank two glasses of wine, escaping into the fantasy of television with Bill Cosby and Sam Malone. Her doctor's appointment was tomorrow after school. "Tomorrow, and tomorrow, and tomorrow…"

Usually, there was never enough time for Brigid to teach everything she wanted in a class, but the day of her doctor's appointment presented her with a seemingly endless drag of hours. Even Duke Ellington's "Such Sweet Thunder," couldn't move fast enough. When the final bell rang, she was out the door before the students, leaving them confused, as Ms. Nagy never missed their final high five to end the day.

Dr. Schultz's office was crowded, but the nurse ushered Brigid into his office before she sat down in the waiting room. The doctor was waiting for her in his office, wearing a calming, kind smile. He began the conversation.

"Hello, Brigid. I imagine you have had a restless night."

"Rather unsettling, yes. Very anxious to hear what you have to say."

"Of course. So here we go. I see in the notes that you have

already been informed that your biopsy indicated you have Lobular Carcinoma In Situ. This is, simply put, abnormal cells in the milk glands. My practice treats this as cancer. At stage zero, it is not yet invasive, but we recommend treatment so it does not become invasive. In other words, our main goal is to nip this in the bud, so to speak. The word cancer is horrifying, and you are right to be concerned. Some oncologists don't refer to your condition as cancer, but whatever the label, it needs to be treated. And I can assure you that this is treatable."

"So what are my treatment options?"

"OK, right to the point. I will explain all the options; give you a day to research and consider. But I recommend we get started as soon as possible."

The doctor proceeded to gently and thoroughly explain the options, from surgery, to chemo, to radiation, to pills. Brigid's head was spinning, but she made her decision before she left the office. She would choose what she thought to be the least invasive and least poisonous option: a daily pill of tamoxifen. She would tell her mother, but no one else.

Brigid never tolerated drugs well, and as the weeks after her diagnosis passed by, the side effects of the drug began to ravage her mood and body. Sweats, mood swings, insomnia, and a general feeling of lethargy became the norm. She was hoping no one would notice, but little goes unnoticed among lifelong friends.

Her condition came to an emotional peak during a seemingly innocuous conversation. There was one subject that Rosie, Babs, and Brigid did not discuss. Abortion. As usual, Babs stayed non-committal, but Rosie was an adamant pro-choice advocate, and Brigid was an even more adamant anti-abortion activist. Although there were lengthy and respectful exchanges of opinions, they would never agree. With Rosie, all consideration focused on the woman; she could not understand Brigid's insistence that a woman did not have a right to decide what to do with her body. With Brigid, all consideration focused on the human life that the woman carried; she could not understand Rosie's insistence that a woman had the right to kill that life. It was an argument that could not be won; two perspectives that would never compromise. The friends decided to respect each other's opinions. Respect, not accept. Neither would agree with the other's opinion, but both would agree to see past the difference and respect the heart from which it came.

On a cool, early November evening, as the friends enjoyed a glass of wine and a burger on the outdoor patio at Heck's bar, not far from Brigid's school, Brigid began to sweat profusely, and became agitated. Rosie was relaying the news that their high school friend, Ellen, just gave birth to her fourth daughter. As Rosie began to describe the baby, Brigid broke out with a harsh, unrelated comment.

"Jesus, Rosie, almost twenty years ago you were trying to save the fucking snail darters. Now you support killing babies. How do you rationalize fighting for the survival of a tiny fish, advocating abortion, and celebrating a life all at the same time?"

Rosie and Babs sat in astonishment.

Babs spoke. "Brigid, where the hell did that come from?"

Brigid, now flushed with sweat, left the table, and went to the parking lot, where she got into her car, and started crying. Babs paid the bill, and Rosie ran to be with Brigid. Rosie wanted to lash out, but she knew there was something terribly wrong, so she entered the passenger seat of Brigid's car.

"OK, Saint Brigid. The F bomb, an irrational outburst, and, I must say, a disgusting sweating exhibit, are very uncharacteristic of the woman I know. What is wrong?"

By then, Babs had entered the back seat.

Brigid told them of her ordeal with her breast problems, admitting she was embarrassed that such a low risk of cancer trouble was stressing her so much, and that she had no control over the side effects of the medicine. She apologized to Rosie, begging forgiveness for her unfair lashing out. For a moment, they reminisced about the snail darter incident Brigid had referred to, when they bombarded the legislature with calls and letters to save the fish and halt the Tennessee Valley's dam project. They sat in the car, discussing the delights and dilemmas of being women in their forties, each promising to share both the merriment and misery that come with age.

As Rosie and Babs left the car, Rosie whispered something to Babs. They turned around and knocked on the driver's side window.

When Brigid looked, they lifted their blouses up to their necks, and flashed their breasts, Mardi Gras style, as they shouted, "You got this!"

November winds off of Lake Erie soon began to hint at the Cleveland winter that loomed in the coming weeks. Babs was working long hours, communicating with the Jet Propulsion Lab, and the meticulous workings of the Wide Field Planetary Camera 2, as well as COSTAR. It was becoming evident that she would have to visit the lab in California to adequately address her work and make a more detailed contribution. NASA was still paying her a generous salary, and it was expected that she should participate in person before the end of the year.

Adam had requested to see Annie over the Thanksgiving holiday, and although he relinquished visitation rights to the actual Thanksgiving Day, he still had several days a year when he was awarded time to spend with her. Annie herself had indicated that she wanted to see her daddy, and she was also mentioning that she missed the warmth of the California sunshine and the balmy breezes of the Pacific Ocean. NASA offered Babs an all-expense-paid work trip to the coast, which included plane fare for herself, her mother, and Annie, as well as a week's rental in an ocean-view condo not far from the lab. David was not yet ready to give up Thanksgiving in New York, so the three generations of women headed to the West Coast.

Earphones playing music from the Big Band era calmed Barbara through the entire three- hour flight, and Annie enjoyed the movie *The Never Ending Story 2*. Babs took the time to rest and enjoy the uneventful trip through the clouds, during which no one asked anything of her.

They arrived at the Los Angeles airport at noon on Sunday, November 18. The temperature was 83 degrees, and the warm air caressed their faces like a welcome massage. An old friend of Babs's, Christine Sandoval, met them at the airport. Christine would look after Barbara while Babs went to work. She was one of many engineers who received pink slips after the Apollo 11 moon landing mission and was now teaching at Berkeley. She had no immediate family and agreed to stay with Barbara, and help Babs with Thanksgiving dinner. Babs had hoped Barbara would be in a mindset that was easy to handle, and that she would remember the friend, who had visited frequently when they lived in California. Lately, Barbara had retreated into a silent mode and did not speak very often, but Babs never really knew what to expect.

They settled into the spacious three-bedroom rental home in El Segundo, and then immediately went out to the shore to take a walk. The Pacific Ocean reflected the brilliant blue of the sky, punctuated with the soft lapping of waves. The women and child walked in silence, becoming one with their surroundings, and each other. They walked for about a mile, when Barbara sat in the sand, reached her arms toward the sky, and said, "Oh, it's wonderful to be back in Cape Cod."

Annie looked quizzically at Babs, and Babs quietly explained that when she was a little girl, the family would vacation in Cape Cod. It was Barbara's favorite place.

Barbara beckoned her daughter and granddaughter to sit beside her. For the next hour, Annie heard stories about the summer retreats to the Cape and the important work of her grandfather, who also loved the peace of the sea. Then, Barbara abruptly stopped the narrative and retreated into silence. Babs took both of their hands, and they again walked quietly in calm meditation back to the house.

Adam stopped by in the early evening to pick up Annie. Babs was both surprised and somewhat irritated at the warmth of the embrace he shared with Annie. When he approached to embrace Babs, she backed away and spoke quietly, so Annie would not hear: "You will never touch me again."

Forgiveness had not yet dissolved her anger.

Annie said her goodbyes and skipped to the silver Porsche that waited in the driveway. Babs trusted Adam enough to take good care of their daughter, as she waved goodbye.

Barbara stood by the window, with her middle finger raised.

The disease that was ravaging her mind, sometimes was a source of sad amusement to Babs. Growing up, Babs was not even permitted to say "crap," and she never heard her parents utter anything foul or crass. So when her proper, brilliant mother now spontaneously expressed vulgarities, Babs could not prevent a laugh.

Adam lived in Glendale, halfway between the lab and where Babs was staying. Annie would be with him Sunday through Wednesday, and Babs would pick her up on the way home from work on Wednesday. Babs had made it clear to Annie, if at any time Annie felt like she wanted to leave, Babs would get her immediately. When Annie called Babs Sunday night, she gave her report.

"Daddy's house is fantastic. It has a pool, and he brought some video games for me. We are sitting on the patio now looking at the San Gabriel Mountains and he is being very nice. Tomorrow we are going to Forest Lawn Cemetery! You know how I love old movies, Mommy, and we thought it would be fun to go where so many of those old actors are buried. I have to go now. Love you the most."

Babs was happy to hear Annie giggling and having fun. Knowing Annie was enjoying herself would make Babs's leaving for work less stressful, and their signature goodbye, "Love you the most," was especially poignant now.

When Babs left for the lab the following day, Barbara was helping Christine with breakfast. She was in normal mode and remembered Christine from when they had lived in California. Christine gave Babs a wink, and for the first time in several months, Babs was at peace.

NASA had provided a brand-new royal-blue Chevy Corvette ZR-1 for her to use during her stay, which would make the hour-long ride to the lab much more enjoyable. She was never a car aficionado, but she did love 'Vettes.

She soaked up the red-carpet treatment she was getting from NASA. It stoked her self-esteem, which had been dwindling since Adam's infidelity came to light. So, there she was, soaked and stoked, driving the highways and byways in the California sunshine, blasting the Beatles' *Revolver* album, actually enjoying the feeling of being forty years old and free.

When she reached the lab, there was a parking spot reserved for her, and when she entered her former work space, there were hugs and applause. They had missed her, and more significantly, they respected the contribution she was offering from home. It had been less than a year since she had left, but it seemed like she had not seen these people for a much longer time.

As it turned out, there were several she had actually never seen. Several new, young faces approached her and said how happy they were to meet her. She had thought that being confronted with the infiltration of youthful colleagues might somehow diminish her, but instead, the respect that they showed her made her appreciate, once again, the perks of middle age. Her welcome back was both professional and emotional, a satisfying beginning to her week. She assumed her duties as Senior Scientist in the program office, managing the development of planetary science instruments.

Once again, however, professionalism covered an underlying sexism. After one of the meetings, where she was the main presenter, one of the scientists approached her, lightly grabbed her backside, and whispered, "You look better than ever, honey. My wife is out of town; how about coming to my place tonight for a hot toddy?"

"Only if we make it boiling hot, so I can pour it down your pants," Babs responded, as she broke away.

The rest of the day was filled with meetings and lab work, and hopeful predictions on when the mirror would be repaired, and other tweaks would be completed, so the Hubble could launch. Optimism was the mood of the day — a significant change from when she left in May.

"Human interaction beats long-distance communication in ways I didn't imagine," she said to Christine and Barbara as they dined on fresh seafood and hush puppies that Christine had prepared.

Barbara nodded her head, and an engaging discussion ensued about the work on the Hubble, and also the seeds of Barbara's work on Mars' exploration. Annie called with a report on her trip to the cemetery and their plans to visit the Neon Art Museum the next day. Babs was surprised that there were not more natural excursions like the mountains, or stargazing, but Annie sounded like she was having fun, so Babs did not allow any hints of skepticism.

NASA filled Babs's week with long days of calculating, testing, discussing, and planning. She enjoyed every moment. She eschewed the after-work dinner and drink invitations, not wanting to overburden Christine's time with Barbara, who thankfully had few lapses in cognizance. It was Barbara's change in language that both amused and concerned Babs. Tuesday night, when Babs was settling her mother in bed, Barbara asked, "Have you run into the prick and his whore at the lab?"

Babs did not stifle her laugh, as she answered, "No, Mother. The prick and his whore have the week off."

Barbara smiled and fell softly to sleep.

Wednesday went at a slower pace at the lab, as several of the staff started their Thanksgiving holiday early. Babs was thankful for the quiet contemplation of working alone, examining and writing reports. It also gave her time to have personal chats with some of her old friends, the chats at times turning to philosophy and fate.

Lawrence Roman, an engineer from Shaker Heights, whom Babs had become friends with only when she moved to California, explained his insights.

"The revelations I am seeing in the cosmos are uncovering so many spontaneous and incredible formations and cellular interactions. I'm convinced more than ever that the universe has popped up through chance and randomness."

"Popped up?" asked Senior Engineer, Gail Jankovich.

Lawrence continued. "Gravity had to already exist, since something had to be holding that singularity together. Not a stretch to theorize that somehow gravity started the whole burst, and then chance and random bombardments took over, offering probability, but not predictability. Discovery after discovery gives evidence to that."

Stephen Simpson, a Postdoctoral Fellow in the Microdevices Laboratory, added, "The more we know, the more possibilities arise. We are postulating that gravity is, in fact, infinite, and that it precipitated the 'Big Bang.' Or there was no big bang at all, and the universe always contained material of extreme heat and density, which gravity eventually pulled together."

Gail questioned, "So, basically, the theories seem to lean in two directions. Either material that makes up the universe, along with gravity, is eternal, always was and always will be? Or … these materials, along with gravity —'popped up,' as you say, out of nothing?"

Babs interjected, "That's straight out of Catholic Catechism. The definition of an eternal God, 'always was; always will be.' And the definition of theological creation: 'God made something out of nothing.'"

Lawrence visibly scoffed at the mention of God. "Sorry, my beautiful, brilliant, Catholic girls. God is out of the equation."

Babs questioned, "Even with the something out of nothing theory? Nature can create from nothingness?"

"Ya know, the problem with our professions is that we are so myopic in our focus that we often don't look out of our own specialties," Lawrence said, smugly.

Babs sighed, thinking of all the doctors she had taken her mother to, none in agreement. "Like doctors," she said. "There's so many specialties and a patient has so many specialists prescribing pills and tests; no one knows what the other is doing."

"Yes, something like that." Lawrence continued. "So, back to the point of nature itself, creating something out of nothing. There is fascinating research that indicates, in fact, a particle-antiparticle combination can actually come out of nothing. Both Einstein and Heisenberg provided the foundation for this occurrence."

Lawrence again looked smug, thinking he had knowledge the women did not. Gail popped his bubble.

"I am well aware of that research. In order for that to happen, a phenomenal amount of energy is required."

Lawrence shot back. "Yes, but it is a possibility, and that negates the need for a supernatural creator. The universe can exist without it."

"Not really," said Gail. "The energy and the dense material, and gravity that is necessary for the particle-antiparticle occurrence, had to be created. They could not 'pop out' from nothing. So we are back to the question of eternal. Either the materials of the universe always existed, or they were created by something or someone else. I'm not trying to persuade you to believe in the existence of God. I'm just saying that, in the end, it's a question of choosing which eternal scenario we want to believe. Scientists need to stick to the observable, natural world, and not comment on what cannot yet be observed."

Steve re-entered the conversation. "We need to get together and discuss this when there is more time. By the way, what, exactly is time? Does it really exist? Nevermind, don't get started on that."

They all laughed, and Babs said, "I truly miss you all, and these stimulating conversations. But now, I have to pick up my daughter, and go stuff a turkey."

Gail and Babs walked to their cars together.

"It amazes me," Gail said. "That these guys can, on a daily basis, observe the wonders of the universe, and chalk it all up to chance and randomness. For a while, I got sucked into their way of thinking. When my husband died suddenly, I lost all sense of wonder, all sense of meaning. None of this, I thought, makes sense. Randomness rules everything. And then, I forced myself to pray. And I found a group of scientists who prayed. I began meeting with them, and before long, my eyes were open, and I felt the spirit of God that transcends all. I'm telling you this, because I know the changes that have happened in your life. I know how ugly the world can be. And I know how useless going to church can be. Keep the faith, Babs. There is an eternal truth, and that truth is God."

Babs was only thinking ahead to the scenario that awaited her at Adam's. She dreaded seeing his house, and his new life. She appreciated Gail's words however, and she would remind herself of them when needed.

As she drove to Adam's, she did pray for peace of mind, but as she pulled into his winding driveway, she began to seethe. His house was a beautiful sprawling ranch, with solar panels, wraparound porch, and perfect landscaping of a meticulous lawn, with numerous rows of purple, red, pink, and white hibiscus surrounding the perimeter.

And there, an ugly blot on the tranquil scene: the whore, sitting on the porch with Annie and Adam. She hated the word whore. It was an unfair, misogynistic judgment on women that had no comparable language for men. However, her mother's words stuck to her heart, and from now on, Adam and his new young woman would be known to her as the prick and the whore.

But, for now, Adam was Annie's father, and in front of her daughter, she would treat him as such. She felt no responsibility, however, to treat the whore with anything but a frigid courtesy.

When Babs got out of the car, Annie came running to her, Adam trailing behind, carrying her suitcase and a large stuffed teddy bear. The whore wisely remained seated on the porch.

"Whoa," Babs said. "Not sure how we are going to get Teddy on the plane. Adam, why don't you UPS him to our place in Shaker? Is that OK with you, Annie?"

"Sure," Annie replied as she thanked and hugged her father, and opened the car door to get in.

Adam touched Babs's hand and said, "We had a nice time. Thanks for not making this difficult."

Babs wanted to slap his hand, and his face for that matter, but she knew Annie was watching, so she forced a smile and closed the door. As they drove back to their house, Annie shared some of the things she had done with her father. She never mentioned the whore, and Babs was satisfied that Annie enjoyed herself, and that was all that mattered. Other topics would be discussed when Annie brought it up. Babs did, however, recognize that perhaps she focused too much on academics and science with Annie. She made a vow to herself to open up more doors of activities for her daughter.

That night, they broke bread for stuffing, chopped vegetables, removed the innards from the turkey, and readied the side dishes so they would be ready to cook. The next day, Thanksgiving dinner was peaceful and delicious, and ended with a walk on the beach and a good night's sleep for all. The remainder of the week consisted of a furious work schedule for Babs, and a lazy, sea breeze enhanced bonding between grandmother and granddaughter.

When they returned home, Babs touched base with Rosie

and Brigid. Rosie reported she had a fun holiday in DC, the boys "becoming more American every day." Brigid had a stress-free New England Thanksgiving with old friends. Now, they had to appease their mothers and spend Christmas with their respective families. Even with their daughters in middle age, Mama Vanetti and Dar Nagy still had a stronghold on the apron strings of their treasured eggs.

The following year, 1991, was a settling-in period for the three friends. Brigid continued to teach at her high school, growing closer to Paul, but only in friendship. His intelligence and kind demeanor reminded her of Martin. She was also still in high demand on the lecture circuit from colleges who studied her feminist criticism. She tolerated the new doses of Tamoxifen very well, and all signs indicated she would defeat any onset of the cancer that may have lingered beneath her breasts.

Rosie and Sammy also firmly settled in, as their reputations (Sammy as a writer and Rosie as an animal expert) earned them a local celebrity status that was accompanied by excellent salaries. Their oldest son, Ricky, decided to attend the alternative high school where Brigid taught, where he enjoyed the gentler atmosphere of freedom and choices that it offered. Rosie felt relieved that Brigid would quietly assure that he was taken care of with the best teachers and schedules.

NASA continued to employ Babs, as the entire staff worked constantly on the equipment and mission that would fix the Hubble Telescope so that it would work to capacity. Her mother was becoming more difficult, as she more frequently had irrational outbursts of crying, and laughing, and spewing vulgar language. Babs could not have handled it without the caretaker, Charlene, but even she was showing signs of concern and fatigue. Babs noticed that Annie asked more often to spend the night at a friend's house, and seldom invited anyone over to her own home.

As the friends celebrated their forty-first birthday in June, at Sokolowski's Restaurant, where the views of Cleveland's bridges and buildings and waterscapes still brought them joy, they reflected on their current conditions, as well as the changing conditions in the city of Cleveland. The conversation started, of course, with the most pressing matter. The Cleveland Indians.

"God, I don't know how we can be so awful. We're already sinking well below .500."

"And we have players like Alomar, and Bell, and Baerga, how can we not win?"

"No pitching."

After they exhausted the topic of Major League Baseball, Babs began the more serious topics.

"My mother is rapidly accelerating her descent into madness. I'm not sure I can give her the care she needs. Her living with us is affecting Annie's life, and the caretaker is at her wits' end, trying to keep up with outbursts, strange behavior, and frequent verbal abuse. It's becoming impossible for me to give my work the focus it requires, and you can forget about my having a social life."

"We never really imagined this scenario, did we?" Rosie mused. "Especially with your mom, Babs. She was the most brilliant woman I have ever met, and to see her mind be slowly eaten up with this condition is sad and bewildering."

Brigid had been sitting in silence, then finally spoke. "Babs, how can Rosie and I help? I know you are hanging on to the hope that you will not have to put her in a home, so let's try to come up with a plan to ease some of your burden, so you can keep her as long as possible. I can bring my mother and father over once a week to be with Barbara. They have always enjoyed each other's company, and ..."

Babs interrupted. "That is so kind, Brigid, but at this point, it's a fifty-fifty chance that Mom would have no clue who they are."

"Doesn't matter. My parents could still be with her, while you and Annie leave and do something fun together, and we would come during the week, so the caretaker could have a day off too. Dar and Miklos haven't even hit seventy yet, and they have more energy than I do. Once a week, Babs, think about it."

"Mama Rose just hit seventy-two, and she would love to have Barbara and you and Annie come over once a month for dinner. Annie could spend the night at my house, and my mom and Sammy could bring Barbara home and stay with her for a while, during which time, you could have a date, and get boinked," Rosie said, with no hint that she was not completely serious.

"Oh my God, Rosie," Brigid exclaimed, her expressed dismay cloaking her thoughts that Rosie had a very good idea.

Babs, exhausted with continued bouts of worry and weary, said, "I'll think about it. And, damn, I love you gals."

The evening continued with exchanges of thoughts and theories about their lives and the visions of what was to come. They ended, as always with a toast, "To our mothers, who carried the treasured eggs that resulted in ... us!"

They put the plan into action for the rest of the year, which reduced some of Babs's stress level and allowed Annie to escape some of the pain of watching her grandmother become a different, often frightening person.

Dar and Miklos, and Mama Rose enjoyed helping this woman whom they had admired for so many years. The arrangement provided an outlet for three generations of friends and families to support and love the people they cared for most. For a few months, this small circle of loved ones nurtured Barbara and each other.

But within a year, Barbara's condition grew more ominous. She often would find a way out of the house and began wandering the streets. Her bouts of irrational screaming were increasing in number and intensity, and her presence in the household was destroying any sense of peace or normalcy.

When the three friends met at Babs's house for their annual birthday lunch in June 1992, Babs shared sobering news.

"Charlene has given her notice that she can no longer remain as Barbara's caretaker. I have until the end of the year to make other accommodations for my mom. Annie has finally broken down and told me that she doesn't sleep well. She withdraws to her room more often and is now asking to spend the entire summer with Adam. David comes home when he can, and he, and well, all of you have given so much of your time, but, I... I..."

Babs put her hands over her face, as tears became visible. She continued in a shaky voice. "I am going to have to find another place for her. I can't keep asking more and I can't do more. I have to put this woman who made me what I am, who helped put men on the moon, who laid the foundation for landing technology on Mars, who wrote critically acclaimed papers on Martian biology — I have to put her in what our parents used to call a 'nut house.'"

A numb silence stilled the room.

Brigid spoke. "These places are not the nut houses of old, Babs. They are run by caring, professional people, and often the grounds and rooms are beautiful and peaceful. You have done everything possible to hold on, but now you must do what's best not only for you and Annie, but for your mom. She will be safer, and you, too, will be safer."

"My mother has connections all over the city, Babs," said Rosie, as she reached for Babs's hand. "We'll find the best possible place."

Babs, not wanting to exhaust the conversation with sadness, changed the subject to politics. "Brigid, are you going to try to see Bill Clinton when he stops at your favorite Parma pierogi place in August?"

"I doubt it. My sisters are ga-ga over him, but there is just something about him and Hillary I don't trust."

"Lord, here we go," Rosie harped. "What is it that doesn't appeal to you, Brig? Is it intelligence, or his good looks, or his command of the language?"

Brigid had to laugh, but she was serious with her distrust. "Kennedy fooled all of us with those same charming characteristics, didn't he? I can't reconcile being a snake in private life with being a good president. And somewhere in my intuition, I think Clinton is a snake."

Babs, the logical peacemaker, added her insight. "It is ironic that the politicians who seem to advocate for women are often the ones who treat the women in their own lives with disdain. I wish one of these days we can choose a man who is consistent on both a private and political level."

"Better yet," Brigid said, "hopefully one day we can choose a woman."

And that statement provided the closing toast.

Chapter 6

* *

*"what i want most / is to look into my child's eyes /
and / see / that i have given birth / to / a / heart."*

Nayyirah Waheed

Feminism continued to proceed in a direction that many women in the '60s generation found disturbing. When Annie decided to dress up as Madonna for Halloween, it became one more distressing angle in Babs's life. Madonna had just released her latest album, *Erotica*, and her latest book, *Sex*, both of which glorified sadistic and masochistic sexual activity. Not wanting to judge something she did not know much about, Babs bought both of those items, listened, read, and then slipped into full-blown mother craziness.

Annie, now twelve years old, was dancing with the same blast of hormones that all girls eventually deal with. Babs recalled her own rebellions at that age: smoking, "necking," sneaking around instead of going to church. She cringed at the hell that she put her parents through. Her parents came down on her with groundings and a strict curtailing of her activities. But now, things were different. She was the mom.

Babs bemoaned her situation at the September lunch with Rosie and Brigid. "Why is it that I am afraid to tell my twelve-year-old daughter that she cannot walk through the neighborhood with black fishnet stockings, a skirt that climbs her butt crack, and a shirt that hangs below her pubescent cleavage crack? She's a good girl, gets good grades, I like her friends, blah blah. And yet, she wants to imitate the fashion of sex maniacs. It should be an easy 'no, you cannot go out like that, Annie.' And yet I actually have fear of the scene it will create. Have I spent too much time with work and my mother that I missed some sort of twist in values in my own daughter? Am I so worried about losing her respect that I won't dare discipline her?"

"I talk to so many mothers of students who are facing the same thing," Brigid said. "Parents are actually afraid to confront their kids. It's an amazing turn from when we were younger. Even when we were doing bad things, there was always the fear of death that our parents would find out. Nowadays, it seems like the kids just do what they want, knowing there will be no repercussions."

Rosie offered another perspective. "Having sons, I'm not sure I'm facing the same problems. For one thing, Ricky doesn't give a rat's ass about how he dresses. And they don't chat on the phone. And they don't feel the need to look like Van Halen or Ozzie Osbourne. It seems like girls are bombarded with how to be sexy, how to get a guy, even how to seduce. Look at any magazine and listen to popular songs. I don't know how these young girls escape the Madonna look. I'm sure my boys are doing things I don't approve of, but it just seems like we don't argue as much as mothers of daughters do. As a matter of fact, we found a *Playboy* magazine in Ricky's room. Can you imagine my mother and father's reactions if my brothers brought that stuff into the house? Sammy talked with him, guy stuff, but the bottom line being, any magazine that diminishes women to being sex objects is not a healthy way to deal with desires, and it will certainly not make you into a better man."

"So many of the feminist causes we fought for during our college years have devolved into sexual exploitation. Except now, it's worse, because we're doing it to ourselves," Brigid added.

"Lord, we actually have become our mothers," sighed Babs.

"Don't you ever say that again," laughed Rosie. "Babs, you will handle your situation differently than your mother would, but you will still do it with understanding and love, and one way or another, Annie will grow out of this stage, and you both will be better for it. You should just share a joint with her, mellow out, and have a nice talk."

"A toast to doobies," they said, as they smiled away their woes.

Babs laughed but knew it wouldn't be so easy. She was losing communication with Annie, and, along with everything else, it was taking a toll on her health. She didn't share the information with her friends, but Babs was now taking blood pressure medicine, and her latest appointment with her gynecologist confirmed that she was in full-blown menopause. Dealing with protests, war, and rebellion, now seemed much less stressful than dealing with divorce, child rearing, and aging.

A week before Halloween, Annie had friends over to discuss the costume party they would be attending. Charlene had taken Barbara out for a walk in the Shaker Lakes park, so there were no worries of a "granny episode," as Annie now called Barbara's outbursts.

Babs enjoyed seeing Annie, now a seventh-grader, surrounded by good friends.

Such a tough age, she thought. *On the cusp of adolescence, half wanting to remain a child, the other half wanting to be an adult. And somewhere in between, coping with changing bodies, not sure whether to be shy or flaunt the changes in breasts and hips and moods.*

The girls had decided to attend the party as "Material Girls," a reference to Madonna's hit song, which espoused the physical, material aspects of "romance," where "the boy with the cold hard cash is always Mister Right." *Everything I despise,* thought Babs.

Babs decided not to argue or judge. Although she was unhappy about the idea, she decided to gently give her opinion while still letting Annie know she trusted her. She served the young ladies pop and chips and chip dip, as she eavesdropped on what their costumes would look like.

"My mom won't let me out of the house dressed like Madonna," said a beautiful girl named Maureen Williams, who had become Annie's necessary 'best friend.' "So, I'm just dressing as a flashy rich girl, with tons of fake jewelry, an old prom dress, and gaudy accessories."

Annie gave a glance at Babs, who could not help smiling at Maureen's comment. *I'm happy to see that some moms are still in control,* Babs thought.

Another friend, who had the nickname "Peppy Patty," because she never slowed down, said, "My mom suggested I go as what she called, an "original" material girl — a 1920s flapper. Gonna bob my hair, find a flapper costume, add a long cigarette holder, and there ya go."

Linda, who was undoubtedly the wild one of the group, laughed and said, "I'm going full-blown Madonna, blonde wig, fishnet stockings, short shorts, plenty of make-up with a fake beauty mark, and a tight top. My mom just said, 'Go for it.'"

Surprisingly, when it was her turn, Annie looked at Babs, who was now sitting at the table. "Well, I haven't come up with anything yet. What do you think, Mom?"

Babs stopped herself from hugging Annie, and calmly replied: "I just think as young women, you need to dress how you feel, and not let society dictate to you what you should look like. It's truly heartwarming to me that you shared your ideas with your mothers."

Maureen laughed, "Well, my mom actually did dictate to me what I should look like."

They all laughed, just as Babs and Rosie and Brigid still laughed at the power of mothers.

Annie finished the discussion by saying, "I remember reading about the Beatnik generation in a report I did on the 1950s. The beatnik girls were the 'anti-material' girls. I think I'll get a beret, a striped top, a pair of sunglasses, tight slacks, and a pipe and be an 'anti.'"

Adolescent chat about boys and crushes and whispers now dominated the conversation. Babs left the room, satisfied that not everything in her world was out of her control.

The day after Halloween, Rosie, Babs, and Brigid all received calls from Mama Rose. The message was brief and to the point.

"Your mothers have all agreed that this Christmas time would be a return to our tradition from years ago. Everyone, and I mean everyone, at my house, on Sunday, December 20, at 1:00 p.m. If you play an instrument, bring it, and bring any dish you fancy. See you there." Click.

So, that was that. In the meantime, Babs spent the month of November working and looking for a home for her mother; Rosie continued to visit schools to share a slideshow on her time in Kenya; Brigid immersed herself in her teaching.

∽

Principal Paul read the following announcement over the public address system at Ohio City High School the day before Thanksgiving break:

Transcript of President George Washington's Thanksgiving Proclamation from October 3, 1789. By the President of the United States of America— A Proclamation

Whereas it is the duty of all Nations to acknowledge the providence of Almighty God, to obey his will, to be grateful for his benefits, and humbly to implore his protection and favor—and Whereas both Houses of Congress have by their Joint Committee requested me "to recommend to the People of the United States a day of public thanksgiving and prayer to be observed by acknowledging with grateful hearts the many signal favors of Almighty God, especially by affording them an opportunity peaceably to establish a form of government for their safety and happiness."

Now therefore I do recommend and assign Thursday the 26th day of November next to be devoted by the People of these States to the service of that great and glorious Being, who is the beneficent Author of all the good that was, that is, or that will be—That we may then all unite in rendering unto him our sincere and humble thanks—for his kind care and protection of the People of this country previous to their becoming a Nation—for the signal and manifold mercies, and the favorable interpositions of his providence, which we experienced in the course and conclusion of the late war—for the great degree of tranquility, union, and plenty, which we have since enjoyed—for the peaceable and rational manner in which we have been enabled to establish constitutions of government for our safety and happiness, and particularly the national One now lately instituted, for the civil and religious liberty with which we are blessed, and the means we have of acquiring and diffusing useful knowledge; and in general for all the great and various favors which he hath been pleased to confer upon us.

And also that we may then unite in most humbly offering our prayers and supplications to the great Lord and Ruler of Nations and beseech him to pardon our national and other transgressions—to enable us all, whether in public or private stations, to perform our several and relative duties properly and punctually—to render our national government a blessing to all the People, by constantly being a government of wise, just, and constitutional laws, discreetly and faithfully executed and obeyed--to protect and guide all Sovereigns and Nations (especially such as have shown kindness unto us) and to bless them with good government, peace, and concord—To promote the knowledge and practice of true religion and virtue, and the increase of science among them and Us—and generally to grant unto all mankind such a degree of temporal prosperity as he alone knows to be best.

Given under my hand at the City of New York the third day of October in the year of our Lord 1789.

Go. Washington

The principal and teachers had previously agreed to discuss the contents and/or historical perspective of this proclamation with their students. Each teacher had a specific topic that was somehow related to their content. Math and Science teachers discussed the "increase of science" of the late 1700s. Social Studies teachers discussed the concepts of "government of wise, just, and constitutional laws." English teachers discussed the language, particularly, references to "God, Thanksgiving, and Transgressions."

The conversation in Brigid's class was lively, with diverse opinions and comments spewing forth with little or no coaxing from Brigid. She gave control of the discussion over to the students, only intervening when the comments became too heated or derogatory.

"I think this is a beautiful proclamation. I wish we would talk more about God in our country today."

"Yeah, well, I wonder what Washington's slaves were thankful for."

"Or the Native Americans that were being killed off and having their land stolen."

"We were still a young country. Those were probably the transgressions he was talking about."

"The whole point was to ask God for help in making things better."

"For who?"

"For the citizens of the new country."

"Exactly. Again, who were those citizens?"

"But he does refer to 'all mankind.'"

"So, I do think this is a good message about hope."

"And a prayer that we do better."

"Well, I'm still waiting."

"I'm not ashamed to say that I am very thankful for the United States of America and very thankful that my family and I get to live here. And I think Washington said the right things in this proclamation."

"Me too."

"You are my friends, and I am thankful for that. But I can never forgive what they did to my people."

"Or mine."

"This was 1789, man. It was a different world then. Washington was a great leader and helped start the country that stands for freedom and laws that protect its people. We are still a young country in comparison to other countries. We are still trying to put Washington's words into actions."

"Lotsa trying left to do."

"Can't we be thankful for the great things this country gives us?"

"It's OK to be thankful for our virtues, as long as we don't forget our vices."

The banter filled the period, and Brigid was satisfied with the engagement and participation of students. She told them that she was thankful to have such wonderful students who could disagree with respect and intelligent insights. She also marveled on how different this conversation was, compared to the undying patriotism and Thanksgiving discussions of her time in high school. When the bell rang, they lined up for their daily high five as she wished them a happy Thanksgiving. The last student to leave was a quiet young woman, Maria Lopez, who hugged and said, "Estoy agradecida por usted, Señorita Nagy. Es como una madre para mi." [I am grateful for you, Miss Nagy. You are like a mother to me.]

Women are mothers, even when they are not mothers, thought Brigid, as she locked up her room for Thanksgiving break.

Winter had not officially begun, with just a few inches of December snow, which had melted by the time, on December 20, the Vanetti, Nagy, and Turyev clans gathered at the Vanetti household in the west side of Cleveland. Miklos and Dar were the first to arrive, carrying Irish stew and Hungarian papri-kash — enough to feed a multitude of hungry friends and relatives. One of their twins, Cindy, now thirty years old, and still living with them in their Parma bungalow, came with them. She served as an eighth-grade teacher and Eucharistic Minister at Saint Charles. The other twin, Suzy, was the only family member not able to attend. New York concierges could not take any days off during the holiday season. She would get a family phone call during a break later in the day. Sally, who now lived in Ireland, came in for a few days, but her husband and daughter remained in Dublin. Joan flew in from Chicago, and would soon be arriving with her husband Michael, and their two children. Joan had a music studio where she taught flute, clarinet, and the bassoon. Her husband was the concert-master of the Chicago Symphony Orchestra. Michelle, who married and gave birth to her son, John, while still in high school, was on her way with him and her husband, John Sr.

Babs, Annie, Barbara, and David arrived promptly at 1:00 p.m.

The Scarponis and Vanettis arrived shortly after. Rosie and

Sammy walked in with Ricky, Antonio, and Max. Rebecca, with her husband, George, and son, Stephen, were followed by Robert, still single, working in a successful law firm.

Despite the societal waves of feminism and liberation, the women and girls migrated to the kitchen, and the men hightailed it to the front room to watch the Browns play their last home game of the season. The Browns had a losing record, but Browns fans continued to curse and cheer, this year swallowing their woes in the first batch of a new Christmas Ale brewed by the Great Lakes Brewing Company. Miklos, the last male of his generation within these families, enjoyed the fresh, youthful voices of his sons-in-law, grandson, and Sammy. He took heart that the tradition of Browns' triumphs and defeats would be passed on to new generations. Still a devout Catholic, Miklos truly believed that being a Browns fan was a suffering in Purgatory, and a sure ticket to heaven.

Italian sauces, Hungarian gravies, pasta, juicy meats, marinating fish, fresh vegetables, oregano, basil, paprika, cilantro, turmeric spices, delectable pastries, and all sorts of hearty aromas simmered through the kitchen, as the ladies of the manor prepared a Christmas feast. Barbara was given the task of snapping off the ends of fresh green beans and soaking them in a bowl of sautéed garlic and olive oil. She sat at the end of the kitchen table with a dazed smile. An unspoken feeling of urgency prevailed, that this might be their last feast together. Nevertheless, Mama Rose beamed with joy. Babs and Rosie also beamed as they watched their children enjoy games and laughter along with Joan's. Brigid observed it all, thinking how one day she would research the pure bonds of female friendships and family ties. *Within all of my advocacy for women's freedom, I must never deny that women are women and men are men. We must never give up what is uniquely female. We must never try to become like men. And we must never let society strip us of who and what our sex is — the carriers of the treasured egg, and all that entails.*

During half-time, Mama Rose announced that everyone was to meet at the statue of Saint Ricardo in the backyard garden. During the early years of the Christmas gatherings, the daughters would follow their mothers out to the garden to pray, in memoriam to Ricardo, and the family members who had passed away. This time, decades later, Mama Rose insisted it would be a family affair, including the men, women, and children. Twenty-one members of the three families gathered in the cold drizzle to pay tribute to the great-grandmas and great-grandpas, and aunts and uncles, and husbands and fathers, and brothers and friends, whose history and family ties would never be forgotten. After the reading of the names, Mama shared the history of the statue, and invited each of the matriarchs to share a story from their family lore.

Dar started with an unexpected tale of an Irish ditty.

"When Brigid returned from Ireland, she asked many questions about the Travellers of Ireland. She wanted to know why neither her Grandma O'Malley, nor I, never mentioned those people of our culture. Well, the stories I had heard as I was growing up, and the stories my mother knew first-hand, were not suitable for young ears. My Irish relatives never called anyone Travellers. The people who roamed the land were just referred to as beggars, and they were not treated kindly by our clan. I do remember a little song that my grandmother used to sing, about a little beggar boy who would steal from her garden. So, here is a bit of O'Malley Irish culture… sung to the tune of 'Turkey in the Straw.' I don't think this is what you expected, Brigid, but it's authentic."

Dar then proceeded to tap her toes, tap her Irish brogue, and take center stage with the following:

Oh, ye darty little beggar, does yur mudder know yur out,
  with the hole in yur pants, and yur pecker hangin out?
  Well, I'll lock ye a box, and I'll throw away the key.
  Fir all the darty tricks that ye pulled on me.
  Keep the ol' boy rollin, rollin down the hill,
  and if I don't play it on me old banjo.

The young boys lost their composure at the word "pecker," and the rest of the group, young and old, clapped to the beat, then howled with laughter and applause when the song ended. Brigid, Michelle, Joan, Sally, and Cindy doubled over in amazed guffaws, having never heard their mother engage in anything off-color or demeaning. Dar enjoyed the merriment and blushed when Miklos whispered in her ear, "I like this side of you."

When things came to a lull, Barbara blurted out her thoughts.

"The damn Nazis stole my husband's mother and father. He learned that they were buried in the ditches and ashes of Auschwitz. Then he tattooed their numbers onto his skin. Then he buried himself in his work. Someone told me my mother and father are dead. Are they? Someone told me I have a daughter. I don't know. I don't know who I am or where I am."

Babs placed her arm around Barbara's shoulder, and Annie placed her arm around Babs's shoulder. And then, Mama Rose began a hushed, gentle singing of "Silent Night," and within seconds, the voices of each person there echoed the melody and lyrics of the century-old hymn, as the December mist evaporated into the eternal flame of family love.

The festivities again grew boisterous inside as the house burst with final preparations for the meal. Muffled curses emerged from the living room, where the men suffered through yet another Cleveland loss.

Miklos, shouting over the noise coming from the kitchen, said, "Between asshole Art Modell, Bill Belichick, and Nick Saban, I don't know how we'll ever win."

Sammy joined in, "Modell will never win a Super Bowl."

John Corrigan, Michelle's husband, added his opinion. "And Belichick will never coach a winning team. We need to dump his butt."

"What about the defense?" asked Joan's husband, a closet Bears fan. "Saban isn't gonna last in football very long."

Rosie interrupted this expert, completely inaccurate analysis, with a call to the dinner table. Those sitting at the "kids'" table started the prayer, and all joined in to say grace. Barbara ate heartily but remained in a foggy silence for the rest of the evening. The scene was jovial and loving and stress free, a moment of everyone getting along and getting their bellies full. Pumpkin pies, Black Forest Cake, kiflis, and cannolis finished the feast, swallowed down with coffee or punch.

Everyone contributed to the clean-up. Soon, they gathered around the piano, where Dar played the piano, Joan the bassoon, Brigid the sax, Sally the flute, and Ricky joining the gig on drums. They jazzed up every fun Christmas carol they knew, as the children danced and sang with parents and cousins. As they finished their rendition of "Up on the Rooftop," four-year-old Max added his own toot with a burst of loud flatulence that brought down the house.

Giggles and chuckles accompanied the hugs and goodbyes. Mama Rose and Dar helped Barbara, who was still silently dazed, to the car, adding extra embraces as they said good night.

Chapter 7

. . . .

"Stepping onto a brand-new path is difficult, but not more difficult than remaining in a situation, which is not nurturing to the whole woman."

Maya Angelou

Babs quietly moved her mother into a residential home for Senior Citizens suffering from Alzheimer's disease, in February of 1993. There had been several inches of snow the day before, which prevented David from flying in from New York to help, but it also created a white blanket of serenity, which Babs embraced. Barbara seemed to enjoy it too, as she kept repeating, "I love winter; I love winter. I hate California. I hate California."

The Alzheimer's home was located in Beachwood, Ohio, close to Babs's Shaker Heights house. Babs had brought her mother here to visit almost every day during January and the early days of February. During each visit, Barbara seemed more comfortable, and even occasionally recognized some of the workers, although never their names. It was set on four acres of beautiful grounds, owned and managed by Catholic Charities with an excellent staff of doctors, nurses, and caretakers (including two nuns in traditional habits and veils), providing twenty-four hours of care, seven days a week. Because it was run by Catholics, there was not only a chapel, but also three enclaves where Blessed Virgin Mary statues, arms outreached, greeted the residents in the halls and garden. The grotto setting in the garden was dedicated to Our Lady of Lourdes. *Hello,* Babs thought.

Babs had read that this place subscribed to the guidelines and resources of Alzheimer's Disease International and offered care based on the latest research into dementia and Alzheimer's. The facility was immaculate, and the rooms were small, with private bathrooms. Babs had brought her mother's favorite family pictures, bedspread, and wintry wreath to hang on the door of her room, along with clothes that her mother found comfortable. While driving to the home, Babs fought back tears and the feeling of dread and guilt that filled her body and soul. Although she knew it needed to be done, she never thought she would do it. She seldom prayed anymore, but today, every thought was a petition to Jesus and Mary to please bless this place with the peace that her mother deserved.

When they walked in, two caretakers greeted them with warm hugs and warmer smiles.

"Hello, Barbara, we are so happy to see you here again. We would like you to stay with us a while; would you like that?"

"I like you," Barbara replied.

They started walking to the room, passing fast-paced walking patients who smiled aimlessly, just walking around the circular paths of the halls. They passed rooms with women sitting on their beds, suddenly sobbing, then just as suddenly, grinning. One patient came up to Barbara and said, "Hi, will you be my friend?"

Barbara began to show obvious signs of apprehension.

"This is not my home. Why are you taking me here? Where is my mother?"

Babs had hoped that this moment would be easier, but she had prepared for the worst.

"Mom, your mother passed away. Your home is with me, your daughter, but my house is being painted, and you need to stay here for a while, in this beautiful place, with these wonderful people. Look at this lovely room. Will you help me make your bed, and make it pretty?"

Barbara, even in her worst moments, always liked to help. After Babs fitted the sheets to the bed, Barbara put the bedspread on, and folded the towels. Babs hung the wreath on the door and told her mother that if she felt lost, she should look for this wreath. They took a walk around the halls, where they both stopped to pray at one of the Mary statues. Then one of the nuns held Barbara's hand, and said, "It's time for lunch. Let's see what's on the menu today."

"OK, Sister," Barbara said, passively.

"I have to go now, Mom. I'll be back soon to see how you're doing."

Barbara just stared at her, but when Babs turned her back, and headed for the door, Barbara moaned the most sorrowful words Babs would ever hear.

"You're leaving me? Please don't leave me. How can you leave me here? Come back. Please come back!"

Babs almost fell to her knees in grief, but one of the caretakers held her elbow, and whispered, "Keep walking. I promise you, she will be fine. Try not to come back today; it's important that your mother begin to trust us and start to feel safe."

For one hour, Babs sat in the parking lot, and cried to the point of exhaustion. She finally resisted the temptation to go back and swoop her mother into her arms and take her home, because the thought of Annie, and the increasing stress it would bring to the household, forced her to leave.

She and Annie shared a peaceful but sad dinner. Annie looked at her mother's tear-streaked face, and said, "Oh Mom, I'm so sorry for you to be so sad. But, Mommy, I am so grateful to you for giving me my life back. I love Grandma so much, and I will always remember what a smart, great woman she was. But I need you, too. Please don't think I am selfish. I pray she likes that place. I will visit her. I love you."

"I love you, too, Annie. And thank you."

Annie cleaned the kitchen, while Babs fell into a deep early-evening sleep. She had set the alarm, because, at 9:00 p.m., she was going back to tuck her mother into bed.

Barbara was sitting on a bench near the door. The workers told Babs that her mother had tried to get out several times, but the door, of course, was locked. When she couldn't get out, she resigned herself to just sitting by the door. Waiting.

When Babs opened the door, Barbara yelled to the people at the desk, "I told you she would come back. I told you! I know you. I know you." Then suddenly, she got very quiet.

She looks so scared and helpless and tired, Babs thought, overwhelmed once again with sadness.

"I am Babs, your daughter, Mom. I would like to get you ready for bed and pray the rosary with you. Are you tired?"

"Is your father here?"

"Dad passed away several years ago, Mom. But I am here. And I will help you."

"Oh, I'm so sorry he is dead. I'm tired. Can you take me to my room?"

Babs guided Barbara to her room. Her mother had no idea where she was. After Babs helped her wash and get in pajamas, she tucked her in, and they began to say the rosary. Barbara jumbled the words, but Babs could tell she recognized the structure of the prayers, and she eventually fell asleep. When Babs went to the desk, she instructed the nurse to contact her anytime her mother wished to speak to her, or anytime there was undue stress or frightening behavior. She also said that the Mary statues and the rosary seemed to quiet her mother down. The nurse wrote those insights on a notepad that had Barbara's name, which gave Babs hope that her mother would get personalized care.

When Babs returned home, Annie was waiting for her. She had poured her mother a glass of Merlot and served her chips and chip dip as they watched the 11:00 p.m. news. The broadcast did not provide any relief from the day's unhappiness as mother and daughter watched in horror the reports from the World Trade Center, where a terrorist attack killed six people and wounded hundreds more.

"What a damned world we live in," Babs sighed.

Annie snuggled next to her mother and smiled. "Don't worry. Dick Goddard, the weatherman will be bringing us a sunny forecast."

He did. Then, the young daughter and the middle-aged mother went to bed, both holding the old grandmother in their thoughts and prayers ... as the old grandmother wandered around a strange place, holding her rosary, crying.

∽

The next few months brought challenges for all of the families and the world around them.

Cleveland had one of its heaviest winter snowfall accumulations, which led to numerous school snow days. The snow days gave Annie chances to visit her grandmother, sometimes spending hours just walking around the facility with her or sharing lunch and dinner. Babs would drive her, stay for a while, then leave to get some work done, grateful that her mother was not alone. Barbara, most of the time, did not know who Annie was, but there were frequent flickers of recognition, and Annie treasured every moment. Babs still visited every night, said the rosary, and tucked her mother in. Barbara, for the most part, was complacent, but her frequent crying outbursts and her continuous mental degeneration were painful to observe. Babs's work with NASA intensified, as a December date had been set to send a crew aboard the shuttle *Endeavor*, to repair the faulty mirror and make other improvements on the Hubble telescope. Babs planned to visit the lab in summer, and in December. She would again take Annie to see "the prick and the whore." David agreed to come to Ohio during that time to spend the days with Barbara.

Many of Rosie's professional activities were canceled because of the snow, which prohibited her ability to help at the zoo. However, a 1993 performance appraisal of the Cleveland Zoo indicated very high scores in the categories "variety of animals and quality of exhibits," two areas where Rosie's expertise was evident. These evaluations did not go unnoticed by the Metroparks' authorities, and Rosie was offered a new and substantial contract for the 1994-95 fiscal year.

The winter snows slowly thawed, and in April, during

Easter break, Brigid visited friends in Milwaukee, where she became very ill from a cryptosporidiosis outbreak. The main Milwaukee water source had become contaminated, and Brigid was one of almost one half a million people who fell sick. The agony of AIDS victims also came to light, as most of the deaths from the outbreak occurred in those patients who suffered from that disease. Because her own immune system was also weakened by cancer treatment, she spent most of her time in the hospital. She returned home, thin and weak and fatigued, but continued her teaching, never missing a day of school. Dar brought her soup and tea twice a week.

When Brigid, Babs, and Rosie met late in June for their forty-third birthday at the 100 Bomb Group Restaurant near Hopkins airport, there was much to talk about. The first topic was mothers.

"Well, Mama Rose took a tumble down the front porch steps last week," Rosie began. "No broken bones, but she is banged up pretty good. Between Rebecca, Robert, and myself, we try to keep an eye on her, but I'm afraid it may be time to look for a smaller, maybe ranch house for her. But I can't see her ever wanting to leave that place. I think she is half expecting one of us kids to move in. She comes from that generation where multiple generations lived in the same household. I would welcome her to live in my home, but I'm not sure she would be happy away from her parish and that neighborhood where she, and my dad, and all of us, grew up. She is a spry seventy-four-year-old, but her body is showing some very significant signs of just wearing out. I just don't know."

Brigid offered her scenario. "My mom is in better shape than I am. She is turning seventy in a couple months, and she is still giving music lessons, walking five miles a day, and babysitting for my sisters' kids at least once a week. And, believe me, they don't put anything past her. She also took care of me when I was sick, which I was grateful for, but it made me sad to think that I should be the one taking care of her."

"Watch what you ask for," said Babs.

The women smiled in sympathy.

Brigid continued. "The fact that my dad is around is a huge bonus. They take care of each other, which takes the pressure off of the kids."

"Are you having a seventieth party for her? asked Rosie. "You should ask my mom to cook or bake something for it. It would give her something to do. She loves your mom."

"It is cool how our moms have stayed close. I'm not sure whether we are going to have a party, though. My mom is pretty adamant about just having a family dinner. She said her only wish is to have all of her kids and grandkids under the same roof, and that would make her so happy."

Rosie mumbled, "Sounds like a frickin nightmare."

"You are incorrigible," Brigid laughed.

"If I knew what that meant, I would probably be angry," Rosie laughed back.

Babs then gave her report, with regret and worry resonating in her voice. "It seems that for the most part, my mom is adjusting to her new place. But she is bewildered most of the time, and she still cries out when I leave. The caretakers say that during the day she helps fold towels and things. Well, mostly, she keeps refolding the same towels, over and over. I'm rather upset that they don't have time or access for music. I've read numerous research that music awakens a lot of memories and stimulates brain function."

"Are you at peace that your decision was the right one?" Brigid asked.

"I have to admit that yes, I am getting much better sleep. Annie has benefitted the most. She has friends over the house more often and does not spend so much time in her room. And we share a lot more because we have private time. She visits my mother often, which is truly heartwarming to me. But yet, we still feel guilt every time we leave her. Sometimes, the haze is lifted from her eyes, and she recognizes me, and for brief moments, we talk about my father or David. Then she gets agitated and goes back to the nether world."

The friends knew that there was nothing they could say to soothe the situation, so Rosie began a new thread.

"So, I start a new position in September with the zoo. In addition to lecturing in schools, I will be an administrator in charge of animal safety and habitat. I can do this and still be available to the boys before and after school and have weekends free."

Brigid and Babs gave a quiet applause. Brigid asked, "I'm curious, Rosie. If they demanded more conventional hours, say evenings, weekends, or nine to six o'clock, what would you do?"

Rosie was annoyed at the question but answered honestly. "I don't think I would have the energy to devote all that time to work and still give the kids the attention they deserve. I admire women who can manage that. I am very lucky that Sammy makes enough income that I never have to make that choice. So, in answer to your question, I guess I would become a stay-at-home mom if that scenario ever occurred."

This time, Babs changed the subject. "Hey — what about Ruth Bader Ginsburg being approved for the Supreme Court!?"

"Fantastic!" Rosie shouted, not noticing the attention she was getting from the other diners.

"Fantastic, with reservations," Brigid said, not so enthusiastically.

"What reservations?" asked Babs.

"I'm guessing that abortion is Brigid's reservation. But seriously Brigid, what can you argue with about Ginsburg's opinion?" Rosie spouted off a quote from Ginsburg. She had memorized it, anticipating this discussion. "'The decision whether or not to bear a child is central to a woman's life, to her well-being and dignity. ... When government controls that decision for her, she is being treated as less than a fully adult human responsible for her own choices.'"

Brigid sighed, and Babs said, "I thought we agreed not to ...'

Brigid interrupted. "I am thrilled with Justice Ginsburg's appointment. She is intelligent, fair, articulate, and just the type of woman — the type of person — who should sit on the Court. In answer to your question, Rosie, that is an admirable opinion she has. And she will be a welcome, fierce advocate for female equality. But her opinion only covers women. I will never give up advocating for the 'well being and dignity' of the baby girls — and boys — who are being aborted by the millions. I will always be their voice."

"And I will always be the voice of the women who refuse to let men make choices for them," answered Rosie.

Finally, Babs spoke. "Well, I will always be the voice who draws the line on this continuous no-win discussion between you two. A toast to Ruth Bader Ginsburg. May she be a voice of wisdom, both for choice, and for life."

Rosie and Brigid clinked their glasses, then with Babs's, as they said, "To Ruth!"

Later that summer, Babs and Annie flew to California. Annie stayed with Adam, and Babs stayed in a hotel near the lab. Babs still enjoyed the respect from the staff and the scientists as she reviewed plans and revisions to the Hubble Endeavor project. Unlike last year, she was able to participate in the social gatherings after work and on the weekends. Knowing that Annie was having fun with Adam, and David was visiting and caring for her mother, Babs finally allowed herself to have some relaxation, and refresh herself in conversations ranging from the Universe to the Unabomber. Annie still called her every night, but Babs resisted communication with David; she needed a clean break from the torment of her mother's situation. She knew things would resume when she returned, but for now, it was completely David's turn to be tormented.

After Babs completed two full weeks of hard work and light play, Adam brought Annie to the hotel. Babs met her in the lobby, happily avoiding any contact with the prick. On their last night in California, Annie and Babs dined at a five-star restaurant, which sophisticated Annie described as "fancy shmancy." They then saw the movie *Jurassic Park*, which sparked a dinosaur craze in Annie's choice of attire and bedroom decor.

Both napped on the flight home to Cleveland, each relishing the mother-daughter time, and peace that the trip provided. Significant decisions awaited them in the coming months. Annie had to make a decision on which high school to attend next year, and Babs had to decide if her mother was truly in the best place. In December, she would also have to decide if she would remain with NASA or change careers — not an easy path for a woman in her forties.

For the next few months, Babs, Brigid, and Rosie sailed through time on cruise control, as national and world events occasionally blew into their calm waters. In addition to the stress of her mother's steady decline, Babs had to face NASA's loss of contact with the *Mars Observer*, which she had worked on. Although valuable data was still retrieved, the main focus of the mission was considered a failure. It pained Babs that she could not discuss it with her mother, who had contributed extensive research toward NASA Mars projects.

Mama Rose lost a cousin in the Big Bayou Canot rail accident. Rosie told her friends that the incident thrust Mama Rose into "an obsession with death," frequently talking about Baby Ricardo, Reynaldo, and her late husband. "She's losing her flair, and it worries the hell out of me."

Brigid, inspired by the recently passed Arkansas Civil Rights Act, increased her integrated curriculum of jazz and language arts to include reading biographies of the brave men and women who spoke out against the Jim Crow Laws. Her class consisted of a diverse group of students of African, European, and Hispanic descent. The discussion was lively.

"Damn, oops pardon me, Ms. Nagy, I mean darn! I always

heard about the Jim Crow stuff, but I never really knew how bad it was."

"They beat the hell out of us, couldn't vote, couldn't get school books, couldn't get legal protection, couldn't even get in the same line as white people in an amusement park."

"And it was the Democrats that did it to us."

"Southern Democrats."

"Potato, potawto."

"I'm proud that so many black women and black mothers were so active in fighting all this. Ida B. Wells is my new hero."

"And Charlotte Hawkins Brown."

"I kinda liked Isaiah Montgomery's idea. He took a lot of black folk and settled in Mound Bayou, Mississippi, in 1887, and said, screw the whites."

"So, are we hating white people now? I mean, we have tried very hard to set things right, haven't we? None of what happened with Jim Crow Laws is happening today. None of that stuff is legal. We have laws that forbid any kind of discrimination, don't we? We're all sitting here together in the same classroom, with the same books, with the same teacher. Am I supposed to be hated because of what happened a hundred years ago?"

"Well, thank you, Massa, for letting us be in the same room with you."

"That's not fair."

"Well, think about it. Think about Rodney King, think about Arkansas, where they are just now passing laws to protect minorities."

"And it wasn't till the 1960s that laws were passed to

protect us. This shit ain't over. Sorry for the language Ms. Nagy."

"And, let's face it, you can pass all the laws you want, but people are still gonna look down on us for the color of our skin."

"Well, it sounds like you are looking down on me for the color of my skin."

"You ain't got no color, bro."

The class erupted in laughter, much to Brigid's relief, because the discussion was proceeding with raised and heated voices. She ended it by saying, "I hope we can begin to appreciate each other's perspectives."

She was not sure, however, that there was much appreciation going on. There was, in fact, a palpable anger emitting from both the black students and the white students. The Hispanic students were unusually quiet. *Even when we are hearing each other, we are not really listening,* she thought. *These kids are our future. This does not bode well for America if the past cannot be reconciled in the present, by these young people.*

December brought a slight reprieve from familial worries. Babs once again traveled to California, this time to discuss with her colleagues the *Endeavor* repair mission for the Hubble. Annie asked if she could stay with a friend for two weeks; she did not want to miss Christmas celebrations and exams before semester break. Babs was hesitant to leave a thirteen-year-old with another family for that long, so Rosie graciously offered to have Annie stay at her home. Sammy was engaged in writing a piece about the Western Reserve

Historical Society whose headquarters was, ironically, on the east side — a point which Sammy would explore in his article. Since he passed close by Saint Dominic's, he offered to drive Annie to and from school, for the school days that Babs would be in California. Annie pouted about the arrangement, but Babs stayed firm, and in the end, all enjoyed the set-up.

Dar and Miklos made a commitment to visit Barbara every day, and Brigid promised to visit in the evenings. Babs knew that this would be difficult for everyone, perhaps especially her mother. She had decided that this would be her last trip to California. She planned to leave NASA in January. Now, however, for the first time, in a long time, she was putting herself and her career first. She wanted to be with colleagues, and to be a part of a project that would open up the universe in all its clarity and wonder for all to see.

Hubble and *Endeavor* did not disappoint.

The mission took eleven days, and with the exception of a falling screw (which the astronauts daringly recovered), every task, all of the five spacewalks, all of the repairs, all of the improvements, all of the upgrades, and all of the replacements, were performed with a precision that scientists described as "a remarkable, spectacular success."

Babs arrived at the lab on December 8. The mission had already been deemed a success as far as procedures, and the astronauts would soon be on their way home from their historic journey. Staff conversed about how they watched the astronauts train at the lab on how to install the Wide Field Planetary Camera 2. They took pride that everything was completed with pinpoint accuracy. Until the images appeared with clarity, however, the celebration would not be complete. Babs waited, alongside her peers, with bated breath for the space travelers to return and data to come back from the Hubble.

Endeavour returned safely on December 13, and five days later, gasps and tears filled the screening room as images from the Hubble filtered through the image-processing software. They were clear, and they were sharp. Relief permeated the room, first with loud shouts of hooray, then through wisps of sighs and whispers.

Babs could not hold back tears, not only because of the success, but because of the thoughts of her parents, two pioneers of space exploration, for which their research had laid the foundation.

Babs stayed for four more days, soaking in every picture, every handshake, every hug. It was surreal to be a part of this team, to be a part of this history. The plane ride home gave her three hours of rest, and she emerged invigorated and ready to face her other reality of family.

Rosie and Annie met her at the gate, Annie running to her with a clinging hug and kiss on the cheek. She looked happy, and Babs thought, *The wonders of space cannot compete with the joy of my child.*

Annie wasted no time in giving a full report on her stay at the Scarponi household.

"Oh my gosh, Mom, living in a house with three boys is like being on another planet. It was so much fun. They never stop moving! Running, throwing a ball around, wrestling, and not a quiet moment at dinner time. I'm so glad you made me stay there. I feel like I now have three brothers."

"She got a full taste of a testosterone-fest," Rosie laughed.

"And the boys got to see what it's like to actually have a bed made before seven o'clock in the morning, and to witness someone who actually brushes her teeth before being screamed at."

"Haha, yes, Mom, Rosie screams a lot, and oh, Uncle Sammy is such a peach, so kind and smart, and I loved hitching a ride with him, he was never late. And Mama Rose made the best eggplant I have ever tasted. And, since my Christmas break started before Ricky's, I got to go to school with him and spend time with Brigid. I love that school. I would love to go there."

Annie was beaming with excitement, and happy as that made Babs feel, it also ached her heart that Adam had stolen that happy family life from her. It also made her realize that Annie did need more male role models in her life. David was great, but intermittent, and Adam was unreliable. However, Annie's gaiety was contagious, and laughter dominated the ride home.

Bountiful expressions of appreciation were bestowed upon Rosie, and when Babs and Annie arrived home, Babs immediately phoned Dar and Miklos to express even more bountiful expressions of appreciation. They reported that things went well with Barbara, but the underlying caution in their voices warned Babs that there were things amiss.

Annie and Babs decided to have a delivery of Wor Su Gai, Chicken Lo Mein, and veggie egg rolls. They chatted for an hour, as it was Babs's turn to fill Annie in on the spectacular news from California. Annie was genuinely interested and obviously proud.

"So, now, you know what I have to do, Annie. I must visit

Grandma. You are welcome to come with me, but if you want to stay home, I understand. I don't know how long I will be."

"I will stay home, mom. I'll start decorating the house for Christmas — we're a little late. I will lock the door when I go to bed. Being with the boys was so much fun, but I am anxious to sleep in my own bed. I also have lots of gossip to catch up on with my friends. And we will spend all day Christmas with Grandma, so I'm good. OK?"

"Of course it's OK. I love you sweetheart."

"Love you the most."

It was almost nine o'clock when Babs arrived at the home. When she opened the door to the residence area, her mother was sitting on a chair by the door. When Babs walked in, her mother jumped up and grabbed her arm, crying, "Where have you been? Where have you been? My girl. My girl."

Alzheimer's is a strange and most unpredictable disease. Strides in serious research in treatment and physiological causes were being made in the 1990s, but effective help in how to cope with a loved one who had the disease was sketchy. Babs read as much as she could, but in reality, she was alone in her quest to care for her mother.

Although Barbara could not remember names, and frequently lost all sense of reality as to who or where she was, she still had enough capacity to remember that Babs was a special person in her life. Sometimes, she remembered the concept of daughter, but even when she didn't, it was obvious that Babs was her consistent link to any sense of identity. The blessing, a term used ironically and relatively, was that whatever mood Barbara happened to be in could change in a nanosecond. Tears could turn to laughter, agitation could turn to silence …

it was a revolving swirl of moods and emotions — exhausting to caregivers and frightening to the Alzheimer's sufferer.

The nurse on duty told Babs that her mother had not eaten well for the past few days, so Babs took Barbara to the eating area where the nurse brought in some pudding and soup. Barbara ate heartily. They then walked around and stopped at the Mary shrines where Barbara incoherently jumbled the words to the Hail Mary. When they made it back to Barbara's room, Babs washed her, brushed her hair, and dressed her in her favorite nightgown. The staff told Babs that her mother would not accept any other attire for bedtime, and in fact, Barbara would only wear her black slacks and raggedy button-down jacket during the day. She would only allow one specific nun to bathe her and brush her hair. Apparently, when Dar or Brigid had attempted to groom her, Barbara swatted them away and refused their help.

When Babs tucked her in, Barbara snapped into one of her rare traces of normalcy. "Tell me about your trip."

Babs did not know what to make of the request, so she simply told her mother about the Hubble, and the images, and the grand opening of the cosmos that befell them.

"Ah, yes, my husband would have liked that," her mother sighed.

Babs sat in silence, amazed at the mind and woman that spoke these words. The moment somehow filled her with bliss, thankful for this faint connection to her parents and the brilliant people they once were. She said the rosary aloud, as she watched her mother doze into what Babs would pray was a peaceful slumber.

At eleven o'clock, she drove home, basking in the dim

light of the quarter moon, as it shone on the snowy landscape offering a crystallized twinkling of brightness.

Babs, Brigid, and Rosie spent Christmas with their own families. Sammy's parents drove in from DC. The year ended peacefully, with hopes for a happy, healthy 1994.

Chapter 8

· · · · · · · · · · · · · · · · · · · ·

Women who love themselves love good men.

Tracey McMillan

The new year would later become known as the "year of men" for the three friends.

In January, Brigid asked Babs and Rosie to visit some of the science classes to describe their careers and research. They met in Principal Paul's office, and at the first handshake, it was evident that Babs and Paul created some electricity in their touch. Brigid noticed it and smiled. Rosie noticed it and gave a fake, loud cough, winking at Babs when Babs turned to look at her. Paul ignored it, but all signs in his face and his glances at Babs gave evidence that he was smitten.

The students enjoyed Rosie's African videos and photos, especially seeing Baby Ricky in diapers scurrying through the veranda. Ricky sat in the classroom, quietly imagining throwing his mother under an elephant stampede. The African wildlife and the sad pictures of poachers killing elephants kept the students enthralled and interested. Rosie's casual references to Idi Amin and the various ways that Kenyans smoked their way to peaceful bliss raised the eyebrows of the classroom teacher, but opened the eyes of the students a little wider.

Ricky added his own presentation of his bird pictures, especially the flamingoes of Lake Bogoria, where millions of the birds migrated. His classmates applauded Ricky's knowledge of the birds and their habitat. He just smiled, but Rosie burst with a mother's pride.

"Do you miss Africa?" one of the students asked.

"Yes, every day. But I have realized that home is where family is, so I am happy with everything that my family and Cleveland and this great school have to offer."

The words "Yes, every day," lingered in Rosie's heart.

Paul joined Brigid and Rosie and Babs for lunch where they talked about Rosie's African experience. Brigid also re-told the story of Paul's wife, Patti, her childhood "blood sister," and the serendipitous meeting she and Paul had in 1971 when she was doing academic summer work where Paul was teaching at Saint Ignatius.

"I walked into his office, saw the picture of his daughter, and almost fainted at the resemblance to Patti. He told me Patti had passed away of breast cancer when she was very young. I told him several stories from when Patti and I were only seven years old. Paul and I have been friends ever since."

Rosie purposefully asked. "Losing a spouse is so difficult. It's been over twenty years. Paul, did you ever remarry?"

The question was inappropriate, but it was, after all, Rosie, who asked it.

"No, I haven't," Paul responded with no hint of being offended. "Time just got away from me, and neither the opportunity nor the right woman came across my path." He glanced ever so slightly at Babs, but it did not go unnoticed by Rosie and Brigid.

When they arose to go to Babs's presentation, he lingered behind, so as to be side by side with Babs, striking up a conversation about what all people talk about when they do not know what to say — the weather.

The students were spellbound at Babs's report on the Hubble telescope and her work at NASA. Clear pictures from Hubble's camera had just been released to the public. The class gasped at the view of galaxies and space they were witnessing. As they were viewing the pictures, Babs explained how these observations would change or confirm theories of the universe expanding or how galaxies were formed, and an infinite amount of other data and information about the cosmos.

A girl raised her hand, and asked, "Ms.Schwartz, when you are working on all this cool stuff, and seeing it firsthand, I was just wondering, do you believe in God?"

Babs looked at Brigid, then Paul. This was not Lourdes Academy, where a student asked her mother the same question many years ago. This was a public school, and Babs was not sure how to respond. Paul answered with an affirmative nod, which Babs took as a signal to proceed.

"As a scientist, I examine and predict and gather data, physical data, to explain or discover how our world works. When I look at the actions of what is going on in our own world, I sometimes question how God could let this mess happen. But when I look at the universe and the immense wonder of it all, yes, I believe in God. I believe in God because I cannot believe this beautiful, predictable explosion of matter can be random, and that humans are the result of chance."

That triggered more comments among the students.

"Well, what about the mess we are in on earth?"

"It was good, but we just screwed it up."

"Speak for yourself."

The science teacher ended the discussion. "We can talk about all this at a later time. Let us thank Ms. Scarponi and Ms. Schwartz for sharing their wonderful adventures and work with us.

Paul thanked the women for the interesting and educational presentations. He walked Rosie and Brigid to their cars. Babs, having parked the farthest, meant that she and Paul walked together, and eventually away from the others. As he opened the car door for her, he spoke, sheepishly, with a hint of blush in his face.

"Ms. Schwartz, it's been a long time since I asked a woman on a date, and I know, from Brigid, that you have not had an easy time of things lately, but I was wondering if you would possibly care to go to dinner with me this Saturday?"

Babs's stomach flipped. *Good Lord,* she thought. *I feel like a schoolgirl. I mean, other men have asked me out, but, umm, my stomach never flipped like a damn thirteen-year-old's. And somehow I feel even guilty. Why do I feel guilty? I've been single for four years. Annie hasn't seen a man in our house, except David; surely she would not hold this against me. And I think it might be awkward, but still delightful to have a nice evening with a smart, good-looking, successful guy. I mean, he's not a stranger; Brigid knows everything about him.*

These thoughts were a split second in time, so when she answered, "Sure, that sounds nice," Paul had no idea of the turmoil going on inside Babs's head.

When Rosie and Babs and Brigid met for lunch the following Saturday. Brigid stated the obvious to Babs.

"Do you realize that this is almost the exact same scenario

186

as when we fixed you up with Martin, way back in the '60s? Two of my dearest friends connecting like a charged wire. It's rather eerie."

A face-filling smile appeared on Babs. "First of all, we haven't even had our date yet. And second of all, there's nothing eerie about it. And third of all... thank you ... again ... Brigid! I hope you keep having nice men in your life who I can go out with!"

The obligatory dinner-ending toast: "Here's to the good men in our lives!"

To which Rosie added, "And an end to a four-year boink drought for Babs!"

Babs and Paul, did in fact, slowly begin a mutual rapport, and by March were seeing each other on a somewhat regular basis. Annie welcomed her mother's social life, and helped Babs make the transition to dating as easy and non-awkward as possible. Paul, for his part, refrained from being intrusive into their private lives and showed much compassion and understanding of Babs's devotion to her mother.

Paul's daughter, Tamara, who was enrolled in graduate school, studying Gerontology at Miami University in Oxford, Ohio, came home occasionally. She, like Annie, was very happy to see her parent enjoying himself .

While Paul and Babs's relationship was blossoming, fate also intervened in Brigid's orderly lifestyle. Rosie's cousin Beth, now a prominent councilwoman in Cleveland, secured ten tickets to the season opener of the Cleveland Indians. It would be the first game played in the new stadium, Jacobs Field, located on the corner of Carnegie and Ontario. President Clinton was on hand to throw out the ceremonial first pitch. Cleveland buzzed with a life energy that had been missing for some time.

Beth, Brigid, Babs and Annie, and Rosie's family were having lunch at the crowded New York Spaghetti House close by. There was a group of middle-aged men in expensive suits and perfectly barbered hair, dining at the table next to Beth's group. One of the more attractive men kept staring toward the table, which Beth interpreted as flirtation.

"Don't look now, people, but I still got it. That good-looking guy over there keeps looking this way. I'm pretty sure he's a Fed. They're the only ones who still wear suits around here."

One by one, Rosie, Babs, and Brigid looked up to take a look at Beth's fantasy. Rosie and Babs laughed to think Beth was anticipating romance, giving the man a fleeting glance before going back to their pasta. Brigid, however, held her stare. When the man met her gaze, she became ghostly pale. The man smiled meekly.

"Sweet Jesus, Brigid," Beth said. "You look like you've seen a ghost. Better yet, you look like a ghost yourself."

Before Brigid could respond, the man had walked over to the table. Now, everyone took notice.

"Brigid?" he asked, in a deep, soothing voice that strummed through the air like a mellow silk and steel-stringed guitar. "It's Jay Vargo. Do you remember me?"

Rosie dropped her fork, and Babs gave a low gasp.

Brigid, hoping that the palpitations pounding in her chest would not shake the table, answered coolly, "Oh my gosh, Jay. It's been such a long time, but yes, of course I remember you."

"If you don't mind my saying so, you are even more beautiful than you were twenty years ago," Jay said, looking directly into Brigid's eyes.

"You don't look so bad yourself," Rosie blurted, followed by a swift kick from Babs.

Beth whispered to Annie and Ricky, "That's one of Brigid's old hook-ups."

Annie tried not to giggle, and Ricky looked perplexed. They never could imagine one of their mother's friends having a hook-up right in front of their eyes.

Sammy just kept on eating, not at all interested in what was transpiring.

"Well, I'd love to talk, if you have some time. Are you going to the Indians' game?" Jay asked.

"Yes, I am. With my friends here," Brigid responded, sounding normal even as her heart turned to mush.

Jay smiled. "It's been a while, but let me guess... one of these ladies is Rosie, and one is Babs?"

Brigid had to laugh. "Yes. I guess some things haven't changed. I'm surprised you remembered."

"I remember everything," he said softly.

Oh my God, I want to jump into your arms, you gorgeous, smart, Las Vegas-loving rattlesnake, thought Brigid.

Beth took control of the situation. "Hey, everyone, finish up, I want to get to our seats and maybe catch some batting practice. It's going to be a madhouse, so let's get over there as soon as we can. Brig, why don't you and Jay walk over together and get reacquainted. Here's your ticket. See you at the seat before the first pitch."

"That sounds great," Jay said. "OK with you, Brigid?"

Brigid took a quick look to see if there was a wedding ring on Jay's ring finger. When she saw there was none, she said, "Sure," now wanting to hug Beth even more than she wanted to hug Jay… well, not really.

They walked slowly over to the stadium, filling each other in on their lives for the past two decades.

"You broke my heart, Brigid."

"I was a fool, Jay."

"We both were. So, anyhow, here's my story. Two years after you and I broke up, I started dating a woman; we hit it off. She wanted to get married, have a baby, and live happily ever after. Being the fool that I am, I wasn't careful, and pregnancy came before the marriage. By that time, we knew we weren't right for each other, but we married anyway, thinking, for the sake of the child, we would try to make things work. She miscarried at four months. We still tried to make things work, but in about a year, she found someone else, and that was that. I haven't seen nor heard from her for many years. And for the record, I never fooled around while we were married."

They sat on a bench outside the stadium, each wanting to share more.

"I'm so sorry things didn't work out for you, Jay. You are a good man. So, fast forward to where you are now."

"After the divorce, I dove head first into my work. It's been fascinating and fulfilling, and I have climbed the ladder and am now a special agent in intelligence analysis. I never remarried. In truth, I thought of calling you many, many times, but I figured you would be happily married, and I didn't want to cause any drama. I'm in Cleveland now, working on a case, staying downtown. Not sure how long I will be here, but damn, Brigid, if you're free, I would love to see you as much as I can."

This is a road to nowhere, thought Brigid. *But I am going to take it.*

Brigid filled him in on her life at Marquette, her lecture successes, her current teaching position, and her ever-present commitment to music.

"Never fallen in love, in all these years?" Jay asked.

"In and out," she said. "I find it easy enough to love, but very hard to trust."

The moment became silent. Jay asked if she would like to sit in their loge, but Brigid said her friends had been planning this day for a while, and she did not want to seem ungrateful to Beth, who provided the tickets. They parted with a kiss on the cheek, and a promise to see each other again, soon.

Babs, Rosie, and Beth bombarded Brigid with questions, which she answered thoroughly, knowing they would not stop until she did.

Everyone then got caught up in the spirit of Cleveland baseball, each picking their favorite players: Annie, Omar Vizquel; Ricky, Jim Thome; Antonio, Carlos Baerga; Max, Kenny Lofton; Mama Rose, Eddie Murray; and Beth, of course, chose bad boy Albert Belle. Babs, Rosie, and Brigid all remained loyal to Sandy Alomar.

The hero of the day was Wayne Kirby, who smashed a two out homer in the bottom of the eleventh inning to win the game. He gave Indians' fans the first of many exciting wins from this roster of fun and talented players who captured the hearts and loyalty of Cleveland zealots.

Jay remained on the Cleveland case for two months, during

which time he and Brigid dated frequently. At the June birthday lunch, Brigid told Rosie and Babs all of the details, including the fact that Jay was considering accepting a transfer to Cleveland on a regular basis.

Rosie offered the forty-fourth birthday toast: "And just like that, Babs and Brigid are in relationships. Here's to us, and our men! Bada boom, bada bing, bada boink! "

Chapter 9

· · · · · · · · · · · · · · · · · · · ·

Either move or be moved.

Ezra Pound

That summer heralded other changes in the lives of the friends and their families.

Ricky graduated from high school and announced his decision to forgo college for a year. He planned to return to Kenya to work at the Sheldrick elephant sanctuary, where he began his life seventeen years ago. Rosie and Sammy announced that they were taking their boys to Kenya for the month of August to give Ricky a send-off and introduce Antonio and Max to Africa.

Annie enrolled in Beaumont Catholic Girls School in Cleveland Heights.

David moved back to Shaker Heights. He was accompanied by his wife, Jojo, whom he married in a very private ceremony while he was still living in New York. Jojo was of Ghanaian descent, her name meaning "Monday born." It was a custom in Ghana to name children after their day of birth. Jojo possessed a peaceful, quiet demeanor — a welcome addition to this band of rowdy Italians, Hungarians, Irish, and stoic Germans. The love shared between her and David was quietly intense; their joy with each other was contagious.

Babs's and Paul's relationship continued to deepen, and

Paul's daughter and Annie already showed signs of bonding sisterhood.

On July 4, Jay secured a loge at Jacobs Field, and the families and friends gathered to celebrate weddings, graduations, and new beginnings. Sammy's parents, in town for Ricky's graduation, also joined the fun, though the Cleveland gang politely scoffed at their Baltimore Orioles attire. Mama Rose, Dar, Miklos, and the Scarponis enjoyed the generational chit-chat.

Barbara remained lost in her mind at her residence.

The Indians awarded the group with a victory over the Minnesota Twins. As it turned out, attending the game in July was a wise decision — the season ended with a players' strike in August, leaving Major League Baseball with no playoffs or World Series. Cleveland would have to depend on the Browns and Cavaliers for autumn sports' excitement.

Sports were not necessary however, to provide excitement. The friends had much to share at their November lunch, at Z Restaurant on the east side.

Brigid informed them that Jay had bought a house in Parma, and he had decided to remain in Cleveland. "He has fallen in love with Cleveland, and obviously, our love has been rekindled. Absolutely no permanent plans for the two of us, but I have to say, it feels very good to have a strong, decent man in my life. My mother absolutely loves him, mostly because he is a fervent Catholic and drives my parents and me to Saint Charles every Sunday. He also treats us all to breakfast. My mom loves the church commitment, and my dad loves the free breakfast. It's all very nice."

"Is it ALL very nice?" Rosie asked. "Does he need some oranges?"

"Rosie, you still make me angry and make me laugh in the same sentence!" Brigid said as she almost choked on her croissant.

Babs's turn. "First, having David and Jojo in town has been an indescribable blessing. Their apartment is around the corner from me, and he visits my mom every day. Jojo insists on cleaning my house! I just as forcefully insisted that I pay her, even though she does not want money. David is very well off; I think he is a millionaire. He sold all of his gallery artwork before he left New York, and now he has several commissions and contracts to paint more. Anyhow, Jojo says she enjoys cleaning, so, who am I to argue? Other than that, they keep pretty much to themselves."

"How is your mom?" Brigid asked.

"She's been fairly stable; still in and out of reality; memory loss getting worse. Occasionally, we will venture out for a bite to eat. One time, when we were at breakfast, David was being rather garrulous. Mom turned to me, and said, 'When he was a kid, I couldn't get him to talk— now I can't get him to shut up.' We weren't even sure that she knew who David was, but it led to a happy, light moment."

"And Paul?" Brigid asked.

"Well, now. I have some news for you there, Brig. Just this morning, he was offered a Department Chair at Saint Ignatius. He will head the Humanities Department and teach Classic Greek and Latin Literature. He is dying to get back in the classroom and this was too good to pass up. It's literally a few blocks from his house. Please don't say anything yet. He needs to sign the contract first."

Brigid could feel her face getting warm. A tinge of jealousy crept into her emotions. *This is what happened with Martin, too,* she thought. *I was his best friend, then he fell in love with her, and I was demoted. I can't believe Babs found out about this before me.*

The feeling quickly left her. She told Babs how exciting that was, and she was very happy for Paul. She did not express her anxiety about his leaving Ohio City High School.

Babs had one last item on her conversation list. "One more piece of good news. NASA has made me an offer I can't refuse. I have signed an independent contract to engage in research that will help develop instruments to observe Saturn's moons and rings. It's a pay cut, but much less stressful and will not require any trips to California in the near future."

"Well, this is all great stuff," Rosie said. "And now, here's what I got. When we returned from taking Ricky to Kenya, we realized how much we missed having our own animals. The boys fell in love with the wildlife and pets that surrounded the sanctuary. Soooo, Sammy and I started looking around, and we have decided to buy a fifteen-acre horse stables and farm."

"Oh my God, that's huge," Brigid interrupted.

"Where is it?" asked Babs.

"It's in the farthest corner of West Cleveland, right before you get to Lakewood. Developers are hounding the owner to sell it to them to build condos. The guy wants to keep it, but he can't handle it anymore. He's willing to accept much less than the developers offer and sell to someone who will keep the horses and chickens and goats and stuff. There are four structures on the property, including the stables, a barn, a nice country house, and here's the kicker: a very large building that was once a rural hospital. We have no clue what to do with that, but we fell in love with the rest of it. Antonio and Max love it too. I would have to quit my job at the zoo, which stinks because they've been so generous to me, but I'm really excited. It has so much potential."

"Where would the kids go to school?" Brigid asked.

"Antonio wants to go to your school like Ricky did, Brig. Since we will be living in the Cleveland City School District, that shouldn't be a problem, right? I also have to do some more investigating about Max's kindergarten placement."

An animated chat filled the rest of the lunch time. When it was time to leave, Rosie finished the afternoon by saying, "Screw midlife crises; here's to midlife transitions!"

Clank.

December brought another transition for Brigid. Paul resigned as principal, effective in January, and the assistant principal also announced he would be leaving at the same time, to take a job in the business world. The superintendent scheduled an appointment with Brigid, to meet the new principal. Brigid was not known as a person who revered authority — her reputation was that as a dissident. Paul knew how to handle her temperament. She never enjoyed dealing with others of higher authority in the district.

When she arrived at the superintendent's office, she caught her first glimpse of her new boss. "Brigid, meet Dr. Sharon Hutcherson, your new principal. We are meeting to discuss changes at the school, and I thought she should hear what you have to say."

Dr. Hutcherson was a petite African American woman,

fifty years old, impeccably dressed, with an air of confidence and class. Brigid reached out her hand and presented a cordial, "Nice to meet you. I am here today to make sure that everything this staff has labored so long and hard for does not go to shit."

She immediately chided herself for the use of that word. It was quite out of character for her. Before she could apologize, Doctor Hutcherson said in a quiet, but steely voice, "I appreciate your concern, and I assure you I won't let that happen, but I also assure you that in any professional setting in or outside the school building, I will not tolerate vulgar or crass language from neither my staff nor my students. Certainly a Summa Cum Laude English major with a mile-long list of academic accolades can come up with a better metaphor than shit."

Shit, Brigid thought. *I am going to like this woman.*

After discussing every innovation, renovation, and recommendation that Brigid offered, the superintendent and principal shared a glance that was predetermined, reflecting a notion that Brigid was not privy to. The superintendent nodded for Dr. Hutcherson to proceed.

"Before this meeting, I met with numerous staff members and students, and carefully scrutinized your accomplishments in the classroom and in the district. I found your integrity and intelligence to be predominantly exemplary, and your boldness and iconoclastic attitude to be somewhat abrasive, but effective. After thorough consideration, I would like to offer you the job of assistant principal."

Brigid sat stunned, and swallowed the guffaw that was emerging from her diaphragm. She sat, thinking quietly for an awkward two minutes. She looked at the superintendent and at the principal, and finally and firmly said, "I accept."

She waited for the underground chill that would signal that hell had indeed frozen over.

When she met with Babs and Rosie later for drinks, they gave her kudos and expressed a genuine pride and happiness for their friend.

"I wish I could have been there to see you get scolded for using foul language. Seriously, Brigid, you're such a bad influence on me," Rosie said through her laugh.

Babs issued a word of warning. "Watch yourself with those rebel teachers who used to look at you as their leader. Now, you're gonna be seen as 'the man.' Some will be very jealous; some will be angry; and some will kiss your butt and stab your back. Trust me, I've been there."

"I will never be seen as 'the man.' And my friends will never stab me in the back. We've been through too much. They know me."

Babs just smiled.

Brigid spent the rest of December preparing for her move to the front office. Doctor Hutcherson, who asked Brigid to call her Sharon, seemed satisfied that she had made a good choice, as Brigid proved to be hardworking, smart, and a quick learner. Sharon told the superintendent that Brigid's strongest attribute was her devotion to and equal treatment toward all the students. Hopes were high for a smooth beginning to the next semester.

Brigid and Jay spent Christmas with Brigid's family, then visited his family who lived in Milwaukee.

Babs, Annie, David, and Jojo took Barbara home for the day. She was bewildered and confused but managed to eat a little and seemingly enjoy Annie at the piano playing Christmas carols that closed the evening. Babs drove her back to the home at nine-thirty, changed her clothes, and lullabied her to sleep. Paul came over to Babs's later that night.

Rosie hosted a family Christmas at her house, inviting sister and brother and their families, as well as Beth and her husband. Sammy advised her not to mention their plans until the property was officially theirs.

The property would not be theirs for a while. Developers began to lobby Cleveland City Council to claim eminent domain on the acreage. They tried to persuade Cleveland to acquire the property to build a new high school, which they would build, while developing the surrounding area. The property owners would be paid a higher than fair market price, which tempted the current owner. Negotiations took place in smoke-filled backrooms of City Hall, reminiscent of old-time politics. However, Beth and Mama Rose wielded their power and influence to squelch the discussions, and in March, Rosie and Sammy moved into their new home and new life. They called their land "Scarponi's Sanctuary." Sammy jokingly began to parody the theme from the old television show, *Green Acres*, with the husband convincing his wife to leave the city life to a life on a farm.

As they drove the winding road that led to the house, Sammy paused to reflect on the moment. He looked at Rosie, just as he did over twenty years ago, when they landed in Africa.

"Are you ready for this?"

"It's a little late to ask that, Sammy, but of course I'm ready. I'm always ready."

Rosie began to work immediately on making the house her own. As a housewarming present, David painted a beautiful pastoral mural in the large, country-style living room. Babs and Rosie bought a new supply of pots and pans and kitchen necessities. All of the families helped unpack and organize. Miklos, Paul, Jay, and Robert helped Sammy with the animals, each enjoying learning new skills in raising horses and feeding chickens and goats. Dar and Mama Rose kept everyone fed. The sanctuary already was proving to be a pleasant retreat from the increasing hectic chaos of education, government, and business. Rosie and Sammy and their boys slept soundly to the songs of spring peepers and hooting owls.

Mama Rose seemed to be making herself at home, often spending the night. She would sometimes sit on the large wrap-around front porch, looking at the night sky.

"You don't see this many stars the closer you get to the city lights," she would frequently say aloud to herself.

Rosie brought up an idea with Sammy.

"Mama seems really comfortable here, Sammy. What would you say if we asked her to live with us? We have plenty of room, and she could actually be a big help. Please know, I don't bring this up lightly. I am well aware of her personality and her rather dominating desire to be in control. But I've noticed a big change in her. A slowing down. And she has got to eventually get out of that house."

A lengthy pause hung in the air.

"Well, having a mother-in-law live with you is every man's dream."

Rosie punched his shoulder.

"Rosie, we would not have this space without Mama's efforts. She brought you into this world; she has saved your life; she has suffered with and for her family. I have absolutely no objection to her staying here. You are, after all, the product of her treasured egg."

"OK, Sammy, you should have stopped before the treasured egg reference," Rosie said as she leaned closer and hugged and kissed her husband.

When they approached Mama Rose with the subject, she was unusually serene.

"I love it here, Rosie," she said. "I love it more and more. But ... to leave the house where Dad and I raised all of you. To leave the house where Ricardo and my mother died. To leave that neighborhood that we all loved so much. I just always wanted to die in that house."

Rosie, also unusually serene, responded. "I know, Mama. But you have to see that the house has become too much for you to handle. And we can't always be there for you. If you lived here, you could help us; we could help you. You would not have any upkeep, and you could spend nights at Robert's and Rebecca's whenever you wanted to, without worrying about leaving the house alone."

"But to think of strangers living in that house ..."

"Just think about it, Mama. Weigh the pros and cons."

"I will. But if I decide to do it, I insist on paying you and earning my keep. I vowed never to be a burden on my children.

I have a monthly social security stipend, and the money I got when I sold the store."

"We will discuss all that." The following week, Rosie discussed the idea with Rebecca, Robert, and Beth. They all liked the arrangement. Beth came up with an additional thought.

"I would love to buy that house. I will never move out of the neighborhood, and it would be so much roomier. I'm with Mama Rose; that house just has too many memories to just hand it over to strangers. And she could come and visit and stay for a while anytime she wanted to."

Mama Rose agreed to the arrangement. The entire move was bittersweet. The old house had been cleaned, with three large dumpsters filled to the brim as evidence. Beth and her husband had already begun to modernize the layout and the landscape. It evolved into a very good deal for all.

Rosie's household was about to become fuller after Ricky wrote that he was coming home.

April 20, 1995
Dear mom and dad,

What a wonderful experience this has been. I have grown up quite a lot. I am in love with this amazing Africa. It is my motherland. I have learned so much about animals and the world we all share. I will definitely return.

But now, I felt as you did, Mom and Dad, when you decided to go back to Cleveland. I miss you. I miss my brothers. I want to be there to watch and help them grow up. I want to be there as Grandma Rose grows old. I want to hear her stories.

So, I have applied, and been accepted into the Cleveland State

University Pre-Veterinary Program. It's a two-year program. After I complete it, I can decide what to do next. If you don't mind, I would like to live at home, our new home. What a bonus that would be to work firsthand with all of our own animals.

I will call you on Mother's Day, May 14, at three o'clock p.m. your time. We can discuss further. Can't wait to talk!

"Nakupenda sana,"
Ricky

༄

Brigid, Babs, and Rosie celebrated their forty-fifth birthday at an Indians game, where they dined on hot dogs loaded with stadium mustard, and beer.

"The Indians are red hot this year! I think this is our year!" Rosie exclaimed.

They watched the Tribe beat the White Sox 7-4. Talk was all about baseball and fun. The conversation did not get serious until they met for drinks at Slymans.

Babs began with a show-stopper.

"Paul has asked me to marry him."

The announcement struck like a lightning bolt and created a charged silence.

"Whoa, whoa, and whoa. That's all I can think of to say right now," said Rosie.

Brigid, looking confused, laughed and said, "Gosh, Babs, how are you feeling about that? Should we be happy? Should we be nervous? Tell us what to think."

"Well, first of all, let's drink!"

They did, and then Babs continued. "There is no way I will

commit to marriage right now. The main reason is that I will not hit Annie with another huge adjustment to her life."

"To motherhood," said Rosie, as they had another drink.

"I'm also in a maelstrom of emotions and decisions about my mom. Everyone is obviously cuckoo there…"

Rosie interrupted. "Love that scientific medical diagnosis."

"The thing is, most of the residents seem to have predictable behavior. Some just walk aimlessly. Others sit in complete silence. Others are rambunctious, and still others are quietly in constant fear. With my mom, I just never know what to expect. Her behavior is different day to day. Until I have some degree of normalcy, I just can't commit to anything but Annie, my mom, and my job."

"Do you think you love Paul?" Brigid asked, still being darted with a tinge of jealousy.

"I'm definitely falling in love with him. He is wonderful. But I just don't know him well enough to say I love him. And although it's been a few years now since my divorce, I am very hesitant to take a chance."

"Will he wait?"

"Well, if he doesn't, then the problem will settle itself. But I do believe that he will, and eventually we will end up together."

"OK, then, we will wait with you!" Rosie said, and Brigid agreed.

Rosie filled her friends in on Ricky's return and her decision to send Max to Our Lady of Mount Carmel for kindergarten and elementary school.

"It's not that far of a drive, and since I have no work schedule outside of home, I can drive him and pick him up. It also helps Mama connect to our old neighborhood in a very real way. She cried when I told her."

Brigid expressed her approval, and then became reflective. "I wonder if you'll feel like I do sometimes. When I go to Mass at Saint Charles, I feel like I'm living my childhood all over. Although so much has changed, as I look around the Church and the grounds, and I see the school buildings, I'm removed from the present. I saw a movie once, and the character, struggling to find her way in the world, proclaimed, 'All reality is consumed in our youth — the remainder of our lives is memory.' I believe this. As I watch my body change and my life take different turns, my mind still stays with the 'me' that was at Saint Charles, and Lourdes."

"You are so frickin' weird," Rosie said as she chugged her Merlot. "But I hate to admit, I kinda know what you mean. I find Mama staring at the mirror sometimes, just looking, and saying, 'I just can't believe that old lady is me.' She's not cuckoo like your friends at the home, Babs; she knows who she is, she just can't believe…"

"Lord, Rosie, we get it," Brigid said.

Babs offered some insight. "There's actually some research that indicates how we process images and situations changes as we grow older. Slower processing actually may give the perception of time going faster. That's why our younger memories seem more vivid, because we processed quicker and retained more images, which actually made time seem to go slower. And explains why we can often remember things from childhood more distinctly than we can remember things from a few years ago. And the older we get, the more pronounced this becomes."

"I don't get it," Rosie said.

"Same," Brigid said. "I understand the result, but definitely not the process."

"It's all in the early stages of research and discovery. I read a great deal of this information now, to help me understand my mother's condition. It's fascinating and depressing at the same time."

"Well, enough about getting old, we are still kicking it with gusto. So here's to being forty-five and whatever it brings," Brigid exclaimed, as she lifted her glass.

"Bring it!" Rosie shouted.

And, the year of being forty-five did, indeed, "bring it."

Their own worlds evolved in a natural rhythm of work, caregiving, romance, and pleasant social lives. Rosie and Sammy were becoming experts at raising horses: mucking, grooming, feeding, treating, keeping the acreage clear of poisonous growths. The list of "to-do" things seemed endless, but their love of animals and their work ethic provided a sure path to success. Sammy was still being well paid for articles, and they had saved a large sum of money from their time in Africa and Rosie's work with the zoo. They also accepted funds from Mama Rose, who insisted on sharing the nest egg she and Papa Vanetti had accumulated over the years. Ricky provided significant aid through his connections with Cleveland State. The University arranged to have students come to the sanctuary to examine and observe the animals to learn about their physiology and health needs. They paid a monthly stipend to the Scarponis for this program.

Brigid enjoyed her job as assistant principal, feeling confident that she was an advocate for both the students and the teachers, while still fulfilling her duties as administrator. Her main duties were the special education and English as a Second Language curricula. Special Education presented the most difficult conflicts. Some teachers were adamant about having the students totally immersed in regular classrooms with aides and tutors, although the main task of differentiating the curriculum would rest with the regular classroom teacher, who was ultimately responsible for the grade. Others wanted to continue unit classes where students in the program would be separated and put into classes taught by a special education teacher. These were much smaller classes, and the curriculum was adjusted according to the student's needs. Brigid saw the advantage of both options and worked hard with teachers, parents, and students to make sure that the school was providing the "least restrictive environment," in accordance with the Individuals with Disabilities Act and the Elementary and Secondary Education Act. There was much to consider and much debate on how to implement the requirements of these laws. Brigid knew it was going to be difficult, and at any given moment, she could feel the anger toward her from all sides. Nevertheless, her working and personal relationship with the staff seemed to be intact, as they continued to invite her to the Friday Happy Hours at the local pub. Jay lived close to her in Parma, which gave them more time together and served as a break from her professional duties. Dar called this proximity an "unholy convenience," because she knew Brigid spent many nights there. Brigid would just smile and say, "Mom, I'm forty-five years old."

Babs was quite sure that if her mother knew how her relationship with Paul had developed, she, too would not be happy with a similar "unholy convenience." When Annie visited Adam in California for the month of August, Paul stayed every night at Babs's home. The feeling of security and shared responsibilities from a man she enjoyed being with, and who genuinely cared for and respected her, rejuvenated her. He told her he would wait to get married until she felt comfortable with the changes it would bring to her life.

She told Brigid and Rosie, "And the best part about it is ... he loves to cook!"

David and Jojo spent the month of August in New York, visiting her family and seeing old friends, so Babs spent many more hours with her mother. Paul always had dinner waiting for her, no matter how late she came home. When school started, Paul was less free with his time, but he and Babs made it a point to speak with each other every day and see each other at least a few times a week. He never spent the night when Annie was there, to which Rosie said, "Do you really think she's that stupid?"

The lives of the families settled into a steady pattern, but the sports scene in Cleveland exploded with a delirious flurry of excitement — first with a frenzy of exhilaration, then with a frenzy of disappointment and anger. The Indians made their way to the World Series for the first time in a half a century. Attendance records were set at almost every home game. Miklos and his son-in-law and grandson, Sammy and his sons, and Rosie's brother Robert, along with Jay and Paul, attended every playoff and World Series game. When Miklos insisted on "testosterone-only" outings, the women just laughed. The "progesterone" group of Mama Rose and her daughters, Dar and her daughters, Babs and her daughter, and Brigid, disregarded the whole testosterone order and took their place at several games.

"Little do they know how much we enjoy their testosterone fests, and how nice it is to be with just the matriarchs of the family," Babs told Annie one evening while they visited Barbara. Barbara had no idea what they were talking about, but she laughed anyway. She often pretended to be in their world, even though her own world was very far away.

The Indians lost to the Atlanta Braves in game six of the World Series, 1-0, in a game where the Tribe's bats froze with just one hit. The city, accustomed to disappointment, once again had their collective heart broken, as the Cleveland Plain Dealer headlines screamed "Oh, So Close," accompanied by a large photo of pitcher Julian Tavarez sobbing in the dugout.

Just when the pain of that headline began to subside, another more ominous, more shocking, more despicable headline greeted Cleveland fans on November 7: "BROWNS BOLT."

Although rumors had been swirling through the season that owner Art Modell (known as "jackass" in the Nagy and Vanetti households) was moving the team to Baltimore, no one believed it would happen. When it was officially announced, the city and the team sank into a funk that permeated throughout Northeast Ohio and beyond. One of the most touching and unexpected tributes came from Cleveland's most bitter rival, the Pittsburgh Steelers. Steelers fans protested the departure of the Browns. A special edition of Pittsburgh's famous Iron City Beer was issued, showing the helmets of both teams and the words: "Iron City Beer, 45 Years 1950-1995, Saluting the greatest rivalry in football, Cleveland Browns vs Pittsburgh Steelers."

The Browns, who, before the announcement had a promising record of 4-4, lost six of their seven last games. Their final victory came at their final home game when they defeated the Cincinnati Bengals. An attendance of over 55,000 fans said farewell to their treasured team — as they ripped apart seats, demolishing and taking other pieces of Cleveland Municipal Stadium as souvenirs. When the game ended and the team left the field, the crowd became more rambunctious. The anger dissipated into a sorrowful bonding when the team came back onto the field, saluting the fans and reaching out to shake hands. Gratitude and respect temporarily replaced anger and loathing. Miklos attended the game with two of his firefighter friends. When his daughters asked what memory he would carry in his heart of this last game, Miklos, never a fan of Modell, responded, "The 'Muck Fodell' rally in the parking lot."

Dar had given him a raised eyebrow look, usually reserved for misbehaving children. Miklos never mentioned that part of the day again.

Chapter 10

· · · · · · · · · · · · · · · · · · · ·

O, what a noble mind is here o'erthrown!

Hamlet

When Babs opened the entrance door to her mother's Alzheimer's home, for her first visit of the year on January 1, 1996, she sensed an unusual atmosphere. A feeling of unrest pulsed through the halls. Her mother was not in her favorite chair by the door. The nun on duty smiled nonchalantly, slightly easing Babs's trepidation. However, as she entered her mother's room, her sense that something was amiss was confirmed.

Barbara sat huddled in a corner, rocking back and forth, saying repeatedly, "He was in my room. He was in my room. He was in my room."

Babs immediately sat on the floor next to her mother, cuddling her and assuring her. "Everything is alright, mom. I'm here."

Barbara squeezed her arms around Babs, calming down, and within a few minutes rested her head on Babs's shoulder and fell asleep. Babs did not move for an hour while her mother slept soundly, her head nodding heavier as her sleep deepened.

What happened? Who is 'he?' My God, was she attacked or is she just hallucinating about father? These thoughts tormented her, but she dared not move while her mother slept. As she sat there, she noticed the sound of men's voices in the hallway. Men were not housed on the same floor as the women, but twice a week they engaged in mixed activities such as walking in the garden, or "exercises" like balloon tennis or ice cream socials. They were never in the halls of the private residence areas. Until now.

Barbara woke up, seemingly refreshed, but very quiet.

"Why am I on the floor? Where have you been?" she asked Babs. No mention of men.

"Hi, Mom. We decided to take a nap on the floor for a change. Are you OK?"

"Why wouldn't I be OK? No, I'm not OK. I'm never OK. I'm hungry."

They stood up, and Babs watched as her mother, bent over and holding onto the walls, struggled to go to the bathroom. When she finished, they started walking to the cafeteria. Barbara clung tightly to Babs's arm, not saying anything, but with an obvious element of fear. As they passed one of the resident rooms, Babs saw a man sitting on the bed and crying with deep sobs. Her mother did not notice, but the sight mortified and angered Babs.

It was after lunch time, so the cafeteria was almost empty. Babs brought Barbara some soup and crackers, which she began ravenously to devour. A caregiver walked by, and Babs took the opportunity to motion to her to come to her. She stood far enough away from Barbara, but she did not disguise the anger in her voice, and she could be heard at the front desk.

"Why are there men in the hallways of the women's

residences? And why was there a man on a bed in my mother's wing? Why was my mother saying a man was in her room? What is going on!?"

The caregiver, obviously confused, said politely, "Please wait while I get the manager on duty."

The nun came over, looking annoyingly placid with a forced, phony smile. She was petite and diminutive — Babs towered over her.

"Ms. Schwartz, please be seated."

"I prefer to stand. Why are there men here?"

"There was a frozen pipe in the men's quarters, so we had to give them temporary housing on this floor. There was water damage, and they will be staying here until repairs can be made. Please…"

"Don't you know how upsetting it is to disrupt the routine of these women? My mother hasn't seen another man near her bedroom besides her husband, since … since maybe never. And I know she is confused, but when she says that a man was in her room, I believe her. Who is supervising this situation? Are they free to roam the halls and enter anyone's room? Are they as looney as the women?"

"No need to be rude, Ms. Schwartz."

Babs felt her face begin to burn. Before she spoke again, she noticed her mother walking away. Wanting to stay close, she followed her, but first turned to the nun and said, "You have no idea how rude I can be. My mother naps during the afternoon. Make time to meet with me. I know the owner comes in later also — make sure she's at the meeting."

"I will arrange it," said the nun, grateful that the encounter was over.

Barbara settled in for a nap. Babs took three chairs from the television area and placed them in the hallway by her mother's room. She wanted to make sure there were no unwelcome visitors while her mother slept.

The owner, Cynthia Crowdun, who recently purchased the home, was a dull-witted woman in her late forties who dressed like a teenager. Her bleached blonde hair and heavy make-up made her look like a shriveling Barbie Doll. Her demeanor was transparent; she was here to soothe the situation. Babs immediately pegged her as not being very bright but obviously successful. Rumors abounded that she was having an affair with the treasurer of the company that possessed a large portion of shares in the business. Cynthia began the meeting.

"I am so sorry that your mother had a disturbing incident. We tried to reach you..."

"That's a lie. I have been working at home all week. Don't lie to me, Ms. Crowdun. That is the worst thing you can do right now. Now, tell me, why wasn't I notified about this change, and how are you protecting the women from unwanted attention from the men? How are you preventing men and women from going into each other's rooms?"

"I do apologize. I was told that all of the families were notified of the change. As you know, we are very diligent about the safety of our residents. We cannot, however, lock the doors to their rooms, for safety reasons."

"You did not answer my question. How are you controlling the interaction between the men and women?" Babs fantasized about strangling this woman.

"We have had family members express their concerns, and

we have hired new employees to sit in each hall to make sure residents do not go into or near the wrong rooms."

"Is this in effect now?"

"It will take two more days to put everyone in place. Until then, as I said, we will be extra diligent in monitoring the situation."

"I found my mother cowering in a corner on the floor of her room. I expect better 'diligence' than what you have been providing."

"Again, I apologize. I will have our caretaker, Tracey, keep a special eye on your mother. It is in the reports that Barbara has a special liking for her."

Babs knew, for a fact, that was true. "That's fine. I will remain here until I put her to bed this evening. I will expect an hourly report, assuring me that she has been checked on and is fine. Even through the night, leave a message on my answering machine."

"We do not ..." Cynthia stopped herself. "Under the circumstances, I will make sure that is done."

Babs fed her mother some dinner, then settled her in, hopefully for the evening. The caregivers did give an hourly report through the night. She no longer trusted them, however, and she definitely disliked the new owner.

Her situation at home gave her little respite from the day's happenings. Annie had dinner waiting. She had eaten but sat down with Babs to have what she called a "mother-daughter chat."

If she tells me she is pregnant, I will kill her, Babs thought. She quickly admonished herself. The events with her own mother continued to upset and worry her. She had lost her characteristic, stoic serenity.

"What is it, Annie? Are you OK?"

"Well, I am and I'm not, Mom."

Annie's eyes filled with tears. She, like her mom, was not prone to emotional expression, so the tears caused Babs to push away her meal and reach out.

"Annie, whatever it is, we will work it out." She went over to Annie and placed her hands on her daughter's shoulders, then sat next to her.

"Well, I know how stressed you've been with Grandma, and I know that you and Paul are making each other happy, and I know that your work can sometimes be stressful. I never want to add to that stress."

"Annie, you are what I live for. I hope you know that by now. You never need to hide anything from me. What is bothering you?"

Bad grades? Drugs? Boy troubles? Babs's mind ran wild, as she thought about her own teenage years and the stupid, bad decisions she sometimes made.

"Well, I know you're paying a ton of money for Beaumont. And it really is a great school. But, well, umm, I hate it. I know how much your high school and your high school friends mean to you. And I wanted to have that too. But, Mom, I'm just not feeling it."

"Has anyone hurt you?"

"No, Mom. The teachers, the girls — they're all OK. I don't know, I just don't look forward to going there. I love the Cleveland neighborhood where Brigid teaches and where you went to school. The West Side Market, being close to the city, the restaurants, and also the gritty diners. I just think I'd be happier there."

Babs hugged her daughter. "Are you miserable?"

"Not totally. I'd just like to be somewhere different."

"Friends?"

"I have friends. I get along OK. And you know Maureen. But she goes to Shaker now, you know that. So, my going to another school wouldn't hurt our friendship."

"Tell me the truth, Annie. Do you want to live in California? Is that what this is about?"

"Oh, Mom! No, no, no! Dad is great and all and I do enjoy visiting there. I love California. But, gosh no. That is not it, I promise."

"Annie, we can't change your school now, in the middle of the year. And I don't think you can even get into a Cleveland school, living here. There's much to consider. You'll have to finish this year at Beaumont, and during the next few months we will explore other options."

"Are you mad at me?"

"Of course not. Thank you for telling me. We'll work it out."

"Thanks, Mom. Now eat your dinner," Annie said with a smile.

"Daughters taking care of mothers. That seems to be the order of the day."

Later, Paul called, and Babs shared everything with him. He comforted her with strength and assurances. *God, I wish he was here right now. I can't do this alone. I miss having a mate, and I miss my mother and father so much.*

The next day brought a cold, Cleveland sunshine. Annie was still on Christmas break, so mother and daughter had breakfast at a local cafe and then spent the day with Barbara.

Men were still roaming the halls, but Babs noticed there was constant monitoring of the hallways.

Barbara was especially quiet but seemed to enjoy Annie's presence. Annie would walk around the building, hand in hand with her grandmother. Barbara would smile at the caregivers and then retreat into silence. When she took her afternoon nap, Babs brought Annie home and then returned to Barbara.

If not for Paul's steady presence, Babs thought she, too, would go insane.

School resumed a week later. It was now Brigid's turn to face adversity. Brigid had delved into her administrative job with gusto, and within a year had assured that all Individualized Education Plans were in compliance, that all department chairpersons were meeting regularly with their departments, that teachers had all of the supplies they had requested. Students knew she would discipline and give consequences for bad behavior. They also knew she would hand out this discipline with fairness and compassion. She worked until 8:00 p.m. almost every night and slept soundly, smugly at peace, thinking that all were happy with her performance. Occasionally however, she would have a strange sensation in her back — a sensation of being stabbed. As she soon discovered, it was more than metaphorical stabbing in the back. It was a betrayal.

One morning, Principal Hutcherson called her into the office for a meeting. It started marvelously and Brigid grew very comfortable and cocky with the successes that the principal was discussing. Then the principal got up, shut the door, and addressed Brigid.

"You're not going to like what I have to say, and I know you well enough by now to know that you are going to want to slit someone's throat when I'm done. But I want you to sit there, quietly, take it, think about it, and come back and talk to me in the morning."

Brigid lost all feeling in her toes; her heart started palpitating, and her shoulders started sinking. *What on earth had she done? Whom had she angered ?*

She had been so careful to curb her sarcasm and hold her tongue at administrator meetings. The central office staff was loath to see her succeeding, she thought. Well, she was ready for a fight — she had documented every move she made and her record was impeccable. But when Dr. Hutcherson continued, the stabbing pain in Brigid's back pierced to the bone.

"Two days ago, four department chairpersons from our building came to see me with concerns about some of your actions. They ..."

"What?!" asked Brigid. "My own people? My friends? They came to you to complain about me? Why didn't they just come and talk to me? I ..."

"Let me finish," the principal said, obviously annoyed. "I will tell you that the discussion was led by someone who is obviously jealous of your success, and for the most part the others just let her talk. But they joined in with comments of their own. However, whatever their personal feelings are toward you, they made some valid points."

Brigid sat stoically, burning with hurt and anger.

"They think that you are making decisions based on the

input from a small circle of friends and advisers. They requested that you go to department chairs first. They ..."

"Why the hell couldn't they just tell me that," Brigid mumbled.

"They also commented that your wearing tennis shoes demeans the seriousness of your administrative position."

Brigid groaned in disbelief.

"And finally, they questioned your administrative expertise and knowledge regarding some of the special education decisions you have made in student placements."

She paused and waited for Brigid's response.

Brigid choked out the words. "You are my boss, ma'am. I would like some guidance as to how I should respond to these criticisms."

"Professionally, Brigid, these are easy fixes, and frankly I disagree with their professional evaluation of your work with special ed. You have improved that department significantly. Personally, you have now faced a crisis common to those who move from the classroom to the front office. You have handled the transition better than most. So far, I think you have done a spectacular job, but also with a couple spectacular blunders. At any rate, you need to finally take your teacher shoes off, physically, and metaphorically, and walk the line of an administrator. You are going to lose friends. Teachers are a cornerstone of our society, but they are impossible to please. I respect them more than any other profession, but they are complainers, and impossible to deal with sometimes. Toughen up, compromise when you can, stand firm when you must, and follow your intelligence and your conscience. Your ultimate responsibility is to the students."

Brigid thanked the principal and went back to her office. Two of the department chairpersons were waiting outside her door. She invited them in and closed the door. They proceeded to apologize and told her about the meeting with the principal, saying that the conversation had taken a turn that they had not expected. Brigid listened and nodded and expressed her appreciation that they now had come to her.

When they left, she sat back in her chair, lifted her feet, and rested them on her desk. She would leave her tennis shoes firmly on her feet and her teacher shoes firmly in her heart ... but she would walk the walk of an administrator more cautiously, aware of who was walking with her and who was creeping behind her. She vowed never to lose sight of the students' needs that guided her every step.

Instead of seeing Jay that night, she decided that she needed to be with her mother.

At the June forty-sixth birthday lunch, the friends agreed that they were happy that year forty-five of their lives was over.

"It was a tough one," Babs said. "Mom declined quickly this year. I bless David and Jojo and Paul every day for helping me get through it."

"I'm so happy you have help, Babs. But we know you carry the heaviest burden. I know I speak for Rosie, too, when I say, please, please, let us know how we can help."

"Right now my main problem is Annie. I don't know why she is so unhappy at Beaumont, but she really wants out. I'm afraid I built up Lourdes Academy and the benefits of an all-girls school so much that the expectations were too high, and Beaumont ended up falling short of those expectations. She wants to attend your school, Brigid. I haven't had time to investigate, but Annie said she could open enroll."

"She may open enroll, after the neighborhood lottery is complete. I am permitted to enroll two students out of the neighborhood and city boundaries. I arranged it for Ricky when Rosie and her family lived in Lakewood. It was an administrative perk I demanded, for situations just like this."

"What's the criteria?" Babs asked.

Brigid smiled. "Whatever the hell I want it to be. She's in, if that's what you decide, Babs."

Babs started to snivel. Then cry. Then blubber.

Brigid and Rosie looked at each other, stunned at the emotional outburst from the friend who almost always "had it together."

"Thank you so much. I just want her to be happy. I don't know what I would have done. I can't move, because I have to stay close to mother. Annie wanted it so bad, she even offered to move in with Paul. I worry about my mother; I worry about Annie. I cry so much I do not even recognize myself. I went to my gyno yesterday — haven't had my period for a while. Can you imagine what that scenario could have been?"

"What did she say?" Rosie and Brigid asked simultaneously.

"She said … she said…" Babs burst deeper into tears. "She said I'm in full-blown fucking menopause."

Brigid looked at Rosie. Rosie looked at Brigid. They had never heard Babs say anything that resembled that word. Although they tried to hold it in, they both released an uncontrollable, boisterous laugh. No matter how hard they tried, they could not stop. The more Babs shed tears of menopausal melancholy, the more they shed tears of maniacal mirth. Babs stared at her friends, and soon she was laughing too. They sat like fools, tears streaming from their eyes. Laughing at madness; laughing at motherhood; laughing at men; laughing at menopause; laughing at Babs dropping the F-bomb. When the waitress came to take their order, they could not talk, so she politely said, "I'll come back when you're ready." That set off another round of laughing fits.

Finally, they settled down, and as they dabbed their eyes, they ordered their food.

Rosie, trying to have a serious conversation about a serious subject, asked Babs. "Did you have any other signs besides your missed periods?"

"Well, you know I have always prided myself on my German stoicism, but lately, I just cry at anything."

"Oh, we haven't noticed," Brigid said.

Another round of hysterics.

"So, go on…" Rosie coaxed.

"This will put you over the top, so brace yourselves. I was listening to an oldies station a few weeks ago, and *Tie a Yellow Ribbon Round the Old Oak Tree* started playing. When it got to the finale, I had to pull over because I knew what was coming, and I started crying uncontrollably."

Rosie spit out her drink; Brigid snorted so loud the other diners stared, and for the next five minutes, the friends experienced a phlegm-loosening, ceaseless-chortling, teeth-hurting, convulsive bout of laughter. They could not stop.

They eventually became embarrassed by the looks from the others in the room, and they gathered themselves together into a semblance of sane behavior. When the waitress served the coffee, Rosie started a conversation that would eventually change all of their lives.

Brigid first beseeched Rosie. "Please do not say anything funny. My face actually hurts from laughing so hard."

"Nothing funny, I promise. It's actually something I've been dying to tell you. Here goes. You know we have that old hospital building on our property. Well, Sammy had some inspectors and electricians come out to look at it, just to see what we had. It turns out it's in pretty good shape. We started thinking maybe we could do something with it."

"Like what?" Brigid asked.

"Here's another piece you need to know first. Antonio brought a friend home a couple weeks ago. Someone he knew from Lakewood. She is about five months pregnant. Her parents kicked her out of the house. She has no other family. The father of the baby is a rattlesnake. She was a mess."

Babs sighed. "I cannot believe parents are still like that in this day and age."

"Yep. Apparently more than we think. So, of course we took her in. We're giving her a place to stay until we can settle things. Her parents are having second thoughts. We're hoping she can go back home."

"Totally cool of you," Brigid said.

"It got us thinking. What if we can make that building a place for girls like her. Or even for women who need help. Our sanctuary could be a great place for them to retreat to a natural, peaceful life — at least for a while. Ricky has done some research on animal therapy, particularly horses. There's so much we can do, even with Alzheimer's patients, Babs.

We could have a small medical staff, and maybe volunteers. I don't know. The more Sammy and I talked about it, the more excited we got."

"How would you pay for it?"

"There are an unbelievable amount of resources for women starting businesses, or from the Right to Life organizations. Even Planned Parenthood could possibly help with doctors or education on pregnancy prevention. There's also monies available for care of the elderly."

Brigid bristled at the inclusion of Planned Parenthood, the largest abortion provider in the United States.

Rosie picked up on it. "I said pregnancy prevention, not termination, Brigid. Anyhow, we are just considering all of this. The more we discuss it, the more I'm confident we are going to come up with something good."

"It sounds like a wonderful but daunting task. If anyone can make this work, it's you, Rosie," Brigid said as she placed her hand over Rosie's.

Babs grinned. "Maybe you can give help to women in menopause."

More laughter, and a toast to menopausal women.

It was not, however, the women of middle age who dominated the remainder of the year. It was their mothers.

In early autumn, Mama Rose fell and broke her hip and was admitted to the hospital. While there, she developed a staph infection, which lengthened her stay. Rosie visited her frequently, but the exploration of building plans forced her to lean more on her sister Rebecca and brother Robert for support. They made sure that Mama Rose was getting the best of care and was never lonely.

Babs's situation became more dire. Barbara's home was under renovation, so the male residents still lived in close proximity to the females. This continued to disturb Barbara, and now, each time Babs visited, she found her mother crying about men being in her bedroom and touching her during mealtime. The administrators assured Babs that nothing inappropriate was occurring. New staff was hired, and her mother was constantly being observed and protected. Despite these assurances, it was obvious to Babs that her mother was slipping further away from reality.

Barbara had been a working mother and a renowned scientist, in an era when neither of those life choices dominated the culture. However, her attitude toward modesty and the female body were very much in line with the 1940s mores of what was proper maternal attire for women. Babs had never seen her mother in dresses above the knees, nor spaghetti-strap tops, or tight-fitting slacks. Although she possessed an academic and superior vocabulary, she still referred to her female organs as her "private parts." Babs was certain that the activity that produced her and her brother had been done under the cover of darkness, and blankets.

One day when Babs entered the wing, she heard a horrifying screeching. Despite the beastly sound, she could tell it was her mother. She ran to the source, and there she found Barbara, naked, holding one hand over her shriveling breasts, and the other around her most private part. Standing next to her was a large, male nurse, trying gently to shower her.

Babs was certain there was nothing unprofessional about

the episode, but the total disregard for her mother's privacy, and the frightened scream that came from her mother's soul, convinced her that her mother could not survive here.

She wrapped her mother in a towel, took her to the bedroom, and cradled her in her arms, just as her mother did to Babs so many years ago. When the fear passed, and Barbara settled, Babs dressed her, looked into her glazed eyes, and said, "I'm taking you home, Mom."

Babs phoned Jojo and asked her to please clean out the spare bedroom and prepare it for Barbara. The room had nothing but a chest of drawers. Everything else had been previously removed, less Barbara find a way to hurt herself or others.

When Babs and Barbara arrived, David and Jojo were waiting. Not wanting to alarm Barbara, they did not rush to hug or engage in conversation. Both mother and daughter looked exhausted. Barbara was subdued and quiet. Babs tucked her into bed and soothed her with German lullabies until the heavy anchors of sleep forced her eyes to close and drift into slumber.

Babs sank into the Queen Anne chair in the living room and mused out loud. "Now what the hell am I going to do?"

David came to her side and said, "We will work this out, sister. We have money to hire help, and time to make sure mom is taken care of properly."

"Oh my gosh, David, could you possibly pick up Annie from school and explain the situation? I do not want her walking into this unprepared."

"Of course."

Barbara slept for several hours, which gave Babs time to

settle herself and compose her thoughts. Annie came home and hugged her mother. "Mom, I love my new school. I am so happy there. Please don't worry about Grandma being here. It'll be OK. And Dr. Nagy, Brigid, said you know you can count on her if you need anything."

Paul stopped by, and once again Babs appreciated his presence in her life.

While all this was happening with Babs's and Rosie's mothers, signs of dementia began rippling through the behavior of Brigid's mother, Dar.

Brigid's sister, Cindy, informed her that their mother had been becoming more forgetful and doing strange things.

"We are finding keys in the refrigerator, and the gas stove being left on. Dad says she's just getting older and careless. There's no doubt he does not want to admit that Mom is losing it."

Brigid, too, had noticed that her mother's cognitive abilities had been changing, particularly in her forgetting names and not recalling what certain items were called. Once, when asking Brigid to bring the toaster to the table, she could not remember the word toaster. She just said, "You know, that thing over there, that you put bread in."

Most of the time, lucidity did dominate, sometimes with wit and humor. Dar had always kept her house spotlessly clean: daily dusting; weekly floor washing; monthly scrubbing of cupboards. Brigid noticed that Dar had let up on the cleaning. Visible dust on the furniture, and scuffs on the kitchen floor were evident. One day, she sarcastically asked her mother about it.

"Mom, I noticed the house actually has some dust floating around. Are you getting too old to clean?"

Dar replied in the same sarcastic tone. "I just take my eyeglasses off, dear, and everything looks spic and span."

The family decided, for now, just to keep a closer eye on both parents. The Nagy women kept in constant conversation with each other, and their parents. Michelle, Suzy, Sally, and Joan planned to visit more to help Cindy. The sons-in-law and grandchildren would also do their part to make sure that Miklos and Dar were safe and the house did not fall into disrepair. Jay, too, often visited to help, and maintained the Sunday ritual of 11:00 a.m. Mass, followed by breakfast at the Whip Coffee Shop, a favorite dining place on Pearl Road in Parma Heights.

Situations in all of the households seemed to be under control. And yet…

Barbara had become almost completely withdrawn. A palliative nurse came in once per week to check on vital signs, and a healthcare worker also came in to help with sanitary needs and exercise. David and Babs shouldered most of the care. Barbara had begun to show signs of Sundowner's Syndrome, a condition common in Alzheimer's patients. She became extremely irritable as nighttime drew near, wandering the house, hallucinating that she was being attacked, and constantly pulling at invisible strings that she said were hanging from the ceiling. Nights became a horror.

The change in behavior was taxing, but Babs and the caregivers were persistent with their gentle care and attempts to soothe Barbara's anxiety. David and Babs alternated taking her on walks around the court, but soon that became too difficult for Barbara to achieve. Her stamina and physical condition were deteriorating now as quickly as her mind.

By November, Barbara refused to get out of bed, lying there, almost completely non -responsive. The visiting nurse tested her, using the criteria for the Glasgow Coma Scale, which assesses motor, verbal, and eye-opening responsiveness. She informed Babs and David that their mother was in a clinical coma, and most likely would not survive for more than a week. She was having trouble swallowing, and she aspirated when she did manage to drink anything. Her body was shutting down. The nurse explained that the blackening of her skin, appearing mostly on her feet, arms, and lips was called mottling, due to the decrease in blood circulation.

The priest from their parish visited the next day, and blessed Barbara with the Sacrament of the Last Rites, which in Catholic doctrine, purified her soul and prepared her to enter the Kingdom of God. Since Barbara could not consume the Holy Eucharist, Babs, David, Annie, and Jojo received it and offered their prayers for Barbara's soul.

Babs insisted on doing all of the sanitary cleaning of her mother when bowels and urine production became uncontrollable. She stayed in Barbara's room throughout the day and moved a cot in during the evening. As the hours passed, she reminisced how her mother had never failed to support her. She remembered the countless hours Barbara sacrificed caring for Babs when she suffered from juvenile rheumatoid arthritis. She remembered when she rebelled with smoking, sneaking out, and engaging in what her mother called "public displays of affection." Her parents gave her strict consequences, Barbara telling her that she "would have plenty of time to experiment with different pleasures, but now was not the time to start. "Respect your womanhood," she would say. "Don't abuse your body or your mind with the misogynistic messages that lull you into degrading yourself." She remembered when her mother and grandmother supported her through her first heartbreak when her neighbor, her first major crush, Lou Pentello, left for college and said a permanent goodbye. "The essence of who you are is independent of any man — or anyone else for that matter." The memories flooded her mind as tears flooded her eyes. *I hope you know how much I loved and appreciated you, mom. You wonderful, beautiful woman.*

Barbara Anne Turyev passed away on Wednesday, November 13, at approximately 1:00 a.m. She died, as they say, peacefully in her sleep. When Babs awakened and saw her mother's pallid skin, she touched her cold hand. She kissed her mother's forehead, placed a rosary on her hands, and called Annie into the room. They embraced and said a Hail Mary. David and Jojo were notified and began the preparations for the wake and the funeral.

Annie phoned Rosie, Brigid, and Paul, who arrived with a buffet of food and drinks by noon. Paul asked the building substitute teacher to take his classes, and Brigid received permission to take the afternoon off. Brigid volunteered to write the obituary. Babs gratefully accepted, since there were so many other tasks to perform. Feelings of friendship and love filled the household, and Annie soaked it all in, hoping that someday she would have friends such as these. She asked her mother if she could call her dad, and Babs gave her permission. Adam feigned sympathy, having never really cared for Barbara, knowing that she felt the same toward him. He casually asked Annie if she wanted him there. She told him that was not necessary; she just thought he should know. That was the gist of the entire conversation, leaving Annie with a glimpse of the icy heart that lay within her father's outward geniality.

The obituary appeared in Thursday's *Cleveland Plain Dealer*, accompanied by a beautiful photo.

Barbara Anne Turyev (Schneider) passed away peacefully at her residence. She is survived by her daughter, Barbara, and son, David (Jojo), granddaughter, Annie, and numerous friends and colleagues. She is preceded in death by her husband, Richard; father and mother, Karl and Barbara Schneider. Barbara was a loving mother and grandmother, and an active member of Saint Dominic's parish in Shaker Heights, Ohio. She was a pioneer of space and interplanetary exploration in the early days of NASA, where she was one of few women on the staff privy to the secret plans of rockets and manned space travel. Her research into the atmosphere and metallurgical components of Mars laid the foundation for scientific discoveries. Barbara's heart and soul nurtured and loved her children, who were always her first priority. She was not only a pioneer professionally, but she also pioneered the concept of work at home mothers, doing significant research at home, while always catering to the needs of her children. Her deep faith in God and the Virgin Mary sustained her until her final breath. Friends may pay their respects on Friday, November 15, from 2:00 to 4:00 p.m.and 6:00 to 8:00 p.m. at Brown-Forward Funeral Home 17022 Chagrin Blvd.

A Requiem Mass will be held at 9:00 a.m. at St. Dominic's Church 19000 Van Aken Blvd. Interment to follow at Calvary Cemetery 10000 Miles Ave.

Former astronauts and NASA officials attended both the wake and the funeral. Current NASA employees were there, and also former scientists from the age of moon landings. The early astronauts who ventured into space in the 1960s chatted with Babs, remembering her as a child, and how her mother and father would bring them home for dinner, then after dinner how they would retreat to the backyard and gaze at the night skies. They reminded Babs and David of the outstanding and critical contributions Barbara made to the exploration of Mars soil and how she predicted the martian soil would most likely have evidence of alien life. Babs and David soaked in the memories, relishing with awe the respect their mother received from some of the brightest minds on this planet.

The remaining winter months passed in somber reflection for Babs and her family, but Babs allowed a break in the mourning for Annie to have a Sweet Sixteen sleepover with a few of her friends. It served as a harbinger for better days ahead.

Mama Rose came home from the hospital, with a walker and a weakened body. Beth invited the entire Vanetti family to celebrate Christmas at her "new" house. The family returned to their old home at W. 61st and Detroit, to celebrate their traditional Italian holiday.

Traditions also continued with the Nagys, but Brigid and Jay began their own tradition, by spending New Year's in Vienna, Austria, courtesy of the Federal Bureau of Investigation, who staffed an office there.

Winter months and 1996 passed, and when the snows

began to thaw, the buds of Spring awakened. Babs and Annie spent Easter break in Cape Cod, where Babs showed her daughter all of the beautiful places she visited with her parents when she was younger. Annie was happy to see, first-hand, the peaceful refuge that Grandma Barbara talked about. She loved the lighthouses and the little villages bursting with art and antiques and handmade clothing.

When they were walking along the Stony Beach in Buzzard's Bay, they shared a mother-daughter cathartic moment.

"I don't know why, Mom, but I love the East Coast better than the West Coast. It's just quieter, and I get a cool sense of history. For some reason, though, the Atlantic doesn't seem as peaceful as the Pacific. Crazy, the thoughts that run through my head."

"New England is my favorite place in the world, I'm so happy you like it here Annie. I wanted you to see Cape Cod for many reasons. To connect with my past, and my parents, and for one other reason. You need to be honest with me when I ask you something."

They found a soft, sandy spot to sit, and for a while they just listened to soothing sounds of the splashing waves and the soft purrs of the seagulls.

Finally, Babs spoke.

"Annie, you probably have observed that I have fallen in love with Paul. I can't imagine how strange that must be to hear your mother say that she is in love."

"Oh my God, mom," Annie interrupted. "Do you really think it's stranger than seeing Dad living with someone almost half his age? You've done things right, mom. You've always considered me first, and I am just fine. And I love Paul, too. Don't think I haven't noticed how he's taken care of us in a lot of ways."

"He has asked me to marry him, and …"

Annie jumped up. "Yay, yay, and yay! Please tell me you are going to say yes. I would love to live in Ohio City. I could sleep for an extra hour. And I would love to be Tamara's sister. And I would love to see you be happy!"

"It's going to be a big change, and you've had so many changes in your young life. It might be weird having a man in the house all the time."

"Mom! I'm good! Before you know it, I'll be off to college. You've been divorced for seven years. It's time."

"I am so grateful for you, Annie. I love you."

"Love you most."

The drive home from the Cape was filled with conversations about wedding plans and getting the Shaker house on the market. Babs was excited to share the news with her friends, and of course, to tell Paul of Annie's reaction.

Rosie, Babs, and Brigid had not met for lunch since January. They spoke on the telephone and used America Online to send messages, but it was a few months since their last detailed gabfest. There was much to talk about. This time they ate in Parmatown, at one of Brigid's favorite restaurants, Antonio's.

Babs was the first to talk. She announced her engagement and showed them her marquise diamond ring. She also shared the conversation in which Annie approved. Rosie and Brigid did not let out the whoop that Babs thought they would. Instead, they expressed sincere happiness with streaming tears and hearty hugs.

"All I can do is cry because I am so happy for you, Babs. You deserve happiness. I'm so glad we can share it with you."

Rosie was blubbering. "Lord, we're all in f'ing menopause.

"We are traveling to Cape Cod in June to be married in a seaside chapel. Since I am divorced, the Catholic Church insists on an annulment before I remarry. Rules are rules, and I respect that, but I will not play their game. So, a chapel it is, in a beautiful setting, and goodbye Papa John Paul — I am excommunicating myself."

"A toast to Babs and Paul, and a curse on Papa John Paul," shouted Rose.

"I can't drink to that. My toast will be just for Babs and Paul," growled Brigid.

Babs and Rosie took an extra swallow to make up for Brigid's half toast.

Brigid then shared her adventures with Jay in Vienna.

"We attended the Vienna New Year's Concert by their Philharmonic Orchestra. They performed in the Musikverein concert hall in a beautiful room called the Golden Hall. Girls, let me tell you, it took my breath away. The acoustics were mind-bending. I haven't been swept away by sounds like that since I saw Judy Garland in concert way back in 1961. And one of the greatest bonuses was that this was the first year they had a female member in the orchestra!"

"Bravo!" Babs and Rosie said in unison.

"Jay and I stayed a couple extra days to tour the city and to take a day trip to the Alps. It changed my view of the world and myself. For a brief moment, I was truly one in spirit with the earth. I imagine that's how you feel when you look at the cosmos, Babs."

Rosie just had to ask. "Were you one in body?"

Brigid replied as any internationally known Doctor of English would have done. She stuck her tongue out at Rosie.

Babs asked, "Any wedding plans for you in the near future, Brig?"

"We do talk about it, and at forty-seven, I do think it might be time. I do love him. I think I always have, which might explain why I never did get married. I'm just not sure I want to give up my totally free lifestyle."

"You'll know when the time is right," Babs said.

"Good Lord, fifty is right around the corner, Brig. Give it up already."

Again, the tongue stuck out.

"Your turn, Rosie," Babs said. "What's new on the ol' homestead?"

"First of all, I need to say how happy I am for my dearest friends. Really, here we are all starting another chapter in our lives, and we are still here to share it with each other."

"To us," Brigid said.

And the glasses clanked again.

"Here is how my new chapter has progressed, and it astounds me. It turns out the zoning is in place to keep the building as a medical facility. They never changed it, so that was one hurdle we did not have to jump. We have secured documented pledges from several organizations to provide funds for one half of the facility for girls who are pregnant, with no place to go. The other half will be for women with near to end Alzheimer's disease. These monies will fund salaries and medical professionals and food services, and they come with a five-year commitment. The thought of all this is overwhelming, but I knew from the start that something big was going to happen. It's actually falling into place, except for one last piece, and it is a whopper."

"I am stunned, and so impressed, and so proud of you, Rosie."

"Same for me," Babs agreed. "It's simply amazing. Now, tell us the whopper that is the last piece."

"Welp, we need one and one half million dollars to do the necessary renovations and to build the wall and partitions necessary to separate the girls from the women. Also, to purchase bedding and decor to make it as homey and comfortable as we can. I can't believe God would let us get this far, and then stop it all."

"Is there a deadline as to when you have to have the money?'

"Yep. July."

The women became silent in thought.

Babs excused herself for a brief time and went to her car to use her car phone. When she came back, she could not control her beaming smile, or her outburst of news.

"OK, are you sitting down? Yes, I know you are sitting down."

"What the hell – out with it." Rosie was on the edge of her seat.

"I have told you before that my brother, David, is a millionaire. Actually, a multi-millionaire. One would never guess it by his lifestyle, he and his wife are both so frugal. When my mother died, he said he was going to donate a million dollars to Alzheimer's research. I just went to my car and told him about your plan and your current situation."

"Oh, my God, Babs," Rosie whispered.

"Yes, Rosie. David said he would give you the full amount with only one string attached."

"I will give him my limbs."

"Haha. Not a limb, but a wing. He would just like one of the wings to be called "The Barbara Turyev Hall.""

Rosie, now truly overwhelmed with emotion, said, "It would be my honor."

The women sat in silence — all engulfed in the momentous decision at what just happened, and what will happen. They ate their lunch but could not find words to chat with. Between wedding plans, world travel, a colossal undertaking and unfathomable generosity, they just let the moment fill their spirits.

Rosie led the final toast, "To David."

Babs and Paul married in the Chapel at Cape Cod. Annie gave her mother away, Tamara served as maid of honor, and Paul's brother, Mark, served as best man. The bride and groom stayed in an oceanfront condo, while Tamara and Annie stayed in an old, quaint hotel in the middle of town. Mark flew back to his family in Milwaukee after the ceremony.

The house in Shaker had sold in a week, so when the families returned home, they settled into Paul's house in Ohio City. He had renovated a large Victorian home, with four bedrooms and three bathrooms. Tamara described the house as "simply glorious, an architectural masterpiece."

Later in June, Rosie and Sammy hosted a surprise reception for the couple at the Sanctuary. Members from the

Vanetti, Turyev, and Nagy families, as well as several friends, gathered to celebrate both the wedding and the progress of Sammy and Rosie's grand dream come true. David had asked for his gift not to be mentioned, and they honored his anonymity. Sammy, however, invited David to walk with him to see the facility, and expressed his profound gratitude.

"What you have done, David, is generous and magnanimous beyond words."

"Right back at you, Sammy. I gave money; you are giving your heart and soul. You will never know how much it means to us to have our mother honored this way. The dignity you will be giving to girls and women is something my mother would treasure."

Day turned into evening. After everyone helped clean up, some sat on the porch, while others visited the horses and goats. Dar, Mama Rose, and two of Mama Rose's friends from her church group sat in the living room. All were in their mid or late seventies, and their topic of conversation leaned toward growing old.

"My chin sags down to where my breasts used to be."

"And my breasts hang down to where my belly button used to be."

"And my belly button hangs down to, well, you know where."

"Thank God, we don't use THAT anymore."

Giggles filled the room, as Mama Rose concluded the topic by saying, "Yeah, but we're still damn cute."

Rosie, Babs, and Brigid listened from the kitchen, enjoying the wisdom and humor of these old friends — old friends who in many ways were still young.

The topic of Dar came up.

"I'm not really sure where to go from here," Brigid said. "She's still functional, and most of the time, lucid. The worst part is, she knows what's happening to her. When I stopped in yesterday, she was sitting in her rocker, pulling her hair, saying, 'I prayed this wouldn't happen to me. I prayed this wouldn't happen to me.'"

"You should have Miklos bring her down here to the horse farm. I'm telling you, the research is clear regarding the soothing effect horses have on people, including people with brain issues," Rosie offered.

Just as sound traveled from the living room to the kitchen, so did it travel from the kitchen to the living room, and the old ladies in the living room heard every word that was said.

Dar cackled a shout: "You're not sending me to no darn whores' farm! That's for girls like you!"

Laughter exploded from both rooms as the daughters sauntered into the living room to join the other women. Rosie played a record, and they all began to dance to Perry Como singing "Papa Loves Mambo."

The remainder of the year held no surprises. The Indians made it to the World Series ... and lost in the eleventh inning of the seventh game. There was no Browns team, so as Miklos said, "fans were at least spared those heartaches." He jested, but the heart did still ache, because there was no team.

Chapter 11

• • • • • • • • • • • • • • • • • • •

*Although the world is full of suffering, it
is also full of the overcoming of it.*

Helen Keller

L ourdes Academy Class of 1968 hosted their thirtieth class
reunion on *The Goodtime* cruise boat sailing the Cuyahoga
River and Lake Erie, on June 6, 1998. Brigid's first roommate at
Marquette, and the President of Student Council at Lourdes,
gave a welcoming speech, and mentioned Rosie's Sanctuary
project and its commitment to helping women in trouble,
through pregnancy or dementia. The Lourdes women applauded, and by the end of the evening, Rosie and Sammy
had been offered over twenty thousand dollars in pledges.
Their generosity flabbergasted Rosie as she promised that the
money would be used wisely and effectively.

Warm emotions and sincere respect filtered through the
atmosphere for all of the classmates. Again, the cadre of
women shared their success stories as well as their failures.
Homemakers, mothers, authors, scientists, CEOs, CFOs, doctors, nurses, educators, activists, social workers, women from
all fields of life, reminisced about their special high school
years at Lourdes where women were treasured and nourished and encouraged to meet their potential in whatever life
or love choices they made. Sometimes Brigid would converse

with someone whose experience was counter to what Lourdes was supposed to be. One of the black women, Gabriella, confided that she was devastated by the choice of *Showboat* as the senior class play. Brigid was shocked to hear this, thirty years after the fact.

"Tell me, please, why was it devastating?"

"Do you know how painful it was as a young black girl to have the effects of miscegenation laws blast off the stage of my high school? And the black stereotypes presented in the original script?"

"But we changed those stereotypes, and we did show how those awful laws wrecked lives and loves…"

"Brigid, it was a white play addressing black problems and no one bothered to ask us how we felt about it!"

Brigid did not know how to respond, except to say she was sorry they were not more sensitive to the situation. "I'm so glad you told me, and I'm so happy you are here."

"Me too."

She talked to another classmate, Margie, who had always been very quiet in school. Margie became a biochemist and shared interesting insights into how cells communicate with each other to affect various developments and functions of organisms. In a conversation about life at Lourdes, she mentioned that because her parents were divorced, she was very self-conscious because divorce was never discussed, and most of the girls came from homes with both parents present.

"When I was in grade school, some children were not even permitted to play with me, because my mother was a divorcée. Thank God, my mother was a tenacious woman, and we both came out of the situation strong and confident."

Again, Brigid felt remorse for not being aware of what her own classmates were going through. She hugged Margie and said, "That would not have mattered; we would have loved you no matter what."

When Brigid, Rosie, and Babs met the next day to debrief, Brigid reminded the others how lucky their lives have been, and how ignorant she was of others' suffering while in high school.

"Nobody shared things like that back then," Babs said. "The good thing now is that we do share, and we can be there for each other. I sensed neither judgment nor jealousy at the reunion. There was a genuine feeling of 'we're all in this together.'"

"Talk about 'we're all in this together' — what about that generosity? Twenty grand, without even asking. And I'm guessing there will be more. I've never been so shocked in my life!" Rosie exclaimed.

"To the women of Lourdes Academy!" Clink!

August 7, 1998 would be remembered by the friends as the night Brigid said "Yes."

Jay and Brigid flew to Greece where the FBI, as in Vienna, had an office. Jay attended two meetings, and then he and Brigid traveled the Greek Isles for two days. In the middle of the Aegean Sea, under a brilliant, haloed full moon, on a yacht whose cabin was the size of three of Brigid's bedrooms, Jay, on bended knee, officially proposed to Brigid. He opened up a small velvet cushioned box wherein lay a ring, tastefully set with diamonds in the shape of a fleur-de-lis.

"Brigid Nagy, you are the most intelligent, most beautiful, and kindest woman I have ever met or ever want to meet. I have always loved you and always will. You are already my soulmate. Will you also please my wife? I promise I will always be your faithful husband."

Brigid, her auburn hair glimmering in the moonlight, dressed in a pale green, off the shoulder blouse and white capris which seemed fluorescent in the glow of the lunar light, had never looked more stunning. She took Jay's hand and gently beckoned him off his knee.

"I have never loved anyone else, Jay. You fulfill every spiritual, intellectual, and physical need that I have. I was a fool once, but I am a fool no more. Yes, I will marry you — the sooner the better."

The remainder of the evening was filled with tenderness and bliss, highlighted by a moonlit dance to a recording of *If Ever You're In My Arms Again*, by Peabo Bryson.

Brigid called Miklos the next day with the news.

"I know, Brig. Jay came to me before you left for Greece, and asked for your hand. I told him to take all of you, not just your hand."

Miklos laughed at what he thought was a very funny joke, but Brigid could sense the silent tears streaming down his face.

"Your mother is sleeping. Hopefully, she will understand when I tell her of your engagement. Love you sweetheart."

"Love you, too, Daddy."

Jay's colleagues at the FBI office in Greece hosted a celebratory luncheon the next day. Brigid and Jay both beamed with the look of young lovers, even though he had just turned fifty, and she was closing in on it.

When they reached Hopkins Airport in Cleveland, friends and family were waiting with applause and signs. Babs, the famed doctor of thermonuclear physics, and Rosie, the acclaimed animal behaviorist and businesswoman, toilet papered the car that was waiting for the couple in the parking lot.

Even though Brigid requested no bridal showers, saying, "Please, I'm too old for this frivolity," Babs and Rosie convinced her to allow them to have a very small get-together with close friends.

One hundred close friends attended the "small" get-together. Friends from the Peace Corps, from Marquette (both the college days and professorial days), from Lourdes Academy, current colleagues, and of course sisters and cousins. Michelle, Sally, Joan, Cindy, and Suzy sang *I'm Getting Married in the Morning*, followed by a raucous rendition of *We Are Family*.

The guests presented Brigid with no individual gifts, but rather a collective five-thousand-dollar check.

Jay had no reservations about getting an annulment from his first wife; he never considered it a real marriage anyway. A few weeks later, on December 10, 1998 Brigid and Jay were married at Saint Charles Church. Family and a few friends attended. Since it was Advent, the Catholic Liturgy was minimal, as were the flower arrangements and decor. Brigid's sisters served as bridesmaids, and Jay's brothers and three close friends served as ushers. They opted out of a maid of honor and a best man.

That evening, Brigid and Jay prayed together in thanksgiving for all of the blessings in their lives. Jay suggested donating half of the money gifts to the Sanctuary.

"You are the greatest blessing of all, Jay Vargo."

He smiled and turned out the light.

Sammy and Rosie hosted an Open House at their facility in April of 1999. Brigid and Babs looked after things in the main house while Rosie attended to the Open House.

Suddenly, Brigid seemed harried as she scurried from room to room. She found Miklos in the living room watching an Indians game with Jay and Paul.

"Dad! I cannot find Mom anywhere. Do you know where she is?" Brigid was frantic.

The men jumped up in a panic and began searching the house and the land. She was nowhere to be found.

Finally, they saw Rosie walking toward them, holding on to Dar's arm. They all ran to her.

"Oh my God, thank you, Rosie ! I'm so sorry. Where was she?" Brigid said as she hugged her mother.

"Oh no worries," Rosie answered, laughing, but obviously annoyed.

"Dar was greeting our guests at the door, tearing off strips of toilet paper. She handed the guests their 'tickets,' as she said, 'Welcome to the whores' farm, enjoy your stay.'"

Rosie, Babs, and Brigid celebrated their forty-ninth birthday in the Tremont area of Cleveland's South Side at the

Dempsey's Oasis. The buzz at the table centered around the grand opening of Sammy and Rosie's dream home for young and old women in need of help. It was scheduled to open in September, and the reservations were almost filled.

A major obstacle did present itself, however. Rosie explained.

"Apparently there is another home for women called the Sanctuary, so we cannot use that name for ours. Our farm and stables can be called sanctuary, but not the home for women. Sammy and I are wracking our brains trying to come up with a name, but nothing seems to work. The paperwork needs to be done by July 1."

The women sat in silent contemplation.

Babs's face suddenly changed expression as if an epiphany overcame her.

"Rosie, Brig, what comes to your mind when you think of these women carrying their babies? Or when you think of the wing dedicated to my mom? Or the struggles that Dar is going through after she raised five daughters?"

The light of dawning flickered in their eyes.

The glasses clanked. The women drank.

They shared their toast:

"To the Treasured Egg."

Epilogue

· ·

2010

The Treasured Egg Home for Women proved to be a successful venture. A shrine to the Virgin Mary was built inside the Alzheimer's section. (Rosie wanted to place it on the other side with the younger women, but Brigid convinced her that it might not be an appropriate frame of reference for a population of very pregnant, very non-virgin women.)

The structured and compassionate approach to the care and well-being of their guests served as a model for homes across the country, and funding was never a problem. Tamara, Paul's daughter, who earned her PhD in Gerontology, was the onsite manager of the Alzheimer's section. Sister Mary Hurley, of the Humility of Mary nuns who had taught at Lourdes Academy, managed the young girls' section. Music therapy and horse therapy showed great success both with the younger and older women. Universities from the United States and across the globe came to observe. Lisa Steinway, the clinical psychologist who first treated Barbara, provided cognitive testing for the residents and counseling services for the families. Dr. Hannah Manfred, who delivered Max Scarponi in 1988, served as the onsite gynecologist for the pregnant young women, who received free medical care during and after pregnancy. They were discharged when government monies—or more preferably, family help—became available. When able, they planted and harvested a garden of fresh vegetables which were used in the lunch and dinner menus of the home. Megan Zamusta, now a nationally renowned nutritionist, headed up the food department.

Sammy and Rosie remained happy and content and proud of their contribution to women's health. They celebrated their thirtieth wedding anniversary in 2006. Sammy continued to write, receiving numerous awards for excellence in Journalism. Rosie oversaw the care of the animals and the women. Mama Rose helped with household cooking and small chores, but eventually passed away from a brief bout with breast cancer, at the age of eighty.

Beth still served as a Cleveland City Councilwoman and hosted the family Christmas celebration at the old Vanetti household on W. 61st.

Ricky Scarponi moved back to Kenya, where he lived and worked at the Sheldrick sanctuary with his wife, Jane, whom he met while in veterinary school. He was also a noted ornithologist. They had three daughters.

Antonio enlisted in the Marine Corps and became what is known as a "lifer." He had yet to marry.

Max was in graduate school at University of Cincinnati, studying Zoology.

Paul and Babs still lived in Ohio City, Paul still teaching at Saint Ignatius, and also working as a freelance translator of ancient Latin and Roman manuscripts. Babs continued to work remotely for NASA, using the latest computer technology to communicate. She helped supervise the work of JPL on the Herschel Planck Mission to test theories of the early universe and the origin of cosmic structure. She also supported NASA's 10 Center Team to design the space module, which was later built by SpaceX to go to the space station, and which will eventually go to the moon. She currently provides expertise on the development of the James Webb Space Telescope which will further exploration past the Hubble Telescope. She and Paul continued in their deep love and marital commitment.

Annie could never shake the love for New England that was planted in her soul at her first visit to Cape Cod with her mother. She attended Mount Holyoke, an all-girls college in Massachusetts, where she majored in Environmental Science. She eventually settled in Maine with her husband, a Geographic Information Systems Specialist. They had one daughter, Barbara Ann.

David and Jojo lived in University Heights, Ohio, where he was artist in residence at the Cleveland Museum of Art.

Adam, Babs's ex-husband, still lived in California, with his third wife. He had not seen Annie for five years.

Jay and Brigid traveled the world during the three summers from 1999 through 2001. They moved to New York in 2002 when Jay was appointed to to the Homeland Security Department where he helped in the investigations of the 2001 terror attacks by Islamic radicals. Brigid left her beloved teaching position to become a lecturer and author, in high demand as a speaker on Feminist Criticism.

Dar Nagy entered The Treasured Egg Home for Women in 2000. Her Alzheimer's disease progressed quickly, and she died in 2002 as a result of a brain hemorrhage.

Miklos Nagy followed his Dar, dying of a massive stroke two months after her death.

Rosie, Babs, and Brigid celebrated their sixtieth birthday at Bianca's Restaurant in Brunswick, Ohio which was owned by a Saint Charles friend of Brigid's. As they had for the past forty-five years of their lives, they ended their lunch with a toast.

"To faith, family, and another forty-five years of friendship."

The glasses clanked, and the girls drank. They had more living to do.

Acknowledgments

· ·

Even with a simple story and novel, there are many to thank for its completion. My sincerest appreciation goes to the following:

My reasons for living: Ray, my husband. Phyllis, Jackie, Darlene, and Melanie, my daughters. Megan, Lisa, Tony, Hannah, and Max, my grandchildren, and Angelo and Gianna, my step grandchildren.

Sheldrick Wildlife Trust for taking the time to aid me in my research and introducing me to the marvelous contributions and fascinating life of Daphne Sheldrick.

American Embassy in Dublin, Ireland for providing insight into the Travellers and the relationship between the Native Americans and the citizens of Ireland.

Gail Klein, NASA scientist, Senior engineer, and Manager of the development of planetary science instruments. She is the professional inspiration for the character of Babs. She also provided personal insights into the spiritual struggles that occur while being a Catholic Christian in a cosmic world of many atheists.

Joan Larosa and her husband, Roger Meredith. Joan was Foreign Service Officer with the US Agency for International Development working mostly in Health Population & Nutrition. Roger was known as a Tea Plantation Engineer and was the inspiration for the character Bwana Roger in this book. They provided me with volumes of information and anecdotes on the landscapes, culture, politics, and peoples of Africa where they lived for several years.

My world-traveling sister, Sally Filan, and her husband, John, for information and insights into the landscapes and culture of Ireland, particularly the Travellers.

My New Yorker-at-heart sister, Susan Coyle, for information and insights into the streets of New York, and the life of a concierge.

Louise Quallich Pilz, for being an ever-ready researcher and aide extraordinaire, as well as a much appreciated supporter.

Peggy Zone-Fisher for historical information on Cleveland, and never-dying friendship.

Patricia Bernhardt for marketing management and unconditional friendship.

To all of my friends from Lourdes Academy, class of 1968, for endless support and encouragement, especially my group, "Morning Maniacs," for my daily manna.